Fear is a dangerous emotion. I've seen it bring many to their knees, and yet… it can also be used to a person's advantage. The struggle grows fierce, the need to live pushing past obstacles. The human mind is a fascinating thing. As evolved as we claim to be, it all boils down to 'fight or flight'. Primitive answers to life's trials.

I walk upon hollowed ground tonight. The full moon above is a greenish yellow, yet so bright. It nearly drowns out the stars. A night so eerily beautiful… and I'm sharing it with no one. Shadow has passed over and Nixie is working. Within my mind, I see sparks of emotion. So many run through like the blood in my veins… but not fear. Such abnormality would have me accused of witchcraft in times of old. Especially here, in the midst of a ruined town. Not many know the history of this place, long since lost to time, but it murdered hundreds of women. All accused witches, and all victims of jealousy and gossip.

I breathe deep, catching the scent of burning wood. This place has long since burnt down, yet the smell is still there. The sound of crackling is a whisper on the wind. Without warning, I hear a whoosh and fire surrounds me. Flecks of ash rain down, cinders burning in the air. The heat kisses my skin, yet doesn't hurt. It should, though. These fires are hot enough to melt skin.

The story I've learned, is that this place was set aflame by those that lived here. They thought they had been overrun with dark magic. All the accused were locked within the buildings, and burned alive. Their wailing spirits are everywhere… and nowhere. My first sign of a curious soul, is an opening door. Though hanging on only the bottom hinge, it creaks ajar and a wisp of white peeks out. For their piece of mind, I pretend not to see.

My life has taken so many strange turns, it's hard to keep up. From the old store to 'possible world savior'. Likely an exaggeration, and yet… I *feel* it's accurate enough. Not long after my showdown with Clara, I found another mark on my wrist. It appeared beside the one for fire, yet it's not the same. Whereas they're both triangles, fire is upright and this one is upside down. I have a hunch this new symbol is for water.

Despite the atmosphere, clogging my lungs with smoke, I stand still. My eyes close and I hold out my arms, welcoming the flames. I can't control them yet, my fires, but then… I suppose that's how it *should* be. It's almost like a pet, attacking and defending when needed. You can't control a dog completely either. Fire really *is* alive, and every living thing desires freedom.

A beam snaps and clatters to the ground, kicking up more sparks. I can hear hissed words upon the air, both frightened and in awe. The word 'witch' rakes shivers down my spine. To think, that was the last thing these spirits heard. To be honest, I have no reason to be here. I'm not here to free spirits, or even to practice my abilities. I'm just on a walk to clear my head. Now that I'm here, though, I can't help but reach out to them.

"You don't know me," I sigh. "I've read up on all of you, though. Innocent women accused and murdered. What can I do to ease your souls? What will it take for you to pass on?"

"*You cannot help the damned,*" an elderly woman remarks.

Her spirit comes into view soon after. She's shorter than me, stooped over her gnarled cane, and her clothes are older in style. I surmise she lived when this town turned to ash. Probably trapped by accident. With her presence beaming, the others get brave. I see their forms blink into existence, both young and old… even children.

The old woman moves closer to me, extending her cane to poke my stomach. It passes through, a shock of static tingling on my skin.

"You're not of our world," she states. "And yet you can see us when we hide. You can speak to us. Perhaps we were innocent... but you don't seem to be, witch."

"I'm not a witch," I reply. "Technically, I'm not even human. My job is to save trapped souls like you. What's keeping you here?"

"This is our home," she frowns. "Where else are we to go?"

"You can't stay here, you need to pass on. A better life is waiting for you."

"There is no afterlife for the damned. Not one we're eager to go to."

"You're *innocent*. The sinners are the ones that torched this town, that *murdered* you. If you don't pass on, they'll have won. Do you want that? To be trapped in limbo, reliving your death, for all eternity?"

They seem confused, however I can understand why. They were taught what they thought law, it's hard to go against. For all I know, they could like this place. I'm not the type to push a happy spirit on, but this place is a monument to their tragedy. I can't let them stay in misery, it's just not fair for them.

"We... we were never given a proper burial," a younger woman states. "I know our bodies are no longer, but... maybe a headstone, or memorial?"

"I can do that," I grin. "Now… where to place it."

The search isn't long, though the buildings are only skeletons. In the center of town, like any other back then, is a statue of the founder. It's been worn down and broken with time. I'll admit, I'm not much of a sculptor, but I can do something with it. The next step is to find some tools. A glance around and I see a blacksmith's shop. Although it's charred and only a few beams stand, I can see the sign in front. Ash blankets the ground like snow. I'm wearing light colors, so I'll be filthy when I'm done, yet I still dive into the soot. A few minutes of digging about, some of the spirits watching on, and I locate a hammer and a chisel. They're tucked beside the huge forge, almost untouched by the fire.

When I return to the statue, I have the specters line up. One by one, they give their name and I chisel it upon the stone. It's not perfect, but it's something. Finished with names, I chisel something above those markings… 'Innocent of sins, let them rise above'. It's the only thing I can think. At the relived sighs all around me, I'm guessing there's nothing else needed. I watch them huddle together, reaching to touch the 'headstone' I've given them. That's about the time a thin line of light pierces the night. I expect to see Nixie, however I'm surprised by another. I don't know this Envoy, yet they seem to know me.

"So you're the special case," he chuckles.

"Special case?"

"The one Nixie was assigned to. The Root."

"I suppose I am then. Who are you?"

"Styx," he answers. "At least, that's what the Envoys call me."

"… Um… that's not your name?"

It's here I realize he's not dressed in armor. A long black robe hides his figure, the hood bulky enough to obscure part of his face, and his staff has a hanging lantern instead of a scythe. It's fires glow a light blue. The hand holding it, however, is nothing but bone. When he turns to address one of the spirits, I see an ivory grin beneath the hood. He's not an Envoy, but I would bet every last dime he were a zombie before all this supernatural stuff.

"Okay, ladies," he says. "Time to go. Thank your savior before you leave."

"You don't look like an Envoy."

"Oh, Envoys are typically female," Styx informs. "I'm surprised Nixie hasn't told you about this stuff. Anyway, when I was born no one was here to name me. I was named by a mortal soul, when I ferried them to the afterlife."

"Wait… so you're a ferryman? On the *river* Styx?"

"I'm *the* ferryman, the original. Born of the river's waters. I guess that's how I got my name."

"I thought Charon was the ferryman," I point out.

"Charon is a collective name."

"There are others?"

"Sure, I can't ferry the world by myself."

"How does someone apply for that job?" I wonder, stupefied.

"Ask Nixie, she owes me for this. Leading spirits is an Envoy job."

"Then why do it?"

"… She's the only one I can call a true friend," he states, eyes downcast and voice small. "Thanks for not staring, by the way. She's the only one that doesn't mind the… uh… zombie style."

"Zombies are fucking awesome," I grin. "More people should try that style. If they bother you, though, why not fix it? I mean, can't you guys look however you want?"

"If my mother created me this way, why should I be ashamed of it?"

"Touche," I smirk. "Well, you rock the look. Don't change for anyone."

He bows his head and turns away from me. The lantern is held out before him, vanishing for a moment. Then light spills from a doorway. He ushers the many souls through, and then waves goodbye. I have a feeling I'll be seeing him later.

Chapter 1

The night is too quiet for me. Our small apartment, given to us by Agent Toby Osmond, feels empty and ominous. Since my run-in with Shadow, I find I'm not happy when I'm alone. There's still a few hours until Nixie gets back, which leaves me in this maddening silence. With no other way to drown it out, I throw in some popcorn and one of Nixie's horror movies. Probably not the best way to cover silence, but it's convenient.

As I begin to nod off, the sound of terrified screams surrounding me, I hear a voice. One eye peaks open, glancing at the murder scene. It should be in a basement. The screen flickers between that and something else. I can't make it out. Finally, the scene stays on an orchard. A woman with red hair stands in the center, head bowed. Without warning, she leaps for the screen, mouth opening in an angry shriek. Her face is gaunt and dark with decomposition, teeth yellowed and eyes completely black in sunken sockets.

I yelp and scramble over the back of the couch… just in case. The second I peek over the cushions, the movie has returned and the orchard is gone. My heart beats fast, leaping into my throat. No clue what that was about, however I feel I'll learn more soon. Eager to get away from the haunted device, I go to the bathroom for a shower. When I'm done, I'll just go to bed. Anything to forget this feeling that has my skin crawling.

I'm startled awake by a noise, though I can't recall what it is. It's so dark within my room, I can't even see my hand in front of my face. Without something to garner my curiosity, I'm about to go back to sleep… and then the noise returns. It's soft and distant at first, and then begins to gain strength. Whereas it was in front of me, now it encircles me. The screams of those trapped, tortured…

and lost. My hands dart up to cover my ears. There's just no blocking them out. Just as I'm positive my ears will start bleeding, it all stops. A switch being turned off.

"What the fuck," I utter.

My cellphone rings, scaring me and drawing a scream. Berating myself for the reaction, I reach to answer it. The light from the screen seems brighter in this pitch. Nixie's name shows up, I answer it in relief.

"Hey, Nix," I greet. "On your way?"

"No. I won't be back tonight, so don't wait up. I found out something that might help with our problem. It's kept in the hall of life, though, and that place is about as organized as my closet."

"… You just sent a shiver down my spine."

"It's deserved, I assure you. I'll see you tomorrow, hon."

"Yeah, later."

I hang up before she can ask about my tone. I know it came out downtrodden, but I can't help it. This place has no memories to make it 'home'. With a heavy sigh, I bury myself beneath my blankets. Sleep, however, will have to wait. A voice calls my name, leaving me cursing my curiosity. I slip from my bed and reach for the lamp beside it. The chain is pulled, but the light stays dark. Shrugging it off, I grope my way to the door.

Upon locating the knob, I push through it. My bare feet are cold, but not because of the wood floor. I'm standing on grass. Although covered in most places by leaves, I can see an eerie orange moon. There's not a cloud in the star riddled sky. Unable to help it, I venture further into the trees. Probably not the best life choice, but it'll be another in a long line.

My foot hits something that rolls away. It's only an apple. Down the way, I can see the light of a fire. People are laughing and music fills the night air. I walk toward it, finding a circle of wagons. So many bright colors litter them. It takes me a minute, however I recognize them as gypsies. Gold jewelry clings together as they dance, the fire in the midst of their activity. A soft smile touches my lips at the sight. A few children chase one another, and then… one of them begins to burn.

Wagons are set aflame, people are doused in fire, and their celebration continues. Even as the trees turn to cinders, they dance until they're naught but bone. Skeletons laugh in joy, and then clatter to the ground. Fires devour them as well, leaving naught but ash in their wake. It's like I'm not even here, untouched by this catastrophe. Suddenly, I see a figure in their bonfire. She reminds me of the woman on the television.

"*This is his fault! They will all pay until he's brought to justice!*"

I step forward, about to calm her, and the flames reach higher. A branch falls between us. Distracted by it, my eyes leave her. When they return, however, she's on the move. Her bony body is hurtling toward me, mouth open in a shrill cry. I raise my arms to shield myself. The sensation of knives on my arms tells me her nails found purchase. It's also the thing the wakes me.

I jolt upright in bed, the blanket damp with sweat. When I turn the bedside lamp on, I find it's not sweat… it's blood. On my forearms, are long gashes drawn by nails. The cuts are deep, gushing red fluid and showing a bit of bone on the right. I'm not new to this, yet I am new to the extent of damage. Unable to tend to it myself, I let the fire flow through my veins. It flickers from the wound, and then cauterizes. This will have to do until Nixie returns. Getting out of bed, I pull the blanket off. Now it needs washed. The perfect excuse to avoid sleep.

I load the washer, having already used a cleaner to remove the blood stain, and I hear another noise. The last one led me to injury, so I'm not too eager to follow it.

When a familiar voice calls out, though, I head toward it. My feet take me to the front door… No one is there. I could've swore I heard Nixie in here. As I walk away, I hear a giggle. It's not childish, nor is it malicious… but something in between.

"Oh god, I hope those creepy kids didn't follow me home," I mutter.

With a shaky inhale, I try to locate the source. The living room is quiet, crawling with an ominous presence. they're restless. It's only been a few weeks since Blake was taken into custody, but word gets around fast. I've gotten so many requests for spirits, that I've been forced to rethink my profession. Now my business card reads 'Hashna Investigations (including the paranormal)'. Not what I had in mind, yet it attracts a surprising number of clients. Most are just paranoid, but I get paid anyway.

As I move toward the couch, my laptop screen blinks on. The light is blinding and unexpected. On the screen, word has opened itself. The word 'revenge' repeats all down the screen… and beyond. The pages scroll down as they're filled. I hum to myself in thought. I can't feel the desire to harm, yet there's no sensation of needed help either.

"What is it you want from me?"

"A kiss hello would be nice."

Nixie is standing right behind me, the comment whispered in my ear. I jump, crying out in fear, and move away from her. In response, she laughs at my expense. The moment I calm my racing heart, I hit her shoulder in retaliation.

"Sorry," she chuckles. "I just couldn't help myself. You were so focused."

"I was looking for the spook in here."

"There's no one here but us," she points out. "Maybe you were hearing things."

"… Maybe," I frown. "I just feel like someone is trying to warn me… show me what's to come."

She shrugs, unable to find the words to console me. There are none. Now that she's back, though, the house isn't so empty. It takes the weight off my shoulders. In the early morning hours, there's really nothing to do. Nixie doesn't need sleep and I don't want it… not after that nightmare. We start cleaning up. It's not that it's needed, as we're hardly here, but because we need to keep our minds occupied. As we do the dishes, me washing and her drying, I can't help mentioning my adventure.

"I met your friend," I comment. "I think he said his name is Styx."

"I didn't think he'd go himself," she frowns. "They must be busy."

"You never told me there's a difference between Envoys and Charon. I mean… you really haven't told me *anything* from your life there."

"It's not really interesting," she says. "Women are Envoys, Men are Charon, the purest souls are chosen to do the job. Either that, or you're born into it, like me."

"Or Styx."

"Yeah, or him. He's a really nice guy, but people can't see past his appearance."

"I can understand why, but he rocks the look."

I hand her a plate, both of us stopping at the phone ringing. Drying my hands on the way, I pick up the phone in the living room. There's nothing but dial tone. I shrug my shoulders and begin to walk away. It rings again. This time I hear a woman's voice on the other end. There's a lot of static, yet I can still make out what she's saying. She's probably driving through a tunnel.

"Hello?" I question.

"Is this Catori Hashna? From Hashna Investigations?"

"It is. Who am I speaking to?"

"My name is Adrian Carmichael. I was told you specialize in the paranormal, is that true?"

"Yes."

"I need your services. There's an old road with a rather mysterious history. According to the urban legend, the anniversary is coming. That's when people start disappearing. There isn't much time. Please help me."

"Okay, just send me directions," I offer. "I need to know where you are to help."

"You'll find them in your email. Thank you so much, Ms. Hashna. I can't even begin to explain how grateful I am."

"It's no problem. I'll see you when I get there."

I hang up and glance toward Nixie, who's just putting away the last dish. She wanders over as I pick up my laptop. Both seated on the couch, she picks up the remote. When the television is turned on, she immediately recognizes the paused scene.

"I love this movie!"

"I know, that's why I put it in," I comment, distracted. "Do you know where this is?"

"Um… a couple states over," she informs, glancing at the screen. "I think it's around an old orchard."

"That's where we're going."

With a confident nod, Nixie and I get up to pack. The name of the road seems very old, which is likely why I didn't recognize it. The address, though… it's familiar to me. I can't recall where I've encountered it, nor what it's connected to, but it's familiar. Something deep down tells me this won't go well. I can't shake it, and the longer it holds fast… the more I regret picking up that phone.

Chapter 2

The morning moves slowly. With our bags already packed, there's little for us to do. We can't leave right away, although I would love nothing more. Instead, we're meeting my parents for lunch. Our flight isn't until eight, so we've plenty of time to waste. As we drive through town, I can't help but think of the past. There was so much drama to deal with after the store's curse. Not only did I have to graduate high school, but the incident also threw my house into a war zone. My mother is against magic and doesn't believe in much of the supernatural. My father and I, however… well… at least I learned the 'opposites attract' thing is real.

Nixie watches my features as we get closer to my old house. Mother always wanted a normal life for me, though now I can't really tell what 'normal' is. She's against my business and even my girlfriend. I'm not on good terms with her at the moment. Neither is my father. After hearing of the curse I fell under, he's been adamant about teaching me witchcraft. His mother, and her side of the family, all practiced. He runs her coven from the shadows, even after telling my mother he'd leave it.

"Stop glaring like that, they'll think we've been fighting," Nixie pipes up.

"I can't help it," I sigh. "Mom is so brutal, she doesn't even refer to you as a person. I hate bringing you around her when she acts like that."

"I don't mind it."

"I do."

"Calm down, Cat. She's just old school, that's all. It's nothing new for me. I'm just happy she's not holding a torch and pitchfork. Those days were so grim."

The thought eases my mind a little… but just a little. When I pull into the driveway, I note there's an extra car there. I recognize it as someone my dad works with. I park and turn off the car. Nixie and I don't bother to rush, as we're early anyway.

Inside the house, my father's deep voice carries from the kitchen. There, I find him and his former partner, Ray Hagan. I greet him with a smile. My father used to work with him at the station, but was forced to retire. His new job has strange hours, which made it difficult for him to spend time with his family. To know that both he and my mother are home, makes me wonder if he's between jobs. He's not the type to take long vacations.

"Hey, dad," I smile. "No work today?"

"Nope, I took some time off," he answers. "I don't like to, but… I needed to spend some time with your mother."

"How are you two doing?" Ray wonders.

"Better. It took her a while to come to terms with everything, but she got there."

Nixie greets them both, following me into the living room. My mother is just setting the table for lunch. it's not going to be very fancy, just some sandwiches, but she likes to entertain guests. When she sees us, she sets down the last plate and walks over.

"Hi, honey," she states. "You're early, is everything alright?"

"Yeah, we just needed a little break before leaving."

"… Leaving?"

"I got a job offer this morning," I explain. "It's in another state, though."

"You know I don't like when you go out like that. You're placing yourself in dangerous situations, tempting fate, and one of these days..."

"… I know, I know," I huff, rolling my eyes. "I'll bite off more than I can chew. You tell me that all the time. I know how to handle myself, okay? I've been practicing, too. I'm getting way better at..."

"Stop," she says, firm. "I don't want to talk about that in front of guests."

"I already know about all that, Gwen," Ray waves off. "My mother was a part of a coven, you know. I think the majority of this town is related to them. Besides, it's healthy for her to explore stuff like that."

She frowns in his direction, yet he takes no notice of it. Wanting to get away from the topic, she walks to the kitchen in a huff. Nixie shrugs when I glance at her. Since returning from the store, she hasn't interacted with my mother much. My father and Ray sit in a couple armchairs, regarding me for a moment. It's always been easier to talk to my father, as we're so alike. It drives my mother crazy.

"Another case already?" my father smiles. "Aren't you in demand. Where are you going off to this time?"

"There's an old orchard known for disappearances," I inform.

"... Is there a curse?" he frowns.

"A very specific one," I sigh. "It's not completely random, there are conditions that need met, and they're not difficult to bypass. I should be fine."

"Alright, as long as you're careful. Do you have a name for where you're staying?"

"It's a town called Avalbane," I answer. "Do you know it?"

"Of course, honey, that's where you came into our lives," he grins. "Your birthplace! I bet you're so excited to see it."

"I knew it sounded familiar, but... did we go back when I was a little older? I mean... I don't think I would remember it as a newborn."

"I don't know, honey, you've always been pretty sharp when it came to memory. Anyway, I heard about that old orchard. They have some pretty crazy urban legends there. When we went, I was called on to investigate a chain of robberies. I didn't get to visit the old place, but the rumors sure did fly."

"Mom, did you look into them?" I wonder as she returns with food.

"Those old legends? No, sweetheart, I don't believe in that stuff. You know that. I did, however, spend a lot of time on the main street. The shops are older and it has a lovely vintage feel to it. I swear it's like going back in time."

I can't help but wonder what it looks like. Nixie doesn't seem all that interested, however she's likely been there a billion times throughout history. The name of the town is beautiful, yet also quite odd. Considering the orchard's curse, I would never have given it a name that means 'white orchard'. We fall into silence as we eat, the conversations short and friendly. I try to keep it away from the topic of my next job.

I know it isn't much for them, however I know they appreciate the visits before I go out on a job. They came really close to losing me to that store, and even closer with Damion. My mother, especially, has trouble dealing with this turn of events. It's just become habitual that I see them, spend time with them, before running into the arms of near death.

It's a pastime I wish I could enjoy more. Time always seems to move too quickly, lost in comfort of my upbringing. Much to my displeasure, I'm soon saying goodbye. Our flight will be departing soon, so we need to get moving. I give my parents a kiss before exiting the house. Nixie and I enter the car, sitting for only a moment to gaze upon my old home. I'll miss them, as I normally do, but my place isn't in their world… not really. It probably never was.

"Are you okay?" Nixie wonders, tone soft. "You look a little sad."

"It's nothing, I'm fine," I smile, minute. "I hope this flight doesn't take too long, I hate planes."

"Don't worry, I'll be right there with you," she grins. "And I'll even take the window seat, okay?"

"Gee, thanks."

I put the car into reverse and back down the drive. The airport is only a fifteen minute drive away. The streets aren't too busy, so I don't worry about running late. There are a few people roaming the sidewalks in groups, couples heading to lunch, and even a group of kids heading into the library.

At the airport, we park inside the garage. I won't be taking my car, so we'll have to get a parking pass to keep it safe. We don't have a lot of bags, just one each, so they're checked in rather quickly. After getting through the metal detectors, we search for the right gate. It's a good walk from our current location.

"It would be nice if they picked you up and drove you to the gate," Nixie mumbles.

"With what? We're inside," I laugh.

"A golf cart. Anything would be better than walking."

"Do you think complaining helps?" I tease.

"I don't see why not. Not complaining won't get us there faster."

Her lips twist in a sly smirk, eyes glimmering with fun. The gate isn't much further. When we arrive at it, we take a seat in those uncomfortable plastic chairs. They won't be loading the plane for another half hour or so. I stretch and yawn, wishing I slept in more. Nixie pulls out a book to keep her occupied, so I get up to go to the restroom. There isn't much of a line, which I'm thankful for. Typically, with this many people, there's bound to be a long wait. Today must be my lucky day.

As I wash my hands clean, I hum to myself. There are two other women in here with me, but they're leaving now. Alone in the cold room, an eerie feeling passes over me. The sensation you get when you swear you're being watched. I frown and glance around, yet nothing comes into view.

"*Can you hear it?*"

I jump at the voice that suddenly sounds. A little girl stands behind me in the mirror. Her hair is long and dark, her face obscured by it, and a puddle of water is growing around her feet. I spin around to face her… only to find the spot empty. A second glance into the mirror reveals that I'm still alone. Shaking my head, I mutter to myself and head back to Nixie. When I sit back down beside her, she questions my pale features. I assure her I'm fine, not wanting to risk an eavesdropper listening in. Hopefully, the plane ride won't take too long.

Chapter 3

As we land at our destination, I dodge a child's thrown toy. They've been screaming nearly the entire flight. Now that freedom is only a few steps away, it feels that much worse. The minute we exit the plane, we put distance between us and them. The airport is modern enough, yet when we get outside all I see is the past. This old place hasn't changed since the first building was erected.

"Wow, no wonder this place is a hot spot for tourists," I comment. "I bet they get a lot of historians."

"So, what's the first move?"

"Get a rental car!"

We start toward that building, but we're stopped halfway. A woman is holding a sign with my name on it. she's well dressed, her long brown hair pulled back in a bun, and her smile is so kind. Nixie and I walk over to her.

"I'm Catori Hashna," I inform.

"My name is Adrian Carmichael," she says, extending a hand. "Pleased to meet you."

"Likewise. This is my girlfriend, Nixie. She helps on my investigations."

Adrian shakes her hand as well. She opens the door to an old station wagon, gesturing us in. We both take the backseat, which she seems fine with. As she pulls out, I watch the world outside my window. Spring is so warm here, the foliage thick enough to pass out much needed shade. Sunlight shines in on us, too bright without sunglasses.

"I didn't know how you worked, but I have an old cabin near the road," Adrian states. "I don't live there anymore, so you'd have the place to yourself. There's also an old truck in the garage. It should get you to town easy enough. I imagine you'd get a lot of stories from the locals. Just… don't mention my name, or they'll clam up. I'm sort of the town crazy."

"And… what are you hoping we find?" Nixie questions.

"… Last year at this time, my son disappeared," she sighs. "His last picture was of an apple orchard. It was grown over an old road, the one from the urban legends. People vanish there without a trace. I want you to find out how true the legend is, and… maybe… find my son."

"Then why study the road?"

"If it's true, we can close the road off and save more lives."

"Makes sense to me," I reply. "We'll do our best to find your son, I promise."

She nods, pulling onto a road covered in trees. I could almost believe we're in a primitive place. The road is dirt, likely for wagons back in the day, and the trees are so close together they obscure my vision. Even the town had a rustic vibe to it. Before coming, Nixie showed me where we'd be on a map. This place is at the edge of a swamp. We pass some of those waters now. As dangerous as they can be, swamp lands are just as beautiful.

The cabin looks amazing, I can't imagine why Adrian doesn't live here anymore. It's small, but well kept. Flowers grow in orderly bunches, vines hanging decoratively, and a trellis arches over a cobblestone walkway. The stones are smooth and bi-colored. I walk along them, just behind Adrian, and stare in awe at the landscaping. At one point, this place was her little piece of heaven. I wonder what changed that.

Inside, the cabin is fully furnished. It's décor stays with the rustic theme. So many shades of brown, I didn't even know there were this many. A fireplace is adorned with antlers, but no head. I breathe a sigh of relief. I find bark covered ornaments, live plants, and a clock made from a slice of tree trunk. All in all, the place is very homey.

"The bedroom and bathroom are down that hall," she informs. "I haven't filled the kitchen, but there's money on top of the fridge for that. The laundry is just before the garage, and the truck keys should be hanging in the kitchen. Please make yourselves at home."

"Thank you so much," I smile. "I'll contact you..."

"It's okay, I'll call periodically. I may be unreachable when you call."

"Oh… okay. I'll wait for your call then."

"One more thing. I know you don't live around here, and you don't know your way around, but… please don't use a GPS."

"That's a strange request," Nixie frowns.

"You're not the first investigator I hired," she sighs. "There were three others. I warned them all, but they wouldn't listen. Their cars were found on the road, empty. The GPS was on, but they were never found."

"Okay, no GPS," I comment. "We'll use today to get settled, if you don't mind. I want to gather information on this legend."

"That's fine with me."

She bids us goodbye, leaving us to our own devices. I check her progress from the front window, yet find she's already gone. It's strange, as I didn't even hear the car start. Shrugging it off, I join Nixie in the kitchen. She already has her phone, the notebook app perfect for writing lists. She's been dying to use it since I downloaded it for her. While she's busy, I grab our bags and take them to the bedroom.

Before the bedroom is the door to the bath. Beautiful dark oak is spread on the floor, the counter top a pristine ivory. The tub is a deep claw-foot, set near the wall for the shower head. Towels are folded in a long cabinet, which is where I place our bathroom boxes. Once they're resting on an empty shelf, I finish my trek to the bedroom. As far as bedrooms go, this one is nice. The bed is a queen sized sleigh, a nightstand on each side. There's a large dresser, a roll top desk, and a walk-in closet. For now, I place our bags at the end of the bed and my computer bag on the desk.

Back in the living room, Nixie finishes up her list. She's already got the car keys. Together, we brave the garage. Although the thought is intimidating, as my garage could've been labeled 'hoarding' growing up, it's completely empty. Dust has begun to settle, so it hasn't been empty long.

"Oh my god!" Nixie exclaims. "I was thinking it would be an old rust bucket, but this is awesome! Is this a vintage Ford F1? I haven't seen one of these in years!"

"I didn't know you were into cars."

"I'm not, I just appreciate the titans of the past. This was also my first job when cars came out. It's got a special place in my heart."

I roll my eyes, sliding into the passenger seat. Although I usually drive, I'm just not feeling it today. She backs out of the garage and onto the dirt road, making a beeline for town. The scenery really is beautiful. Trees tower over us, branches waving in the gentle wind. A couple deer leap away from the road. Closer to town, it turns more farmland. More fields of vegetables and pastures filled with cows. Every now and then, a few goats or pigs will be scattered about.

The town itself is warm and welcoming. So many mom and pop shops, filled with people that know every local… and some frequent visitors. As Nixie and myself are newcomers, we're garnering a lot of attention. I don't mind it, it might come in handy. I've found people are always eager to spread their legends to newbies. When we park, the grocery is the first stop. Across the street, an old couple sits in their rockers. I glance at Nixie, trying to envision us at that age… If we ever get to that age. I mean, she probably won't. She's likely passed it, though her body is frozen in time. I don't really know how Roots age. I follow Nixie inside, allowing her the lead. While she scrolls down her list, I grab a cart.

"There are so many people here," Nixie remarks.

"Yeah. Maybe someone might want to talk."

"Hopefully. I like this place, but… I don't thank I want to stay long."

I nod in agreement. Deep in the pit of my stomach, I can feel a storm approaching. By the fruit, I look around. A middle-aged woman is handing out samples. As Nixie wanders to the veggies, I head over to her. The watermelon looks ripe, so I sample one. The woman smiles bright and I test the waters.

"This place is so nice," I comment. "Do you live here?"

"Yes, I do."

"It must be so pleasant. I bet you know everyone in town."

"Just about."

"Are there any urban legends of this place? It's so old, there must be something."

"Ah, you're one of those. We have many stories to tell. The most famous is 'Route 33'."

"Route 33?"

"Yes. I don't know much about it, but then… it was destroyed long ago. If you'd like to hear more about it, I recommend speaking to our historian. He's a supernatural fanatic, so he should know more."

"Where can I find him?"

"Normally, he wanders about the archives near the library."

A shiver travels my spine at the information. The last time I ventured into any archive, someone ended up dead. I thank her, and then begin a search for Nixie. She didn't get far, still debating prices a couple aisles over. At her side, I glance over her shoulder. She doesn't have much more on her list, so it'll go by fast. Afterward, we can search out the historian.

Outside, we set the bags in the truck. When they're locked up, we start our walk through town. It's leisurely, just taking our time to soak it all in. The air is warm, yet the breeze is cool. So many scents are upon it, most from bakeries and some from restaurants ready for the dinner rush. I'm surprised by the many people around us, passing friendly smiles and greetings. At the corner, three blocks from the grocery and next to the library, stands an old building. It looks to be a refurbished warehouse. The windows are cracked in places and it's not really kept up, but the sign says 'archives'. It's a far cry from a library, yet it may only hold this place's relics.

"She said the historian stays here," I explain. "He'll be able to tell us what we need to know."

"So what are we waiting for?"

"… Last time I used the archives, someone died."

"Nothing evil is connected to this place, I promise. He'll be fine."

Although the breath I take is shaky, I trust her judgment. Together, we enter the musty building. There are so many shelves and file cabinets, I could mistake it for a forgotten museum. Dust lays in a thick coat on every surface. As we pass a stack of books, it topples over. We're forced to dodge. At the noise, however, I catch a muffled curse from the back. A short man with wire rim glasses appears. His hair is dark, eyes large, and I can't help the chuckle. He's dressed in a sweater vest… covered in Christmas bows. I'm reminded of an eccentric professor.

"May I help you?" he frowns, crossing thin arms over his chest.

"Actually, I'm looking for the historian."

"That would be me, but I'm far too busy to talk. Today, I've devoted myself to this building. It's haunted, you know. I'm going to get proof."

"… How long have you been trying?" I ask.

"About two years," he sighs, downtrodden. "Nothing ever happens when I'm here, but when I come in every morning… things are stacked, stuff is moved, and there are strange stains over there."

He points to an odd empty space. It's positioned in the center of the room, books and shelves leaving a clean circle. Upon the tile, I catch sight of a black stain. It trails to the side before pooling. A soft cry echoes in the stifling air. Curious, I follow the sound. A little girl is huddled next to her mother, both shot in the head. Not too far away, near the puddled stain, is a young man. He's been shot in the stomach, throat and head.

"Um… would this spirit be… I don't know… three spirits?"

"I… I had theorized that. How did you know?"

"They're right here."

He scrambles over to me, yet stops short. At the sour gaze he shoots me, I can only sigh in frustration. No wonder he hasn't gotten his proof, he can't even see them. I pick up a small notebook, walking to the little girl. On the way, I pull a pen from the spiral binding. She moves away from me at first. When I take a seat across from them, her expression gradually changes to wonder.

"Hi," I smile. "My name is Catori, what's yours?"

"… Taylor."

"That's a pretty name. Did your mommy name you?"

"No, my daddy did."

"Can you help me, Taylor? My friend here wants to talk to you, but he can't hear you like I can. Can you write the answers to his questions?"

She looks to her mother and father first. Their eyes are distant and clouded, far away from their little girl. The thought occurs to me, that they could be figments from their daughter's memory. They could've passed without her, their figures nothing more than a safety blanket. It tears my heart apart.

"Taylor, what's the last thing you remember?" I inquire.

"There was a loud bang and my mommy fell down. I heard my daddy crying, and then... everything went dark. When I woke up I was all alone and I couldn't leave."

"Oh, sweetie, don't you know you died? Your parents went to heaven, you have to find them there."

"I know, but... I don't know how to get there and I'm scared."

She starts to cry again, the loss of concentration banishing her parents. I take her mother's place, holding her gently. As I hush her, I look to Nixie. We really need the historian's help, however I believe Taylor should come first. Nixie must think the same. She pulls her scythe from the air, heedless of our onlooker, and draws it passed her for her armor. Taylor holds me tighter, yet relaxes at Nixie's smile.

"Hello, Taylor, I'm Nixie. I can take you to your parents," she offers. "I'm sorry it's taken so long, but some spirits need time to grasp their mortality. You must've been a stubborn one."

"You know my mommy and daddy?"

"I know every soul, it's my job. Come on now, we need to get going. Don't want them waiting any longer."

She holds out her hand and, with a little coaxing, Taylor takes it. That familiar doorway is opened and they walk through it. When it closes, I stand to face the historian. His jaw is dropped in awe. I wave a hand passed his face, snapping him from his stupor. He attempts to say something a few times, yet nothing comes out. It's understandable, so I offer him a way out.

"I'm sorry I ruined your hobby," I comment. "She didn't belong here, she was just a scared little girl. If you'd like, I can find you another haunted sight, but… well… What sort of evidence were you hoping to get without the ability to see ghosts?"

"I guess… I thought they'd show themselves when they were ready."

"Sometimes it's like that, but Taylor was too scared to play," I remark. "And I'd be extra careful which sites I'd go to. The last two I went to left me cursed and fighting for my life."

"You're a fanatic, too?" he gapes. "Is that why you're here? I've always wanted to visit the old road, but it's too risky… and it only chooses victims on the month of its anniversary. Nothing happens aside from that month."

That's the opening I've been waiting for. As he babbles on about the places he's been, I move a couple chairs over. We sit and he moves on to some experiences he's had. It's when Nixie returns that he quiets. Green eyes stare openly at her, however she brushes it off. She banishes her armor and weapon, retrieving another chair to join us.

"You… What are you?" he murmurs.

"I'm an Envoy," she answers. "I lead souls to the afterlife. How about you? You're a historian?"

"Yes. I'm Jonathan Marley, the town's historian. I also dabble in the supernatural, but I've never heard of Envoys."

"Sure you have, but you know us as the Grim Reaper."

"Fascinating."

"I was told you can tell us the urban legends around here," I cut in, smiling at the nod. "I'd very much like to learn about your haunted road."

"I can tell you all about it," he grins. "It's even older than this town; the story. Back before the town was founded, there was a dispute between the gypsies and a group of settlers. They would be the ones to trigger the event that gave birth to this place. Their leader was the father of our founder."

"Crazy," I frown. "What happened?"

"The gypsies had a camp outside town, where that old apple orchard is. Their wagons were pulled into a circle, they lit a fire in the center, and the night was filled with their music. They were a traveling people, but the settlers… they weren't.

"Among the gypsies was a kind woman. She saw the hardships faced by the settlers, and attempted to help them. Their leader was too proud to accept it, though. When snow began to fall, food was scarce. The women accepted what was offered behind their leader's back. When he found out, he and his men snuck into the caravan. Every door was barred, every gypsy trapped… and then they were burned to the ground. The woman that helped them had been found and forced to watch her people, her family, die before her. She cursed them with her dying breath. When the settlers didn't come home, our founder went to locate his father. They found nothing but the ruins of both camps… and all the personal items taken with the first group.

They built the first part of our town and began a search. No one was ever found. They did, however, find a small grouping of apple trees… right where the caravan was. They gathered the apples, hoping to make it a food source. The first couple people that ate them died. The apples were poisoned. The next day, they set fire to the orchard. When they went back to plant over it, the trees were untouched. There were even more saplings growing… the exact number they lost to the poison.

Ever since, all month on the anniversary, more saplings sprouted. Now, it's a massive orchard no one can use. I imagine it'll eventually spread to overcome the town."

I'm stupefied, unable to think of something to say. Jonathan is truly skilled at storytelling. When I manage to shake myself from my daze, I glance at Nixie. She, too, is astounded. Pleased with himself, Jonathan sits back and grins. The story is very unbelievable, I've heard of gypsies cursing people in the past, yet nothing ever came of it but bad luck. The idea of coincidence nibbles at my mind. Obviously, that's not among the choices I've been dealt. If it were, I wouldn't be here.

"Thank you, Mr. Marley."

"Just Jonathan will do. Please, share any findings you get from there. You *are* going, right?"

"Unfortunately, peril has always been in my cards. Have a wonderful day, I'm sure we'll be in touch."

We rise and Jonathan walks us to the exit. We say goodbye one more time, and then head for the truck. Everything has slowed down a bit, the people inside or just sitting about. The truck is untouched. I move the bags into the truck's bed, taking the passenger seat. Nixie starts the engine, pulling out and heading to our temporary lodging.

The scenery will be burned into my mind for a long time. Swaying branches and bright flowers stretch for miles. The cabin is still just as impressive than my first sight of it. As we unload groceries, I catch movement from the corner of my eye. It's in the direction of the orchard. That's the only reason I pause. The cautious side of me wants to leave it be, but the 'detective' in me wants to follow.

"Nix, I'll be right back."

"You better be," she replies. "I'll start dinner."

I nod and hurry into the trees. It isn't very sunny anymore, the layer of thick branches shutting out the light. I hear whispered giggles and snapping twigs. As I follow, I notice the trees change. This isn't the orchard, the cabin is a good two hour drive according to the map, but it *looks* like it. A figure darts across the thin path, shadowy and small. I reach a clearing, much like the one in my dream. Something rustles the brush behind me. I turn to face them, gasping in surprise. It's a child, clothes singed and tattered. His skin has melted off in places, hair burned to the root in patches, and I can see his entire eyeball on the right. No sound comes from him now, his body still and rigid. Only a few steps back has me in the clearing's center. Between every tree, identical children stand. With twisted grins on their mutilated faces, they raise a hand to point at me. I feel trapped in a horror film, waiting for the jump-scare made worse by anticipation. Just as I start to relax, I'm trapped in a funnel of flames. On reflex, I reach for the nearest water source. Before a connection can be made, something appears in the fires. A pair of eyes filled with such hate and betrayal, it makes my blood run cold.

"They will perish for his crimes!"

"Who's crimes?" I wonder. "Why does *anyone* need punished? I can't help you if you don't tell me."

"You cannot help the damned."

That phrase again. I wonder if, perhaps, it's going to be a theme. Surely they're not beyond saving. Without more information, though, my options are limited. Just as I'm about to press for more, the ground rumbles beneath my feet. It's pulled away and I tumble through darkness. I land on something soft, finding myself in a nest of leaves. The branches around me have a steady heartbeat. This tree is familiar to me... safe. That rhythmic beat calms me, and eventually I close my eyes.

Chapter 4

It's Nixie that wakes me, her worried tone drifting through the trees. Once I shake myself from my stupor, I force myself onto my feet. Nixie is just breaking through some brush. Her eyes are frantic, flooding with relief at the sight of me. I'm groggy, so she pulls me into a hug.

"What happened?" I wonder.

"What happened? What happened! You left an *hour* ago and didn't come back! I told you to come back!"

"An hour? But... it doesn't feel like it."

"You must've passed out. Are you okay? Were you attacked?"

"I don't think so," I frown. "She had ample opportunity, but only seemed to be warning me off."

We begin the walk back, my mind on nothing but the experience. I can feel concern from Nixie, yet I say nothing. If she really wants to know, she'll ask. When she finally does, I recount the events for her. She's quiet the entire time, just soaking in the information. I'm glad I'm not the only one to think it off, as the suspicion in her gaze tips. We're quiet for a bit longer, and then she parts her lips to speak.

"Why is she warning you away?" she frowns. "She wants victims, right? She should be eager to guide you."

"... Unless there's more to the story," I comment. "Maybe information lost to time... or sugar coated? It would be easy to distort history to your liking, after all."

"Wouldn't be the first time."

Back at the cabin, I can smell tomatoes upon entry. I recognize it as Nixie's spaghetti sauce. Although we have to warm it a bit, we sit down for dinner. Work has been hectic for the both of us, so this is our first meal together in weeks. I hadn't realized how much I missed it until now. In the silence of the table, I have time to wonder. I know Nixie isn't used to talking of her other life, but the arrival of her mysterious friend has ignited my curiosity.

"How long have you known Styx?" I question.

"Eons," she comments. "I was placed in his care when mom went on missions. After I turned ten, he would change his age to mirror mine. Still the voice of reason, but more relate-able. When I started training, he was occasionally my teacher."

"But... he's a Charon, not an Envoy."

"When the world was new, the gods and goddesses rising from the earth, Charon did everything. We were created when the world's population grew too much for him... Mainly, a time of war. Besides, his lessons are invaluable, because he's the oldest of us. He's had so much time to deal with spirits, to learn how to calm them and the best methods of breaking the news. That's what I learned from him."

I can only imagine the struggles he faced. To think the young man I saw is actually centuries old... I'm still wrapping my mind around Nixie's age! I'm about to continue my line of questioning, when the lights flicker. It happens a couple times, and then the cabin goes completely dark. I take in a slow breath, my heart beginning to pick up the pace. When the bulb above our table blows, I see a blinding flash of light. Nixie utters a cry of surprise.

Throughout the house we hear the pop of bulbs bursting, the shower of glass on wooden floors. When it dies down, I try to concentrate on the air around me. There's a strange energy in the house, and then I hear water running in the bathroom. Cautious, we walk in that direction. It's still dark and I bump my knee a couple times, but as soon as we turn the corner we can see. A dim light, eerie with a wash of yellow, spills from the doorway.

Against my better judgment, I push Nixie behind me and continue. Like every haunting in horror movies, I wait for the scare. Peeking in, I'm surprised to find nothing. The sink isn't running, the tub is. Holding my breath in anticipation, I brush aside the shower curtain. Submerged in the water is a red haired woman. Her eyes are sunken and opened wide, mouth twisted in agony. The liquid gets hotter around her, boiling and cooking her through. It should smell horrid, like burning flesh, but all I can smell is cooking apples. I'll never see apples the same way again.

"It'll go away," Nixie breathes in my ear. "Come on, let's take a walk."

"They aren't running us out," I state, stubborn. "I don't know what they're after, but I can't keep running away when I get freaked out. I won't get anywhere doing that."

"So... what? Should we have a seance?"

"No, I don't want to rile them more. I think we should just ignore them right now. In an hour or two, I'll head to the orchard. Maybe I can learn more at the source."

"You realize that doesn't always work, right?"

"I know that... I just prefer to ignore it," I answer, sheepish. "We don't have many options now anyway. Besides, at least this site isn't cursed. Might be nice working without a deadline... literally and figuratively."

"Still a deadline. It only acts up one month a year, so we don't even have a few days to prepare. The month is over in a week."

I sigh at the reminder, cursing quietly under my breath. The window of opportunity leaves little time to gather what we need. Already, we've let a day pass with nothing more than a story to show for it. I wish I could've gleamed more information from Adrian, yet didn't want to push too much. Losing her son had to have been nerve wracking enough without me needling her about it. Even now my fingers itch to dial her up. Unable to, as per our agreement, I start to gather a bag for the trip. It'll be short, but there are still some things I'll be needing. A flashlight, for instance, and a rope or two. Something to mark my way. The last thing I want is to get lost there. While I do this, I notice Nixie on her phone.

"Everything okay?" I wonder when she's done.

"Yeah, that was just a friend," she smiles. "I've been looking into past run-ins with the Roots. If this has happened before, we might be able to pinpoint our enemy. It would be nice to take the fight to them for once."

"Have you found anything?"

"Not much," she admits. "A couple sightings, maybe a few incidents, but nothing serious. The book I've been looking for was lost long ago. My friend has a lead on it, though."

"Just be careful, okay?" I warn. "Every time you get close to unveiling the enemy, someone dies."

"... This isn't a movie, Cat," she huffs. "Things aren't always so predictable."

I roll my eyes at her, kissing her cheek before she leaves. For a moment, I wonder who writes the books on Roots. Surely someone knows the history of... whatever I am. With a hum, I grab my bag. No better time to get work done. I head to the garage, picking up the truck keys on the way. Although I'm not eager to go, especially alone, I know this might be the best way to gather information. The orchard began when their lives ended. It's tainted by those deaths, devouring the memories left to replay later. That time is now.

The drive feels like an eternity, the anticipation drawing out each passing minute. When the trees come into view, I'm more than ready to get out.

The scene is foreboding and, while the sun still peeks above the horizon, very dark. There seems to be a tunnel created by the branches. I have my reservations, yet head in anyway. Entering the orchard is like entering an entirely different atmosphere. The air is chilled and stale, the scent of decay in a thin layer beneath grave soil. Guard up and ready for anything, I move into the thick. I stop a moment, and then pull out a rope. Tying it to the trunk of a tree, set right at the edge, I begin my journey more comfortably. The rope stretches behind me, ensuring I won't get lost.

Each tree looks different, the trunks twisted in all sorts of ways. It's intriguing, and yet... ominous. If you only look at the base, they resemble people. A woman on her knees here, a child reaching for the sky there. I'm horrified at the idea. Now that it's in my head, I can't get it out. Getting closer, I catch a couple lines of sap on the bark. It looks like tears of blood it's so red. The sun sets, vanishing with the only light source I have. Before I can retrieve my flashlight, an eerie glow radiates from the tree I'm only inches from. I back up quickly, looking around in surprise. Branches rattle, leaves floating down to the ground. A hand reaches for me, the 'weeping' tree glowing brighter. From the waist up, a woman's spectral image leans forward.

"*Leave this place! The damned roam these trees.*"

"... Yeah... I'm not really that intimidated," I answer. "You must know these trees pretty well, right? Do you know where the center is?"

"*You can't go there, you'll never leave. Even this close to the edge you risk becoming one of the lost.*"

"I can't just leave you all to rot," I frown. "You need to be at peace. I won't leave until I set you free. Where is the center of the orchard?"

"... *Follow the sun, you'll come across an old gnarled tree. Turn right and continue straight. The center is filled with burned soil and odd tree formations. They form a circle.*"

"Thank you."

"*You'll want to take that back in the end, I promise.*"

I ignore the remark, heading west on the lookout for a gnarled tree. The ground is oddly soft beneath my feet, considering the orchard seems dead. Leaves, fallen and scattered, crunch underfoot. It's the only noise aside from my breath. Such dark foreboding all around, I can barely stand it. These poor souls, punished for a crime they'll never know... I need to free them.

After walking for far too long, I reach the end of my second rope. I've also marked a few trees. It seems as though I'm getting nowhere despite my time spent. I glance behind me, noting a marked tree. When I turn to follow it back, giving up for now, another mark shows on a tree beside it... I didn't mark that one. Another look at my surroundings, and I know why that spirit feared me getting lost. *Every* tree is marked. I only traveled a few feet from the rope's end, yet it's nowhere to be seen.

"Shit," I huff. "Well... isn't this just perfect. I never thought I'd have to deal with a labyrinth situation. Now what do I do?"

I don't want to call Nixie, she won't let me live this down. I certainly won't be on my own anymore. With no other choice, I take out my cellphone. There's no service within these slain trees, the battery just as dead. Closing my eyes, I try talking myself out of screaming. If Shadow were here, he'd be able to guide me out. The thought, though saddening, also gives me an idea. I'm the Root of Soul, so maybe I can summon Nixie instead. I take a deep breath and close my eyes.

I haven't had the opportunity to discover this element's power, yet I'm hoping it works like the others. Typically, I can envision what I want to happen, and it will. In my mind, I see my body become translucent. I feel free, lighter than air, and almost drift off. Eyes open, I find my human body gone. In it's place is a specter that more than likely looks similar. I really wish my phone worked, it would've been a wicked selfie! With a calm sigh, I wonder how they're called. As I ponder their system, I feel something around my ankles. A glance down and I gasp. Tree roots are winding around me, trying to anchor me in the orchard. My panic rises, mind searching for any way to prevent this. My brain screams for Nixie.

A thin line of light is drawn down the air. For a moment, I think she heard me. When the doorway opens, however, I'm met with a black robe. Mischief shines in Styx's eyes as he walks over. The lantern that sways upon his staff spills light in the clearing. At my side, he uses it to tap the roots attacking me. With a hiss, they shrivel up and disappear. I'm quick to take my human form again.

"It's not a good idea to become a specter on cursed land," he chuckles. "You're lucky I was listening for lost souls."

"Someone needs to explain this system of yours," I huff. "I had no idea phones died in haunted places!"

"... I thought Nixie said you watched horror movies."

"Those are movies! They're not supposed to be real!" I comment, taking a breath to calm myself. "This orchard just wasted my time. I just wanted to get to it's center, find some clues on how to stop all this. Is that too much to ask?"

"How about I take you there?" Styx suggests. "I can't get lost around spirits, I can see their world and counter their tricks. Afterward, I'll get you back out."

"Fantastic! But... aren't you busy?"

"I've had eons to master getting caught up, I'll be fine."

Although I worry he's overestimating himself, I give him the benefit of the doubt. Together, we begin our search anew. I'm surprised when he moves back to where I started. Shrugging my shoulders, I trust his judgment and follow. I can still feel the phantom roots on my ankles, but it's slowly going away.

"These trees are the victims," I remark to fill the silence. "So many have fallen here."

"True. The thought is a sad one," he sighs. "I hate when spirits get left behind. Too many have suffered through the years."

"I was told this has happened before," I say. "I mean... the Roots being trapped in cursed places like this. Do you remember what happened? Who did it? What was their end game?"

"I know many things, yet some I can't speak of. Stuff like this, meticulously planned over many years, isn't likely to be the work of humans. A cult or coven, perhaps, but no one human. For the amount of time passed, it would have to be an immortal creature."

"Like you and Nixie?"

"Perhaps... even a god or goddess."

"... Figuratively, or literally?"

"Religions are not created without base. There really *are* myth, legend, and higher beings. Their stories may be exaggerated, or even false, yet they exist."

I'm stunned at this news. So many religions, so many possible enemies. The worry is beginning to nibble at my mind. Styx watches patiently, stopping for a moment.

When I glance up, I realize we're at the clearing. The scene strikes me, painting a picture of violence far past.

Chapter 5

I find myself speechless. A rare occurrence for me. In the center of the orchard, a ring of stones sits. Stains of black hint to a fire, yet the coals are cold. Rickety skeletons of wagons are further out, overcome by plants. Trees grow in groups here. One wagon has three, another has six, some infantile saplings or massive trees. They look like family photos, in a way. As we move forward, the scene changes. There's a spark from the stone circle, a bonfire igniting with little incentive. I hear voices on the wind, laughter and excited chatter. Wagons are rebuilt, trees transform back into people, and the eternal party begins.

"This must be that night," I murmur.

"Is this what you were looking for?"

"Yeah. The legend is only a part of this curse, I need to know the rest. What better way than to talk to those that were there?"

"I hate to break it to you, but a ouji board would probably be less dangerous."

I glare over at him, noting something I missed. Set in the trees, covered in moss, is a well. Unbidden, I move toward it. As I get closer, I can hear a small voice calling out. Styx is just behind me, curious as to what caught my attention. Cautious, I set my hands on the stone rim... and peek over the edge. A column of fire shoots up from the bottom of the shallow well. Just before it overcomes me, I feel a cold light on my skin. Styx has reached past me with his lantern, stilling the flames with its eerie light.

"Whoa," I utter. "That's awesome."

"You certainly are curious," Styx frowns. "How are you still alive?"

"Stubbornness and immortality," I answer. "Honestly, I should've died in that store. How did you do that? Can I learn?"

"My will is infinite," he remarks. "As an ancient, my presence demands submission from spirits. I can quell their fury and still their attacks. I imagine you'll also learn how after a few centuries."

"... Do you think you could teach me sooner?"

"Sorry, it's mastered over time. I can give you something to help, though. As soon as we get out of here."

I'm tempted to turn back right away. The only thing stopping me, is the fact it took forever to get here. Going back to the eternal party, I realize it's dying down. The moon overhead is a sickly green. Soon, no one is there but a lone woman. Her hair is red and long, decorated with beads and coins. Her dress is lengthy and colorful. I know at once she's the spirit haunting me. Tarnished emerald eyes watch me as she stokes the fire. Hoping it's an invitation, I warily close the distance between us. I hear Styx mumble some distorted comment, making sure to stay near.

The fire crackles as I near, spreading an odd sense along my skin. It isn't warm, but it isn't cold either. Rather, both at once. These opposing sensations give off the impression of being in limbo. Set at angles around the fire are thick tree trunks. They're cut lengthwise for makeshift benches. The gypsy takes a seat across from us, her eyes glowing through the fire. Styx remains standing, hovering just behind me.

"You've been warning me away," I point out. "Why? What happened here? I want to hear your side of the story."

"*This place was my home*," she starts. "*We lived off this land. When the settlers came, we tried to help them.*"

"I heard all of that," I assure. "And the women took your help behind their leader's back. So he locked you all in the wagons and set them aflame. What didn't they tell me?"

"You know the basics, what more do you need?"

"Why warn me away? Why punish innocent people for his crimes?"

"His blood is cursed," she hisses. "You are not of his blood. Not descended from any of them. Until he's brought to justice, all those related to them will suffer... Just as my family suffered."

She's nothing more than a vengeful cloud now, her form lost in her ire. That darkness spreads, devouring the land. Before I can answer her temper with my own, Styx grabs my upper arm. I'm yanked backwards just as the bonfire explodes. A wash of pure content spills throughout my veins, blinding blue light overcoming my senses. The next thing I know, I'm standing next to my borrowed truck.

"I see Nixie has her work cut out for her," he laughs, the sound just as quiet as his voice. "You really are a magnet for trouble. I'm very impressed with your compassion and conviction, though. Nixie took a century before she could talk to a *placid* spirit. You're already having civil conversations with vengeful ones."

"Well... it started civil," I grumble. "Thanks for the help, I really appreciate it. Nixie never would've let me live it down."

"She won't hear it from me," he assures, taking something from around his neck. "Here, you can have this."

I carefully accept the amulet given. A glowing orb is wrapped in thin gold, pulsing with my heartbeat. Eerie blue light reminds me of Shadow. I've yet to take off the ring I made for him... or rather, *from* him. Hesitant to take such an expensive looking gift, I give him a questioning glance.

"This is a special amulet," he explains. "The jewel is made from the waters of my namesake. Not only will it act as a compass here, but you can use it to contact me."

"How do I do that?" I wonder, amazed.

"What's your phone number?" Styx inquires, seemingly out of the blue.

"I don't know, I don't call... Wait... Okay, I get it," I mutter. "I guess I'll figure it out. Thank you, I hope I learn it soon."

"You're the Root of Soul, I'm sure it'll be child's play for you."

He turns and begins to walk away, opening a door to his river. All alone, I climb into the driver's seat and start the truck. Although I don't want to give up for the day, I know that there's little more I can do. Pulling out of my parking spot, I make my way back to the cabin. The glowing amulet around my neck glistens in the rear view mirror. It was nice of Styx to lend it to me. Eyes going back to the road, I nearly yank the wheel off. Someone is standing in the middle of the road. The truck swerves just in time. It comes to a stop in the grass, where I put it in park once more. The door is flung open as I exit, searching for whoever might be hurt. No one is there. No footprints, no broken twigs... no signs of life.

"Great, now I'm hallucinating," I mutter. "I really need a vacation."

I climb back in the truck, turning the key. A soft sigh to calm my nerves, and then I check the mirror to back up. My heart leaps into my throat. The girl from the road is in the backseat, figure dripping wet and eyes plucked from their sockets. I recognize her as the girl from the airport bathroom. I jerk the wheel in my surprise, foot slamming on the gas. The truck overshoots the street, stopping in the grass on the other side. Thankfully, there isn't really anything to hit. When I come to a stop, the back seat is empty. A puddle of water rests where she sat, wet footprints lay on the floor. This spirit isn't the same as the others. Maybe the same time period, but they aren't burnt like the orchard souls. I wonder, not for the first time, if there's more to the story.

Back at the cabin, I search for Nixie. She isn't back yet, but I don't want to be alone. Too much has happened already, I don't need things to get worse. Debating my choices, I decide to mess around with the amulet from Styx. I take it from around my neck. It dangles on the chain before me, glittering with the shine of the moon. I tap it with an extended finger, gasping in surprise when the glow strengthens. It's responding to my touch. Curious, I lay it in my palm. A line of light appears on the edge. This must be the compass.

"Honey, I'm home!" Nixie calls from the front door. "How'd the orchard trek go?"

"I needed a little help," I admit. "My phone didn't work there, so Styx ended up helping. Apparently, if I'm in a spirit form he can hear my call for help."

"I'll be sure to thank him," she says. "Did you learn anything?"

"Sure did! The victims are blood relatives to those in the settlers' group. Our terrifying gypsy cursed them all. I also met a spirit that might be connected, but died in a totally different way."

"What do you mean?"

"The orchard victims were burnt, but she was covered in water. If she's not connected in some way, why start appearing now? Maybe there's a legend of her as well. If they really are linked, she might know how to end this."

"Tomorrow," Nixie states. "Right now we both need sleep. I know we're in a time crunch, but if we don't care for ourselves, we won't be able to help anyone."

"Did you find your book?"

"She's pinpointing its location now. I'll know more tomorrow."

I nod, leading the way to the bedroom. In our pajamas, tucked beneath the covers, I contemplate our situation. I don't want Nixie to be in danger, yet I'm not naive enough to think she'd leave. Whether I like it or not, we're in this together. As I slowly drift off, I hear a scream in the distance. It sends ice through my veins. Eyes open wide, I look beside me. It sounded just like Nixie. She's already nodded off, though. Calming my breathing, I try to brush it off. Unfortunately, my stomach has gone sour from the shock. I close my eyes and try to force sleep. This mission has warning bells going off in my brain.

Chapter 6

I don't remember falling asleep. There was darkness behind my eyelids, and the rhythmic thud of my heart. Perhaps that's what lulled me into slumber. I'm no longer in bed, in the middle of nowhere. Now... I'm just *standing* in the middle of nowhere. Nothing but black soil and dead plants. The moon looks sickly, battered and ghostly.

"What is this place?" I wonder.

The land looks dead, but a field nearby offers food. A large black dog runs past me. Before I can coax it over, it turns to face me. Fire pours from its eye sockets. Three more dart past to join the first. They eye me, sniffing the air curiously. As quickly as they arrived, they're gone. Not far from my current location, I can make out a structure. That's the direction I head. As I make my way over, I search about in curiosity. Although covered in ashy soil, it appears I'm on a road. Rusted husks of cars lay scattered. Some have been flipped and a couple are newly abandoned. Movement by one reveals a man's half eaten carcass... and the murder of crows feasting. I gag and hurry by.

The building is old and scarred. Graffiti covers three of four walls, boards nailed to cover windows, and the chain-link fence is barred extensively. I frown and reach to touch it. Before I do, I feel a current of electricity. Yanking my hand away, I consider my options. A bit of water can short the fence, or I can use fire to melt a hole. Then again... people use electric fences for a reason. I don't want to endanger lives because of curiosity.

My body takes on a ghostly form. Hoping they really can go anywhere, I close my eyes and step forward. There's a slight tingling sensation, sparks drifting lazily between nerve endings, and then I'm on the other side. I cast aside my form, favoring the solidity of a human shell, and walk up to the door. The knock is hesitant, almost silent, but whoever lives here heard it. The door swings open, after a series of locks opening, and a shotgun barrel is in my face.

"Whoa," I murmur. "Is it too late to leave?"

"Who are you?" the gunman demands.

"I'm Catori," I frown. "Where am I?"

"You're trespassing on *my* land, that's where you are! Now get out of here before the hell-hounds catch you!"

"... Those big black dogs?" I inquire. "They already left."

"It's coming," he gasps. "Leave this place! Now!"

The door is slammed shut in my face. With a frown, I leave the way I came. Outside the fence, I grip Styx's amulet. Hoping I can still use it, I set it flat upon my palm. That thin line of light appears. For the first time since getting it, I follow its compass. Turning away from the north, I realize this compass isn't like others. The line still points the same way, sliding along the smooth jewel as I move.

"Hmm," I utter. "Maybe it shows where I *need* to go."

With nothing else to do, I go where it points. As I traverse, I can't help taking in the dead world. There's a small town up ahead, the houses in various states of ruin. Some as blackened from fires, but a lot still show signs of life inside. All of them are enclosed with fencing. This drastic measure for safety unnerves me. A howl in the distance reminds me of the hell-hounds wandering. I hope they're the danger these people guard against. Unfortunately, deep down, I know they're guarding themselves from something greater.

Children play in a battered playground, watching me with eyes that have seen too much. Although I don't approach them, they scatter and run toward the nearest house. An elderly woman ushers them in. fear and uncertainty is suffocating in the air. Trying my best to stay positive, I check the amulet again. The line has moved now, pointing to the left. A crooked metal post sports dirty street signs. They're so old I doubt anything can clean them.

The road is lined by houses, old stores, and what looks to be a church. The bell has fallen inside the tower, breaking through the wall at the bottom. The gold color is tarnished after so long, dimmed and rusted. It seems unused and abandoned. Colorful shards of stained glass litter the grass, sparkling like gems beneath a punishing sun. It's such a shame, ruining a beautiful work of art like that. With a sigh, I come to the edge of town. Large groupings of trees lie beyond it. It looks so similar to the orchard, I can't help but double-take the town. Though in shambles lost in history, the town looks like a broken version of the one we're camped near.

Slightly confused, I hurry to the orchard. The trees here hold bloody apples, which I do my best to avoid. The ground is littered with crimson droplets. Passing through the trees, the compass changes direction. I follow it, humming to myself in thought. When I enter the strange clearing, I notice an idle fire. The line of light slides to the right. Confused, I go in that direction. I didn't come this way with Styx. Dead and dying brush weaves a nasty barrier, thorns eager to taste blood. No weapon on hand, I let my hand ignite. The fires spread to create a tunnel before I banish them. As my first element, I'm getting a handle on it. I just wish my other two were as easy.

Carefully making my way through, I hear something. My pause is instinctual. Although I strain my ears, it doesn't sound again. With a shrug, my foot moves forward. This time I catch a muffled sigh. It's coming from the end of this tunnel. Every nerve ending is screaming to run away, but I push on. Whatever is at the end, the compass insists on facing it. I hold my breath, bursting into a new clearing with hopes of catching any threats off guard.

I'm the one caught off guard, though. The clearing is a mess of overgrown brush. Fighting through it, my foot catches on something. I'm swallowed by thigh-high grass. A yelp leaves my lips as I go down, and I fight to clear the foliage. My fire won't take here, so I try another approach. My eyes close, picturing a blade of water. I try to ignore the panic rising, as it feels like my lungs are filling up. Picture firmly in my mind, I open my eyes. There's no sword, but the grass is so wet it's been pressed to the dirt. At least the flood helped. It makes it easier to ignore the failure.

Now clear of obstruction, I notice something puzzling. An old, broken sign is sunk into the dirt. It looks to be baring a carved name. The gypsy settlement is a solid hour or two from here, but I hadn't heard of a town before the developed one we visited. It strikes me, the settlers had to have built when they moved. Realizing this is where they started, I pay closer attention.

Beams to log cabin frames are set in four or five places. Picnic tables, rotted and left for time, still have decayed food on them. The larger frame still has a fireplace, although the chimney was knocked down long ago. A few stones are scattered behind it. My eyes fall upon a figure in the trees' shade. It's the dark haired spirit from the truck. Her body drifts deeper into the trees, as though she's on wheels and someone is pulling a rope around her waist. It sends shivers through me. Practically begging my amulet, I glance down to it. The line follows after the spirit.

"Of course it does," I mutter to myself. "Haunted forest, creepy little girl... what part of that doesn't scream 'meet your maker'?"

Steadying my racing heart, I walk toward her retreating form. Quite a ways into the trees, I find her hovering over a well. It looks suspiciously similar to the one that spewed fire. When I approach this time, she doesn't move. I can hear my heart thumping in my ears with each step closer. Near the edge of the well, she parts her lips. I take that as a sign, coming to a stop at once. I can see that she grips something close to her chest. When nothing is uttered, I take the chance to speak.

"I saw you before," I remarks. "What is it you want to tell me?"

"*Find me and save them,*" she answers, voice a near whisper. "*Find me... Find... Can you hear it? Listen... Hear it... save them all...*"

"Where are you?" I wonder, her body beginning to sink into the well. "Wait! How do I find you? I don't even know your name!"

"*Find me... I'm... I'm waiting... so long... the wait. Find me, please... take me home... it's the wishing well.*"

The dark swallows her and her words stop. I'm alone one more time. The amulet in my hand warms, blinking like a warning. I only look away for a moment, but when my gaze returns to it... the well is gone. It's disappearance startles me, but the amulet is enough of a distraction. The glow shifts, drawing a frown from me. I wish I knew how to call Styx, he would know who that girl is. A twig snaps and my eyes dart to that direction. Fog is rolling in, and lights are bobbing within it. An eerie chill rests upon the air. One of the lights pause, and then moves toward me. I'm in the open, nowhere to hide. As a shadowy figure joins the light, I hold my breath.

"Catori?" Styx calls, breaking through the fog. "How'd you get here?"

“I'm sleeping,” I frown. “How'd you get into my dream?”

“... This isn't a dream,” he sighs. “This is one of many afterlives.”

“Seriously?” I gape. “How'd that happen? Did I die in my sleep?”

“No, you're not dead. If you were, I wouldn't wonder how you got here.”

“I think... the girl in the well... that just conveniently vanished... I think she called me here. Is that even possible?”

“It is, though highly unusual. You being the Root of Soul would strengthen the chances, but... this isn't a good place for the living. I know you're immortal, but you'll see things here that will haunt you for the rest of eternity.”

“... Well... that sounds nice.”

“We should get you out of here.”

He opens a doorway in the fog, ushering me through before following. We're outside the cabin on the other side. I invite him in, finding Nixie pacing the living room. I'm in her arms the second she sees me. Styx is about to leave when I stop him. When we're all seated, Nixie thanks him again... although it's exasperated. I understand her tone, but I wasn't exactly *looking* for trouble. Not this time, at least.

“I had told you about a girl's spirit,” I remark. “She was in a well. When I looked your way, the well disappeared. Do you know of her? And... what were *you* doing there? Are you stalking me?”

“I regularly visit cursed sites with my higher ranking Charon,” he explains. “Today was no different... Well... aside from the pull of that amulet.”

“Where did you find her?” Nixie frowns. “And what amulet?”

“He let me borrow his amulet,” I inform, showing it to her. “I think I learned how to use the compass.”

"I found her in limbo," Styx offers.

"What!" Nixie shouts. "How the hell did you get dropped off in limbo!"

I shrug in answer. With everything that's happened to me thus far, I'm not really surprised I ended up there. We attempt to talk her down from a panic attack, only just succeeding. In an attempt to change the subject, she grasps the amulet I hold out to her. Her gaze is studious as she looks it over. With her in a time-out, I turn back to Styx. He must know *something* that can help us.

"The little girl," I press. "The well she was in was the same in the orchard. She wants me to find her... says it will save everyone. What do you know about her?"

"Not much," he frowns. "She isn't much of a talker. Our interactions are rare and she seems to be lost. Not only forgotten like the others, but she *literally* doesn't know where her body is."

"Would there be a myth about her?" Nixie asks.

"You'll want to ask about 'the wishing well'," he offers. "That's all I can tell you. I'm sorry I can't be of more help."

"It's okay," I sigh. "At least we have a direction now. I just hope she has the answers we need."

"I should be getting back," Styx remarks. "Stay out of trouble and get some rest... *Both* of you. I'll talk to you later."

"Styx, keep your ears open," Nixie states. "I'm looking for a book lost to time. The 'history of magic'. If you find anything..."

"You'll be the first to know."

We walk him to the door, bidding him a good night. As we return to bed, I can't help thinking of that girl's words. When she said 'everyone', it sure felt as though it was meant for more than the orchard. If that's the case, perhaps she knows more than I originally thought. I'm still awake when Nixie goes under again. Though I try to fight the hold of slumber, the struggle is futile. My eyes droop, and then close. Right before I nod off, I hear that scream in the distance.

Chapter 7

I'm woken by sunlight peeking through the curtains. Nixie is still sleeping beside me, so I sneak from bed. There's no point waking her. I head to the bathroom to get ready for the day. While I'm in the shower, beautiful bubbled glass doors closing me in, I have a flashback of the store. If not for Nixie that would've been my *last* shower. Calming my nerves, I take a deep breath. The hot water has steamed up the room, so when Nixie comes in I don't bother to search her out. She's at the sink, figure blurry through the glass door.

"I'm thinking of visiting the historian today," I comment, rinsing shampoo from my hair. "I'm curious what he might know. Afterward, I'll check out the orchard again. I didn't realize the settlement was still sort of standing. Maybe I'll find..."

"Who are you talking to?" Nixie questions from the other room.

I pause, shocked. There's still movement in the bathroom. The water feels so much colder than before. I watch frost spread on the glass door, creating the shape of a hand. I breath in sharply, hand slowly grasping the door's handle closing my eyes, I yank it open. No one is on the other side. The relief I feel is like a flood. I wrap a towel around me after turning off the water, walking over to the mirror. One hand wipes off the steam... and my heart drops. Standing behind me, is the drown girl. The scream in the back of my throat is swallowed.

"Cat? You okay?" Nixie wonders.

"Uh... fine," I reply.

"*Find... save them all,*" the girls states. "*Can you hear it?*"

She's gone just as Nixie opens the door. I know my face is pale, my heart still hammering in my chest. Nixie must feel the supernatural freeze, as she shivers and pulls me from the room. I'm forced to get dressed by the bed. As I do, she investigates the bathroom. The frozen hand print has yet to fade, and frost frames the mirror. When she returns, her eyes are frigid.

"Who was it?" she practically demands. "Was it that psycho from the orchard?"

"No. It was the girl in the well."

"Spirits can be so rude," she huffs.

"I thought it was you," I offer, sheepish. "That's why I was talking. I was laying out my daily schedule."

"I wish I could go with you, but there was a natural disaster on the other side of the globe. They're calling as many of us as possible."

"That's fine. I'm going back to the historian, maybe he knows about the girl in the well. I also found the settlers' first home in the limbo orchard. With any luck, it'll be here also."

"Play it safe," she warns. "I'll make sure Styx checks up on you."

"I don't need a babysitter."

"Of course you don't... he does. It gives him something to focus on; keeps him out of trouble."

I can't help but roll my eyes. I gather my things and kiss Nixie goodbye, heading to the garage. The drive to town is lost on me, as I've already begun thinking through my impending conversation. The last thing I need is to ruin his hobby all the more. My guard is on high alert now, unwilling to be surprised once again. Parking next to the grocery store, I lock up the truck and start walking. I may have been able to park closer, but the walk helps clear my head. At the archives, the door is locked tight. It's closed today for some unknown reason.

My mind goes blank, plans erased in this moment of bafflement. The whole day was planned around this meeting. I can only stand here, mouth slightly opened as I try to figure out my next move. Someone stops beside me, their little girl running into the grass to pet a stray cat.

"Excuse me, but are you looking for something?"

"I actually came here to speak with the historian."

"Oh, you'll find him in the cemetery today," she smiles. "I heard there's an elderly ghost he visits, or something. The guy's odd, but sticks to his routine."

"How do I get there?"

"Take this street down two blocks and turn left. You can't miss it from there."

"Thanks so much," I state, hurrying the way she points.

The shops are beginning to thin, giving way to houses. There's a large park next to a school. It's sectioned off and decorated according to age. Tennis courts, a skate park, and swing-sets. Across the street, I see the iron gates of the cemetery. It's a large place, holding generations from this town. A couple cars are parked on the path, their occupants sitting by the graves of loved ones. In the center is a mausoleum surrounded by benches. An elderly woman watches the birds there, seated beside the man I'm looking for.

With hope renewed, I begin the trek there. The sun is warm upon my skin, reminding me of the perfect weather. With a light sigh and a small smile, I relish that warmth. Dealing with the dead leaves a nasty cold about me. The wind picks up, drifting past me in a soft breeze. It seems to wrap around me, lingering a bit too long. I chalk it up to the presence of other souls.

As I approach my target, I try hard to keep from scaring the woman off. She doesn't seem to notice me at first. I sit beside Johnathan, waiting for him to say something. His eyes are distant, filled with sadness, and I realize he knows the woman. Not by word of mouth, or even from the news. He knew her in life.

"Her name is Amelia, she's my grandmother," he informs, never taking his eyes off the ground. "I know she's here, I can feel her... but I could never see her."

"She's sitting beside you," I point out. "She seems to enjoy watching the birds."

"It calmed her," he murmurs. "She died a few years ago, but I still come visit every week."

"You two must've been really close."

"We were," he smiles, sad. "What did you need?"

"I know my timing is horrible, but... do you know anything about a haunted well?"

He frowns a moment, thinking through the lore he's studied for years. I find I'm holding my breath in anticipation, so I force myself to breathe. His grandmother looks over to me, giving a shy wave. Her eyes are expectant, though. As if she knows she'll never be seen by the living. Not wanting her to feel left out, I wave back. Her eyes light up in surprise and cheer. Johnathan narrows his brow in question, and looks beside him. The bitter chill of loneliness has been replaced with warmth.

"How do you do it?" he asks. "See them, I mean."

"I don't know," I admit. "I didn't always, though. When I saw the first ghost, I just kept going back. I wanted to save them, to help them cross. Once I set my mind, more came to me. Maybe it'll work that way for you. Just open your eyes and your heart... but throw away your fear."

"... There are a couple stories about a well," he comments after a pause. "I've come to suspect they're the same one, though. People have reported hearing a little girl calling out. Those that followed the voice to help her, were led to an old well. A little girl sits on the edge, she asks them what they wish for most in the world. If they choose something with good intentions, that wish comes true within a week. Should they choose something born of greed or ill will, however, she jumps into the well. Her heartbreaking screams linger in the minds of the selfish wisher forever, driving them into a horrible insanity.

I found it once... the well. My grandmother was so very sick, she fell into a coma. When the little girl asked me what I most wished for, I told her I just wanted my grandmother to be happy. As if she knew what I was talking about, she asked me, 'even if she passes'? I told her, whatever would make her happy... I just wanted her to be happy. I could've asked for her health, or a longer life, or even a miracle... but I asked for her happiness... and then she was gone. I tried to undo what I did, I looked everywhere for that well. It doesn't show in the same place, though. It's very random. I never saw her again."

"Do you know the girl's name," I question, trying to prob gently. "Her story? Anything to help me locate her?"

"Hmm... my great grandmother used to tell me about a little girl. It was a tale to warn us away from the orchard. She used to say there was once a little gypsy girl that ran away from home. While in the orchard, she came across a well. As she pulled up a bucket for water, she leaned too far in and fell. No one knew to look for her, and no one saw her again."

"How true is that story?"

"I'm not sure," he admits. "I knew the little girl was one of the gypsy children, because of her clothes when I met her. She typically appears close to the orchard's edge, which would indicate she disappeared there. And she fell in that well. The cuts and bruises along her body hinted to that. How and exactly where it happened is a mystery."

The information isn't completely helpful, but it's not a waste. At least I know she's affiliated with the orchard spirits. If that's so, and she appears mostly in the orchard, I just might run across her today. I thank him and begin to stand, stopping at the chilly hand on my wrist. His grandmother levels her gaze with mine. As Johnathan watches, she leans forward and whispers in my ear. Afterward, she smiles and a light shines beside us. A woman I've never met before walks out, dressed in the armor of an Envoy. Her hair is dark, short, and her eyes are icy despite her smile.

"Thank you," she says to me. "I've been trying to get her to pass for a couple years. Since I haven't been stationed on the mortal plain, I can't interact with humans."

"... You have to be *stationed* here?"

"Sort of. Born Envoys are able to walk any world, but appointed Envoys are trapped among the spirits."

"I guess that makes sense, but... it just seems so limiting."

She shrugs her slender shoulders, reaching her free hand out toward Johnathan's grandmother. With one last glance my way, she takes the offered hand. They both walk through the light. The second that door closes, her warm presence leaves with her. Johnathan's face expresses distress, so I'm quick to calm him.

"She's finally able to pass over," I explain. "All she wanted was to find someone to give you a message. She says she loves you very much. You're a wonderful and talented young man. She also told me to thank you for the wish you made, she was so tired of fighting. The only regret she had, was that she couldn't say goodbye to you. You made a very brave and selfless request."

He's crying now, tears of happiness. With the message passed, I leave him to his visit. He doesn't seem to notice that I bid him a good day. The orchard is my next stop, so I'll grab lunch on the go. I may need to picnic with it, but the thought is appealing today.

Leaving the cemetery, I feel eyes on my back. With a shiver at the sensation, I turn to locate them. A shadowy figure lingers around a large statue. When I blink, however, they're gone. Shrugging it off, I walk back to the truck. Before getting in, though, I go inside the store. One sandwich, pop, and a bag of chips later, I start the ignition. Hesitant of a random scare, I check the backseat before putting my foot on the gas.

The streets are just getting busy as the day reaches noon. It's no surprise, yet my guard is up and ready. There have been too many near hits, and a single fatal one, for me to rest easy on the road.

Chapter 8

Outside of town, the roads are clearer. The occasional car passes, but they're few and far between. As much as I approve of the absence, I'm also a bit disappointed. Now I'm utterly alone, facing down death with no one beside me... with no one to protect. Forcing my thoughts onto my current goal, I continue on.

My window is down, so I don't think much of the wind in my face. It has a strange calming effect on me. My head begins to hurt and I'm forced to pull to the side of the road. It feels as though something is gripping my heart in my chest, squeezing without mercy. I tumble from the truck and fall to my knees in the grass. So intense, the pain, I vomit into a nearby bush. As I grip my head and close my eyes to the agony, I hear someone breath my name. Arms wrap around me from behind and my body begins to cool. As the pain starts to recede, I get lightheaded and pass out.

When I open my eyes next, I'm nowhere near the truck. In fact, I can't even see it in the distance. Instead, I'm sitting beside an old Honda. A little boy sits in the backseat, playing with a few action figures. The driver's side and passenger doors are open, a GPS glitching on the dashboard. Near the edge of the orchard, his parents stand. They're still and seem mesmerized by something. I struggle to my feet and wander closer. When I stand between them and the trees, I note their eyes are empty. Pupils are dilated and faces are blank. Slowly, they start to step toward the cursed trees.

"No, wait!" I state, pushing them away. "You can't go in there! You'll never come back!"

Although I use all the strength I possess, the father pushes past me. I manage to hold the mother longer, though. Wrestling her to the ground, I glance back at the car. The little boy is watching curiously. His hand reaches for the handle, cracking open the door.

"No!" I shout. "Stay in the car! It's dangerous out here, you'll be killed!"

There's hesitation in his eyes, and then he closes the door. A scream from the orchard draws my attention, I curse under my breath. The trees have devoured him, his soul beginning to twist into a new sapling. Just as I think the woman has gathered her wits, a branch slams into me. I'm thrown to the side, forced to watch as she's lifted up and added to this sick collection. My only solace, is the little boy that still sits in the car.

The trees have stilled, leaving the car be, and I'm able to stand. With a sigh of misery, I amble over to the car. Opening the backseat door opposite him, I climb in to sit. When I shut the door, he crawls to the front seat and locks them all. Afterward, he climbs back over.

"What happened?" he asks, tears in his eyes. "Where are my parents?"

"… I'm so sorry, honey," I remark. "They're gone now. The orchard took them."

"They're… they're dead?" he cries.

"I'm sorry, I couldn't save them. I tried, but… the pull was too strong. I'm just glad it didn't take you as well. I need you to stay in the car, okay? I'm going to call someone to retrieve you. If you leave this car, the trees will probably try to capture you as well."

"I don't want to be alone."

"I can't stay, but I promise you'll be fine if you just stay here."

"… Okay," he says, quiet and timid. "Please hurry."

"I will."

I hold his hand, trying to assure him as best I can. there's a pull on my back, my body loses solidity, and then I'm yanked back to the truck. My head is dizzy as I stand up, staggering to the truck's hood to lean. Although

I'm still trying to gather my senses, I rummage around for my cell phone. The second I grasp it, I dial Nixie's number. I wish I knew the number for the police station.

"Cat?" she answers. "Everything okay?"

"There's a little boy," I start. "His parents were just taken by the orchard, but I had him lock himself in the car. I can't get back to him, I don't know where he is."

"I'm on my way," she states. "You sound like you need a rest, don't push yourself."

I hum in agreement, hanging up after saying 'goodbye'. My body slides to the grass, and I take a moment to breathe. It takes me a little while, yet soon I'm ready to continue on. I enter the truck, reaching for the key. As I turn the ignition, I feel a chill on the back of my neck. Someone… some*thing*… runs a hand over my hair. It's an affectionate gesture, yet that doesn't make it any less creepy. Trying to brush it off, I step on the gas and return to the old road.

Chapter 9

Near the orchard, I park the car and get out with my lunch. Sitting on the bed of the truck, I eat and take in nature. A few birds sing nearby. The melody only comes from the opposite side of the orchard. From the trees, I only hear a deafening silence. The sun's warmth seems to end abruptly at it's border as well. A rabbit hops about just beyond the tree line. At first, I'm tempted to pull it out. Upon closer inspection, however, I can see its transparency. Nothing living touches that place.

It's a sad thought, no doubt. With a sigh, I look down at my food. That little boy bothers me, I didn't want to leave him all alone. What if the trees lured him out of the car? What if they broke through the car? It makes my stomach sick. Hoping to get some good news, I pull out my phone and call Nixie again. It takes a minute, but she answers.

"Hey, Nix, did you find that kid?" I wonder.

"I did, he was on the far side of the orchard. I'm afraid he may have been a bit traumatized, but I found out he has living relatives. I'm taking him to the police station right now."

"They won't believe what happened."

"No, they won't. But if the child tells them, they'll know his parents were taken… or maybe they'll assume he's been abandoned."

"It's a terrible thought to live with, but at least he's alive."

"Are you at the orchard now?"

"I'm next to it, eating lunch. I can see some animals there… they're all dead. Living on in the afterlife."

"Be careful out there, I've heard some pretty messed up stuff from the other Envoys. No one dares to go to that place alone."

"It's nothing new for me," I shrug off. "A lot of trapped souls, a long warped story, and possibly a demon to destroy. I've already danced this little jig."

"Don't get cocky, that's when the evil wins."

I assure her I won't, and then we say goodbye. I tuck my phone back in my pocket. As I pick at my chips, I can't help listening to the noises around me. A little chorus of grasshoppers are scattered within the grass. Their chirping is lulling me to sleep. I take a deep breath, enjoying the smell of fresh rain and grass. Although previously still, a gust of wind ruffles my hair. It's warm and welcoming.

As I munch on my sandwich, I slide off the truck's gate. My feet carry me along the road, skirting the trees carefully. There's movement in them. Any normal person would chalk it up to the wind in tree limbs, however I know better. I can see the misty figures floating about, I can hear their echoic whispers and suppressed screams. This place is filled with sorrow, regret, and hatred.

"What secrets do you hide from me?" I wonder aloud. "How many souls were innocent, yet murdered anyway?"

"*Asking those types of questions, usually leads one to their end.*"

I inhale sharply, turning to find who speaks. It's the woman from the bonfire. Cautious, as our last meeting didn't end well, I move closer to her. She seems calmer right now, almost accomplished. When I take a seat in the grass near her, she does the same. It makes me feel less threatened, relaxes my guard a bit.

"Why are you doing this?" I frown. "Those people never did anything wrong. Why punish the innocent for the mistakes made in the past?"

"*You are a strong woman,*" she comments. "*Very strong, very brave... and very smart. I have no doubt you shall learn what the others have forgotten.*"

"Why can't you just tell me?"

"*You won't learn anything if everything is just handed to you. This tragedy has been woven around many stories, many lost souls. If you want to learn of a single spirit, you'll need to remember the rest.*"

It's frustrating and I nearly scream in irritation. I close my eyes, pinching the bridge of my nose, and then I look back at her. She's already gone. Throwing my hands in the air, I head back to the truck. The figures I saw before, seem to be hiding now. I wonder if it's because the gypsy showed herself. I know I would be afraid of my captor.

Back at the truck, I pick myself up on the tailgate once more. My food tastes bland now, as I'm too focused on my encounter to appreciate it. If this curse is derived from multiple stories, I have a lot more investigating to do. All I know at the moment, is about the gypsy curse. What other characters are in play here? With a sigh of reluctance, I turn my attention to what I'm eating. I can only hope this trip will be a walk in the park, yet I'm not about to hold my breath on that.

After finishing my lunch, I pack away the garbage and face the trees. Styx's amulet is in one hand, pointing the way. Stepping into the orchard has a different feel this time. There's more static and the temperature has dropped. It isn't much of a difference, yet I can feel it. The orchard is beginning to stir.

Chapter 10

Beneath the shade of the thick canopy, the silence lies heavily upon my shoulders. The amulet in my hand sways, slowly leaning to the right. My feet follow it. As I edge deeper, I begin to feel eyes on me. Ghostly faces peek from bark, hesitant to engage. For now, I allow them that refuge. Shadows of animals, long since decayed, leap between the thick trunks. A pale fox darts in front of me, slipping beneath another bush.

The wind begins to whisper to me. A soft tone upon dead space. The spirits are questioning my presence, trying to learn if I'm a target. The amulet points at a massive tree, gnarled and thick. Something about it is different than the rest. Going around has the needle pointing the other way. With a quiet hum, I reach over and knock on the trunk. It's done as gently as possible. A portly man's face leans out.

"*What do you want?*" he snaps. "*Come to remind us of the lives we lost?*"

"Of course not," I state, affronted. "I'm trying to set you all free. My compass thought I should talk to you. Can you tell me what happened?"

"*What's to know? The chancellor angered that gypsy woman, and then we were dead!*"

"He angered her that badly? Why would he kill them all over a little bit of food? I mean, I could understand if you guys were starving and *took* their food, but... they were *giving* it to you."

"*Is that what they're saying?*" he laughs, humorless. "*I suppose to save face is instinctual. If they knew the truth, no one would follow the family again.*"

"I *knew* there was more to the story!" I cheer. "What *really* happened?"

"... *I don't know as much as his friend, but... I could help you a little. Of course, it's not without it's cost.*"

"Of course," I sigh. "What do you need me to do?"

"*I was on a hunting trip when I died. My wife and son were at home, waiting for me. We had a tradition on hunting trips. She would give me her necklace to wear, so I always had her with me. When I got home, I would give it back to her. I want her to know I'm okay, so could you give her this?*"

One branch dips down, a golden locket with etched roses hangs from it. As I reach for the trinket, thin branches untangle to drop it in my hand. Before I can ask about the information, one thin branch taps the end of my nose. I keep quiet, recognizing the interaction. My father does it, though mostly in my youth, when I get impatient. Seeing my compliance, the ghost nods his approval and continues.

"*I don't have the best memory, but my Betty can remember the slightest detail. Give her that necklace and she'll know you're a friend.*"

"Thank you. I'll make sure she gets it."

He retreats back into his tree. Now alone, I glance down to see the compass has moved. Leading me past the old tree, it shifts to the left. Although it feels like walking in circles, I trust the amulet leading me. When my surroundings change, however, I wonder if trusting it could be a mistake. The fog rolling in is so thick, it looks like smoke around my ankles. Already lacking light from the canopy, the trees are getting darker.

At first, I wonder if the spirits are getting more restless. Perhaps the gypsy woman is getting ready to attack. My body tenses, eyes searching for any threat. The hair on the back of my neck is on end, a feeling of dread overcomes me. When I step up to one of the older trees, something drops from the branches. I scream, falling to the ground in my hasty retreat. My heart pumps violently in my chest, one hand over it, and my eyes are as big as dinner plates. The laughter I hear afterward sets my blood boiling. My eyes shift toward it. Although I see mostly black cloak, the pulsing of my amulet gives him away.

"Styx!" I snap. "You could've killed me!"

"Oh man, I didn't think you'd be that easy," he laughs. "I'm glad I didn't do the whole 'Grim Reaper' act, you probably *would've* died."

"You're supposed to be ancient! How could you be so immature?"

"It's actually a lot easier than you'd think," he snickers, pulling me to my feet. "Nixie asked me to check up on you. Anything interesting happen?"

"My life flashed before my eyes," I remark, expression a pointed glare.

"Was it at least a good part?"

I sigh, catching a glimmer of mischief in his eyes. That alone tells me he's much like Nixie. It doesn't matter what I say, he'll find humor in the verbal spar. Short of punching him in the face, the only way to stop him is to change the topic. I don't know about everyone else, but I'm not even a little curious what happens when an immortal power is attacked. Once he realizes I won't fuel his fire, he pouts and turns to walk away. I note he's going in the direction the amulet points. I can't help but wonder if he's used it so much he can anticipate it, or if he never needed it. I hurry to walk beside him.

"Nixie said you had to check on me, so you'd stay out of trouble. But it seems an impossible task," I say.

"It keeps me young," he smiles. "Literally, not just figuratively. We appear the age we feel, so our appearance can fluctuate depending on our emotions."

"That's so weird," I murmur. "How could you stand suddenly aging twenty or so years all at once?"

"We don't really have much choice, but it's something you get used to quickly. So, any luck yet? Tired of seeing the dead?"

"Why would you ask?"

"It's a blessing and a curse," he points out. "Or so I've been told throughout my millions of years. More-so a curse to the living. Which do you find it to be?"

"It makes life interesting, that's for sure. Like everything else, it has it's drawbacks… but I wouldn't change anything."

"You've done a lot of good for the afterlife. I have no doubt you were meant for greater feats."

I gaze at him a moment. His expression has changed. Age has caught up to him, though not literally. Eyes solemn as he watches the path ahead, a strange calm and air of knowledge surrounds him. His eyes have seen too much for the age he portrays. Even though I have a feeling he knows more than he's telling, I brush it off for now.

"You didn't answer my other question," he reminds. "What have you learned?"

"Well, there's definitely more to the story than history indicates," I smile. "I'm delivering this necklace to another spirit, and then she should fill me in more. I guess you could say your timing was perfect."

"I aim to please."

We walk in silence for a while, trying to rid myself of the creepy image the orchard provides. The air is a suffocating still, growing colder the deeper we go. As ominous as the aura radiating from Styx is, I'm glad he's with me. It helps to be reminded I'm not facing this alone. And, though he's the guide for the dead, I'm comfortable around him. He glances sidelong in my direction, smirking at my attention. I imagine it's rare for him to interact with the living.

"Did you hear about the treasure here?" he questions.

"Treasure?"

"You don't honestly believe all these victims were lured here, do you?"

"Aren't they all related to those first settlers?"

"No, not all of them. The curse didn't start getting picky until a few decades ago. When the orchard was only a few trees in total, random travelers were common," he explains. "Back then, a survivor managed to spread his story. He said that in the very heart of the orchard, he found a tree that held a single apple. The apple, according to him, was made of solid gold. That, of course, led many to their deaths."

"… Was it true?"

"I never saw it myself, but the rumors hold strong with their spirits. Now they insist on seeing it themselves. they're all rather bitter about having no need for it."

"You sure know a lot," I comment. "Is it mostly rumor?"

"The dead like to talk, that's true enough, but no. I like to learn and I learn by listening. The spirits aren't the only ones that like to talk, and I'm very easy to overlook. No one thinks about me being there before speaking. No one talks to me unless they absolutely must, so there's no one for me to speak with."

I almost let a pitied glance escape, yet squash it just as quickly. I don't pity him, that won't help in the long run. The only thing I can do is befriend him. He needs a friend more than misguided pity. I wrap an arm around his waist, as he's too tall for me to reach his shoulders. He seems surprised and hesitant. Although my wrist sinks a bit too far in, I don't move away. I know there's a gaping hole there, my hand settled on bone, but I just smile at his questioning gaze.

"Their loss," I smirk. "So, do you think this tree lady really knows everything? I didn't think about it before, but… that guy could've been full of it."

Styx stares at me a moment, and then we break into laughter. Honestly, I never even thought to doubt the elderly man. I'm just glad my mistake can make him laugh again. Not just because he deserves to be happy, but because these spirits deserve to be reminded what happy sounds like. We wander through the trees, the conversation turning toward more uplifting topics. I tell him about my family, and he tells me about his past with Nixie. He was almost with her more than her mother from the sound of it. A few crows fly overhead, yet their calls are lost to the silence. It unnerves me that this place seems to exist in a bubble, locked away from time. It's a suffocating thought, yet one I can't remove from my mind. Although I thought I hid it better, Styx seems to hear my thoughts.

"This is a lost place," he comments. "They're typically lost in time. Completely removed from the timeline of the living. This place doesn't exist anymore in your world. It only appears there on a single day within a year, taking as many lives as possible… and then disappearing once more."

"How did it happen?" I wonders. "How can a place just... disappear?"

"Although the orchard stands in the mortal plain, it's life force is gone. That life force has passed on to the world of the dead. What stands for humans to see, is nothing more than an illusion. I'm not entirely sure how it happens, I just know how it works."

It's a strange enough idea that it can happen, but to not know how... It's mind-boggling. A few of the spirits are getting curious now, leaning out of their 'headstone' to reach for us. Well... for me. I don't pay them any mind, not wanting to encourage the behavior, but Styx is visibly upset. When a man's hand is inches from touching me, he swings his lantern over to knock away the appendage. In the same movement, he draws it around to herd me closer to him. I can easily imagine him welding it as a weapon. Witnessing a fight between him and another is tempting. I bet he's graceful and skilled on the battlefield. Right after that thought, I have to wonder if battle was something he partook in.

A shiver races through me, a surprise I wasn't ready for. I know it's cold, however it doesn't feel like that's the cause. If it were, I would've been shivering before. The trees seem to be swaying in a nonexistent wind, their branches scrapping against one another. Styx is tense, his gait coming to an abrupt stop just in front of me. Before I can ask what's going on, he holds up a hand to silence me. I catch a spark from the corner of my eye, looking in that direction. Smoke billows up from the foliage, flames licking along trees and bushes. I back away instinctively, gasping when Styx uses that lantern to push me forward. More fire is rushing up from behind. I inch closer to him, the Charon lifting his lantern to cross before me. I close my eyes and hold my breath, the smell of smoke so strong I can taste it. When nothing happens, I crack open one eye to peek. The other follows, both growing large at the sight. We're trapped in an inferno, standing in the midst of destruction, and it can't touch us. I can't even feel the heat upon my skin. I reach out and my hand vanishes within the fires, returning to me without a scratch.

"It's an illusion," I murmur. "Like the flood. But, I thought you could be hurt if you believe it's real."

"You do, but I'm immune to their attacks," he says. "The light my lantern spills acts as a barrier, keeping me in a circle of safety. Even without it I would be unscathed. Unfortunately, that immunity doesn't pass to those I'm with. The lantern is protecting you."

"I don't mind fire," I state, thoughtful. "It stopped hurting after enough practice. I don't even have soot on my skin anymore. This fire couldn't hurt me anyway, I'd just rise from the ashes of my body… like a Phoenix."

"Because that's what you are. That necklace, however, isn't one. I doubt there's another like it here, so I thought it best to use my light."

"… Good idea."

I don't know where it came from, however when we're still standing after a few minutes the fire dies down. I'm released from Styx's light, eyes searching for a source. For a fleeting moment, I catch sight of someone running off into the trees. I don't follow them, it probably wouldn't be the best idea. Instead, I check the amulet in my hand. The second the line stops, I continue toward the tree I'm looking for. Only fifteen minutes later, we step into a thinned area. A tree worn with time stands tall, a smaller sapling beside it. I'm not sure how I know, but that's the one I'm looking for. Styx hangs back when I stand in front of it. One hand settles on the bark, and I try to beckon the spirit out. She's shorter than me, slightly plump, and I can see the years in her eyes.

"Betty?" I question.

"How do you know my name?" she frowns. "And you're living! The living don't stay that way here, child, you should leave."

"I'll be okay, I promise. I spoke to your husband, and he asked me to give you this."

I hold up the necklace, making certain she can see it well. Her eyes light up, tears welling up at the corners. A few thin branches reach over to lift it by the chain, carrying it over to a hollow in the trunk. As soon as it's set within that hole, she smiles at me and let's her tears fall. I want to hug her, yet I know those tears are happy ones. She fights through them, her joy swelling my heart, and then gazes upon me.

"He sent you here for a reason," she comments. "He never does anything without a reason, nor does he expect something done for free. What could have you running errands for the dead, I wonder."

"I want to know what really happened here," I admit. "He told me history's account was false, so I want to know the truth. Are you aware of what led to this?"

"What does history recall?"

"The feud that drove you to your graves, happened because the chancellor killed the gypsies for helping you."

"Ah, no wonder you have questions. The gypsies did help us, that's true enough, however the chancellor welcomed that help. He was a wonderful man when we first came here, thoughtful and kind.

That's one of the reasons we joined him. After meeting the gypsies, we started joining in their festivities. We would share food and dance with them, listen to their stories of travel, and even babysit for one another.

As time wore on, though, the chancellor spent less time with them. Their leader eventually started having things delivered to us by those in her circle. One night, we were in need of medicine rather badly. One of the children took ill. Calista sent her daughter with the medicine, wishing us luck in healing the sick child. She dropped it off and went home... but never made it. Her mother came to us on the next day, asking us what happened. We all saw her go home, so there was nothing we could tell her otherwise."

"So… did they ever find out what happened?" I inquire, enthralled.

"It would've been nice, but... no. Her disappearance led to suspicion and mistrust. Our former friend blamed us, yet it's only natural. We were the last to see her, I understand her frustration and sorrow. One night, however, she came by our small home. She was infuriated, screaming to see the chancellor. He took her away, though I still saw them arguing. The next thing I knew, she was gone and he returned. His attitude was frantic, almost desperate, and he gathered all the men in the settlement. They took off to the gypsy camp. When they came back, they were quiet and distraught... but never spoke of what happened. I only learned what transpired when I saw the ruined camp."

"You went there? Did anyone else?"

"No, just me. I was very close to Calista. We were kindred spirits, her and I. Our children were best friends and we encouraged it. That next day, I went to the camp to check on her. When I arrived, everything was ashes. Bodies laid charred to the bone... and I found her... bound in their fire pit to a post. In the very pit we used to celebrate with them. I fell to my knees and screamed, crying that it was all a nightmare. I wasn't that lucky. I lost my best friend that night, because I trusted the wrong person. I never forgave myself for it."

"If you two were so close, why would she include you and your son in this curse?"

"My son has a tree, but his spirit was never anchored here," she explains. "I chose to stay, so I could be close to my friend until she could release this guilt and move on. She needed support then and I failed her. I won't fail her again."

"You didn't fail her, you're a wonderful friend. I wish I had more like you," I smile. "I think what you did was very brave, I'm sure she appreciates your support more than you know. Thank you so much for sharing your story with me. I hope I can use the information to help free you all of this curse."

"Please, just help my friend. She deserves peace after the pain she's gone through. Thank you for bringing me my necklace as well. My husband was blindly loyal to the chancellor, as all of us were, so he didn't escape her wrath. I'm not angry at her for that. I love my husband, but I know her reasoning. She could've done much worse. I know I would've."

She sinks back into her chosen grave, leaving me proud to have met her. There aren't many people like her around anymore, always too focused on success and greed. I walk back to Styx, giving him a sad smile. I feel for that woman, and I can see that he does as well. The amulet is shifting to the left, and I set a hand on his shoulder to lead him away. Although he gives a look back, his eyes don't linger. We focus on leaving this place. Now that I'm piecing together everything that's happened, the story has unraveled. I wonder if this tale has been passed down to the mayor. If so, I might be able to gleam more information from them. It doesn't exactly tell me why the gypsies were killed, but it does help me understand their mindset.

When the air doesn't get warmer, I begin to wonder if we're leaving at all. Glancing over at Styx, I know we're not. He hasn't relaxed at all, eyes narrowing to give off a harsh look. It unnerves me that he seems troubled. I frown, missing when he comes to a stop. It doesn't matter, though, as I'm forced to stop as well. It happens when I collide with something unseen. Startled, I can only stare at the air. Understanding dawns, and I press my hand to an invisible wall. Although I feel down it for an entrance, there's nothing on either side. Unable to process this, I turn questioning eyes toward Styx.

"You can't pass through to that area," he points out. "You're still living."

"I can take on a soul form."

"No, I wouldn't recommend it. At least, not until you're more skilled in that area. Should you lose that form inside this bubble of death, you'll be killed. I'm not sure if you'll be trapped or not when you rebuild your body. As I'm sure you know, Roots are extremely rare to interact with. In the past, they were revered as gods, or even messengers of them. As time wore on, though, humans began to fear the unexplained. It was just easier to hide within them, or stay dormant within the Source. As such, not much is known about them. I wouldn't take unnecessary chances until you learn."

"... Good idea," I admit, though reluctant. "This is where the amulet wants me to go, though."

"Even the forest is locked away from this place. Whatever is there, is very strong. With this many souls to feed off of, I fear your gypsy stalker might reside in this area."

"If it's her, she's stronger than anything I've come across so far," I frown. "Is there a way to make me stronger than that?"

"Perhaps," he hums in thought. "I mean, it's risky, but... I'll look more into it for you. Should I feel it's a chance worth taking, I'll retrieve you at the cabin. For now, however, I should get you back to your truck. Come, the portal will be faster."

"Nixie said I'm not supposed to go through the portals," I sigh. "I did before, but she said it's not something I should get used to."

"You *should* get used to it, that's a trick I learned from the Source," he informs with a smirk. "Since I was born of the river's waters, I'm technically capable of using magic similar to the Water Root. They taught me to open these doorways, and I taught them to the other Charon and Envoys. It was faster to guide the dead with them, so I kept that magic alive and in use."

"You never told anyone else what it was?"

"No, they didn't need to know. Besides, the Source wished that I kept that tidbit of information out. Not even the Roots were aware I was taught by their mother. At the time, they were all grown and knew their powers. She was feeling that 'empty nest' syndrome with only her Soul Root at home. When she learned I was basically on my own, she took me in. I guess you could say I'm the Root of dark and light."

"I guess that makes sense," I say. "I think it's really cool of her… uh… our 'mother'… to take you in like that. I wish you knew how to teach this stuff to me, though. Learning it on my own is difficult."

"You're doing very well for only having Nixie to teach you. If I had more time, I wouldn't mind taking you on. Unfortunately, this year has been strangely busy. Not that more people are dying, but… more souls are being free from endless wandering. This typically happens when control is desired by the enemy. It's one of the few things I look for when dealing with Roots. Their stories are amazing, yet oddly tragic. I hope you rewrite your story, Catori. I like you. You're not like the others."

I'm surprised by his statement, parting my lips to ask the tormenting questions it brings. He opens a doorway and pulls me through. The wash of euphoria is welcome, though it leaves me feeling drained. I come out next to the truck, turning to see that Styx has stayed within the iridescent doorway. He raises a hand to bid me farewell, and then the door closes. The fact I couldn't ask him about the past is frustrating, though I suspect it isn't something he'd like to talk about. I'm getting a very bad feeling this journey won't end well for me. With a sigh, I climb into the truck and put the key in the ignition. Suspicious, I check the backseat. It's empty and I breathe in relief. Turning back to the windshield, however, has my skin crawling. The girl from the well is sitting in the passenger seat, soaking wet and dripping all over the floor mats.

"I tried to find you," I breath out, voice quiet. "There's a place I can't go in the orchard. Since it moves around so much, I don't know what's in that invisible wall. Are you there?"

"... *Listen,*" she whispers, water running down her face like tears. "*Listen... F-Find me... please... Can you hear it? Please hear it... please...*"

"I'm trying, I promise," I nearly cry. "If I just knew your name... Wait! You're... you're Calista's daughter, aren't you?"

"*Mother... I miss her... so pretty... so nice,*" she states. "*What happened? What... what was it? Did I... was I bad? So much fire... My fault... my fault... all my... fault...*"

I want to console her, yet she's gone. Her body bursts into a shower of water, leaving the seat soaked through and a puddle on the mat. I close my eyes, praying that disappears as well. The last thing I need is for Nixie to see this mess. She'd have my head! Inhaling deep, I open my eyes to look. The exhale is filled with ease. All the water is gone and the seat is in perfect shape. I melt into the chair, looking to the heavens to whisper thanks. The engine roars to life and I start back to the cabin. Time is ticking down, I'm running the race and losing. With any luck, I'll have time to practice my spirit talent. With that, I'll finally penetrate the invisible barrier and find the answers I'm looking for. My gut tells me the way to finish all this is just beyond it. A stone's throw away from where I was stopped... and it's killing me.

Chapter 11

I don't expect company when I return to the cabin. In the driveway, though, a small green car sits waiting. No one knows we're here, so I don't know who to expect. The truck is backed into the garage, and then I get out to meet this new stranger. She also exits, walking up to me with a badge. Tall and slender, I never would've pictured her with one. It identifies her as Officer Gloria Paige. I invite her inside, grabbing a couple glasses of lemonade. When we're both seated, she parts her lips to speak.

"I heard someone was driving Adrian's truck," she comments, sipping from her drink. "She's been so distracted the last year or so, no one has had a chance to speak with her. I called when I heard about her truck, but she didn't answer. Called back, though."

"Oh good," I breathe in relief. "She hasn't called since leaving us here. I was beginning to worry something had happened."

"Why did she bring you here?"

"She asked me to investigate the orchard," I reply.

"You're a supernatural enthusiast?" she frowns, disapproval in green eyes.

"Oh no, nothing like that," I smile. "I come from a long line of officers, so I started my own business. While I can see and interact with spirits, I don't enjoy searching for trouble."

"Do you think you can do what law enforcement couldn't?" she huffs. "Do you have any *idea* how many missing person cases we have here? And you expect to solve them in less than a week's time?"

"I don't, no. I'm not sure how long it will take, nor do I strive to solve every case. All I was hired to do, is study the orchard and maybe give her insight on her son. My hopes going in, are nothing more than helping the orchard spirits move on."

She's quiet for a long moment, eyeing me in suspicion. I don't blame her. There are so many 'psychics' out there, taking advantage of grieving parents. By the casual clothes she wears, I can tell she's here as a friend and not a cop. Her lack of trust is understandable. My features leave no room for hidden agendas, and she relaxes.

"I feel for her," she sighs. "She wants to believe the curse is real, that her boy will magically step from it. I'll admit, so many have been lost in that area. I just don't believe they were taken by spirits."

"Logically, there had to have been a killer in the trees," I agree. "But logic isn't the answer to everything. Many spirits are trapped there, I've seen them. Oh! Perhaps… do you know of a little girl in a well? She would've been alive at the time of the settler-gypsy feud."

"… There was something… Adrian dug up some information on that feud, hoped it would help her find her son. She didn't tell me a name, but she kept the book with her. It might even be here."

"Thank you, Officer Paige," I smile. "I appreciate the information."

"Please… save them," she smiles, sad. "I may not believe in this curse, but they do deserve peace."

She stands and heads for the front door. Although I walk with her, she stops at the welcome mat. Assured she'll find her way, I watch her off. Once the door is closed, my body relaxes. Leaning against the wood, I slide down to sit on the floor. This day has been so taxing, and it's far from over.

I go outside, hoping for a good place to practice. Although it would be ideal to learn before Nixie gets back, I know that won't happen. My fire still hasn't reached perfect control, so water and soul aren't even close. To be completely honest… water terrifies me. When I use it, I feel as though I'm drowning all over again. Panic overcomes me, blinding me and tearing away my control.

I don't like the effect it has on me, so it's not a power I apply often. As a spirit, I get the sensation of floating away. There's always a constant pull to fight, a beckoning from the gates to pass. One more thing out of my control. If only I could be more confident with them.

A few minutes of walking, and I come across a small garden. Wildflowers fill the area, trees growing in a semi-circle, and a small stone bench sits lonely beneath a tree. It's here that I sit. When I inhale, the scent of lavender overwhelms me. It's both relaxing and strong. Every tense muscle melts, me exhale soft and relieved.

This garden is beautiful, filled with life and bright foliage. I can feel an underground stream. It pulls playfully at my senses, beckoning me to join it. I'm not sure how to strengthen my abilities, but meditating while fire helped with that element. Though, Shadow was always with me.

"Nice day out here, ain't it?" a man questions.

Surprised, I turn to face him. At the sight, I'm struck by a wave of conflicting emotions. Sitting in a familiar rocking chair, grinning bright, is the man from the hurricane ruins. He's dressed in a black tee and jeans, a baseball cap sits backward upon his head. I'm lost for words, so I just nod in agreement.

"Stuck again, girl?" he chuckles.

"… Nixie told me you weren't in that town when the waters hit," I blurt out. "That you're not a ghost."

"Sharp as a whip that one," he chuckles. "I'm not a typical spirit, but I was there for the flood. While it didn't 'kill' me, it called me back. Our meeting was in the stars."

"Who are you?" I frown.

"*A friend, I assure you,*" he smiles. "*Now, how about telling me what troubles you?*"

As suspicious as his answer is, I really have nothing to lose from telling him. The recap of my trip with Styx goes by quickly. When I'm finished, the strange man hums to himself and strokes his chin. A moment of thought, and he smiles. He motions for me to scoot closer, which I do, and parts his lips to speak.

"*There's always more than a single path,*" he informs. "*Sometimes, you just need to look outside the box.*"

"I need to strengthen my other elements fast, but I don't know how."

"*The soul is a powerful thing, one that needs to be free. Water, on the other hand, must be led. Whether by creek, or ditch, or even currents. It never disappoints when given a path. Perhaps you should go for a swim, think things over. Who knows, you might even find what you're looking for.*"

"How can I control water, when my lungs fill with it? I always panic and lose focus."

"*You got the wrong mindset, child,*" he says, shaking his head. "*Water isn't just a liquid, not to you. It's your sibling. Don't breathe it in, wrap it up in your arms. Let it hug you, don't fear it.*"

It's easier said than done, but he's gone before I can say it. I'll have to bring this up to Nixie later. Although he says he's a friend, and I don't feel any threat from him, she'll know his true intentions. For now, there's no harm in taking his advice. After all, he was helpful before. I take a breath and close my eyes once again. The dark is welcome, a flame in my mind's eye coming to life. As it flickers, I hear a soft voice.

"*Catori*," they call. "*Catori, come find me. I'm at the Gateway.*"

"What gateway?" I frown. "There's nothing but darkness here. Are you in the cabin?"

No one answers, but the fire ahead grows to an inviting bonfire. I can't help the approach, like a mother caught by a light, I'm pulled in. the closer I get, the further away it looks… until I'm right in front of it. Realizing it just diminished it's size, I reach out to touch it. The flames wrap around my fingers. From just beyond the eerie glow's edge, I can see a small sliver of wood. I thought I was just in the empty space of thoughts, yet as I step up to it… a black fog rolls in. My hand shoos it away, revealing a pale door. Curious, I wave away more of the fog, clearing space at the sides of the gateway. there's no wall, nor is there anything behind it. I can walk all the way around it without obstacles. Humming to myself, I set a hand on the doorknob. It creaks open slowly, a ghostly light spilling from it. Beyond the entrance is a long white hall. Shocked, I close it. Upon opening again, I step around the strange portal. My trek around it is still clear, yet the hall it leads to never wavers.

"How strange," I murmur.

Carefully, I enter the long hall. The door shuts behind me. When I turn to open it, it's gone. Only a blank white wall remains. From it's center, thin tree roots grow. They twist and turn along the flat surface. All the white crumbles, grass and wild flowers breaching the floor. Soon, I'm standing in the middle of a rain forest. The clearing is extremely large, almost overshadowed by the massive tree at its center. It dwarfs the surrounding trees by an unbelievable amount. The roots are so think, I appear an any beside them. As I wander closer, I notice a triangular shaped doorway in the tangle of roots.

Upon entering the enclosure, I see five more evenly spaced in the circular area. It's strange, the sight of them. One has water drizzling from the arch in a thick sheet, another with flowers and vines. That one is caved in. in the center, an ominous fog looms within the doorway. Next is one covered in fire, and the last is empty. Just an indentation in the wood. I draw my hand along smooth wood. It's warm to the touch, a light pulse thumping at my fingertips.

"What is this place?"

"*It's the Gateway*," a bubbling voice provides.

I turn in surprise, finding a distorted image in the waterfall. I know who it is, both in life and death. Meli beckons me closer, holding a dripping hand toward me. When I grip it, I'm pulled into the watery gateway. Meli, my childhood friend, smiles at me. Although I can see the details in her appearance, her form is made entirely out of water.

"Meli," I whisper, eyes teary. "I thought you were gone for good."

"*We'll always be here*," she assures. "*Even though we 'died', we still exist. I gave you my power, the seed of water. It's a core of sorts, the very center of my element… my heart. It's a part of you now, merged with* your soul. This is our Gateway, our connection to our mother."

"Our 'mother'," I murmur. "I know you were found on a beach, but… *my* mother is human."

"The woman that raised you is, but I guarantee you weren't hers by birth. That aside, I didn't call for you to argue."

"Why am I here? Do you know how I can learn my elements faster?"

"No. The knowledge will come with practice. I brought you here, so I can warn you."

As though connected to her emotions, the beach scene changes. Overhead, the skies are filled with storm clouds. Lightening splits the dark, striking the white sands. The waves have turned vengeful. The air, cold. I can't help the shiver that overcomes me. I don't know what might be coming my way, but the look in her eyes… I might not beat it this time.

Chapter 12

My heart is chilled at the sight of her. Whatever she needs to tell me, I can't take it right now. I'm already nervous about this job, I need time to collect myself before facing reality. It would seem she understands, as she moves toward the water. With a small smile, she holds out her hand for me to join her. Although the water isn't my favorite element, a little swim might make me feel better.

The two of us look toward the storming sky, willing away the frightening storm. The sky clears and the sun comes out. Within the warm waters, I sigh. Content to float. A sea turtle surfaces at my side, nudging me with it's flipper. Meli laughs and pulls it away from me.

"*He likes you,*" she states. "*You should visit more often, he would enjoy new company.*"

"… This job is harder than I thought it would be," I admit, staring at the clouds above. "I'm afraid things are going to end badly this time."

"*You mustn't let fear guide you,*" she replies. "*You are better than that, stronger than fear. You are the beginning… and the end. Nothing is above your reach, nothing can defeat you.*"

"Thanks for the pep talk, but I just can't see that," I admit. "I'm not powerful like you guys are, I don't know all the stuff you seem to. Everything is so new to me, so different. Everything is hard."

"*You'll learn throughout your journey, don't lose hope. We're all counting on you, but we don't want you to put yourself in dangerous situations that can be avoided. We're eternal, we have all the time in the world. Take your time, test your footing, and only proceed when the time feels right.*"

A dolphin chatters and jumps over me, droplets of liquid splash my face. A couple more follow it, playing a game of tag. Meli and I grin, diving beneath the water to join them. I can feel the waters around me, churning and twisting as we break through. The game is fast, my body jetting through currents as though I command them. When I surface, I note my skin is gone. My entire being is made of water. Where veins reside, small sparks of electricity flow. I can only imagine it's reminiscent of an eel. Meli appears next to me, a large grin on her face.

We dive again, locating the dolphins and giving chase. Not long into the game, a couple whales join in. I race along their side, circling them in a large loop. Their song is beautiful, carrying through the ocean in vibrations. I can feel it in my core. It makes me feel free and elated, as though I can soar to the sun itself.

Meli and I head back to the beach, where all my fears lay in wait. As we surface, my form has begun to revert back to my human shell. The weight of all that bothers me is back, pressing upon my shoulders like the world Atlas holds. The weather is beginning to answer my inner turmoil. The clouds return and the waters are choppy, nearly pulling us back in when we step on the sands. I fall to the beach, exhausted both physically and mentally.

"*The game was a welcome distraction,*" she sighs. "*But that doesn't change why you're here.*"

"I just want to help everyone," I murmur. "Why is it so difficult? Why should it be hard to help others?"

"*It shouldn't,*" she admits. "*But life cannot come easy either. If it did, no one would appreciate their time here.*"

I can see the wisdom in her words, however it doesn't make them sting any less. There are so many lost souls in the world, so many I may never visit. I can't stand the thought of their eternal suffering. Perhaps, when I learn my abilities, I'll be able to scour the earth for them. I'll be able to save them all. Until then, I have to suffer alongside them. The look in Meli's eyes, however, makes me believe I won't live long enough to see that dream realized.

Chapter 13

Beneath gray clouds and a growing storm, I watch my friend carefully. I don't recall a lot of our time together, yet I know the expression in her eyes. They swim with fear and haunted memories. The look isn't one made for her. Especially with such a young shell. As the rain soaks my clothes, Meli reaches over to touch my cheek. Afterward, she directs my attention to the ocean. The waters twist with her will, forming pictures to the story Meli begins to tell me.

"*Long ago, when time began, there was nothing. Nothing but a vast darkness. In this darkness, a seed of light shown. A tree sprouted, chasing away the dark. As the tree grew larger, more of the pitch disappeared.*"

I watch in awe as the waters commit her dialog to picture. The tree is depicted as a woman, her arms stretching to the sky. I'm reminded of so many paintings, so many interpretations of Gaia, and my heart fills with joy. At the pause in her story, I glance her way. Her eyes are sad.

"*Without the darkness, the tree grew lonely. She bore five fruits, each an element of their own. They were tucked within her roots for safe keeping. When the elements 'hatched' from the fruits, the tree found it difficult to keep up with them. Rooted to her spot, she couldn't* follow her mobile children. Through her instruction, the elements shaped life.

Soon, the world they created was full of people and animals, legends and gods, dead and living. But the world fell into chaos. All strove to control the tree of life. Creatures were hunted, people murdered, and the tree couldn't bear to see it. With her mighty limbs, the wold was split into many. With no world of their own, the dead were separated. The good would rise above her to adorn the night sky, and the wicked were to be held beneath her feet. To protect her five children, the tree wrapped her roots into a cocoon. Separating them and herself from all other worlds. Only one gate remains."

The presentation is fluid and flawless, bringing to light the beauty of this element. I know my expression is one of awe. Meli faces me, waiting for me to speak. I have so many questions, yet they're fighting for the title of 'first' in my mind. Finally, one spills from my lips.

"If she sealed us away, how are we here?"

"The soul was the youngest, so she never allowed it to stray. The others, however, held so much power. As long as we checked in, she let us roam."

"So, I guess the question now, is 'why'?"

"This has happened before, many times," Meli informs. "Each time has played out similar to the rest. This time, however, things have changed. Our enemy has been keeping track of our past encounters, planning to counter our actions. I'm afraid our little family is in serious danger. Your appearance only confirms my suspicions."

"… What am I supposed to do?"

"Fight. Find our missing siblings and fight. We mustn't let the enemy find the Gateway, or all those living will perish. The worlds will become unstable, shattering and killing millions of people. Nothing will be spared."

"How could they even find the Gateway? Isn't this it? It's in my mind, they can't go there."

"They wouldn't be playing so strategically unless they found a way. Be careful, and remember… we're only a thought away."

This is the first I notice the change in the ocean. The waters are rising, thrashing about as thunder cracks overhead. All that liquid is pulled back into the sea, rising to tower over the beach. The wave rushes forward, yanking me into its embrace. I can honestly say, it's doing nothing to build my trust. My air is running low, yet I can't bring myself to breathe. I close my eyes tight, praying the darkness offers escape.

Slowly, I open them again. I'm back on the bench. The only evidence of my mental excursion, is the saltwater soaking me to the bone. I wring out my hair, grumbling to myself. Is it really too much to ask that I don't have to change after using my elements?

"Catori?" Nixie calls from the cabin. "Baby, where are you? Are you back yet?"

"I'm in the garden," I answer, moving to wring out the bottom of my shirt.

"What happened?" she gasps.

She's still in her armor, yet I say nothing. Typically, her armor gleams spotless. Right now, however, it's covered in ash. Splintered wood sticks in her hair, which she shakes free upon my confused gaze. Knowing we're both find and seeing the coincidence, we can't but laugh together. She takes a seat beside me, ignoring the water soaking into her clothes.

"Well, it seems we both had interesting days."

"I found a Gateway in my head," I inform. "Apparently, our enemy has learned over the years. They have a much larger chance at controlling the tree of life."

"… I thought as much," Nixie sighs. "My own research led me to question the past failures. They just never seemed to change their pattern much."

"That ghost I told you about before, he showed up here. The one from the flood. I get the feeling he's more than a wandering spirit. How does he benefit from helping me?"

"With the goal of protecting the tree of life? Everything is connected to it, so even a little instability could destroy life as we know it. It could literally be *any* god-like person. If we're talking about *instant* gratification, though, my money is on Nidhogg. That tree is his only food source. If anyone is helping steer this broken ship, it would be him."

"… Who's Nidhogg?" I wonder.

"He's a dragon that lives beneath the tree of life. He feeds off its roots."

"I didn't see a dragon, I saw a man."

"Dragons are shape-shifters, they can look like anything they want. Being a mythical being, he wouldn't be able to intervene. He can, however, lead you to victory."

I have my doubts, yet I trust her knowledge. I'm not sure why he can't deal with this himself, but I know where I can find out. Styx is a god-like being. There's not better library of myth and legend than him. Right now, I'll be more than happy with a hot bath and a pizza. As we walk inside, I can't help but give Nixie another once over. She blushes, and then scowls.

"I had to rescue souls trapped by a fire," she informs. "The flames grew faster than I anticipated. It took me a few attempts to clear everyone out."

"No one left behind?"

"Now a soul," she smiles in pride. "Styx seemed fairly distracted earlier. I caught up with him before coming here. What happened?"

"I think we found the center of the orchard, but there's an invisible wall keeping us out. He thinks I can enter in a soul form, but I might get trapped there if I lose control. He's trying to think of a way to boost my control."

"… I don't think that's a good idea," she frowns. "He means well, but… he's still a bit old school. Anything he brings up might not be the safest way."

"Nix, I know you just want to protect me, but I can handle this. I know my limits. If it's too much, I'm not proud enough to push forward. I'm gonna bail."

"That's all I'm asking," she states, sighing in relief. "While he's wracking his brain, we should seek alternative approaches."

I nod in agreement, getting up to head inside. Footsteps tell me Nixie is following. The wind carries a strange chill, cutting into me through wet clothes, and I wrap my arms around myself. The shiver is violent enough, the shower is my destination. I kick off my shoes inside the kitchen door, speed-walking to the nearest bathroom. I'm almost there, when the cabin is swallowed by an unnatural pitch. I can't see anything, not even my own hand before my face. Someone is beside me. I can't see them, but I feel their presence.

"Nix?" I whisper. "You better be the one standing next to me."

"I think I am," she answers in confusion. "At least, your voice sounds close enough."

"Good. What's going on? Do you know?"

She doesn't get a chance to speak, as noise begins to drift toward us. The distant, echoic, drip of water. It seems as though it's coming from all around us. I step forward, gasping when I bring my foot down into a deep puddle. The water is ice upon my skin.

"What's up?" Nixie questions, tone wary.

"Cold water," I explain. "I just stepped in a puddle. I think the water is slowly rising."

"Is it the well girl?"

"I don't know for sure, but..."

I gasp again when fingers wrap around my bare ankle. Before I can cry out, I'm yanked into the puddle. Water goes up my nose, surprising me. I'm able to surface for breath, pulled back down afterward. I can't breathe in this water, too panicked to stop the illusion. I hear a voice in my head, whispering echoes of pain and fear. Although I can't see them, I can feel strong hands in my hair. I'm pulled back toward the surface, my lungs burning for oxygen. Coughing and spitting up any water to reach my lungs, I stumble and fall to the ground. I expect to feel the carpet in the cabin. Instead, I dig my fingers into moist dirt. It's an unexpected change. Back on my feet, I search for my attacker. The scene is blurry and I rub my yes to fix it. Unfortunately, nothing changes. I do, however, realize my hands are smaller than they were. I stand and bring them before me. They're most definitely not mine. My clothes are silken and colorful, beaded with gold, and I'm reminded of a stereotypical gypsy.

I find my borrowed body moving without me. Bare feet dig toes into the cool earth, a soft chuckle rising from my lips. I'm a passenger in this memory, so I pay attention. I'm carrying a package, heavy and large upon my back. It feels like food, maybe vegetables. As I wander down a worn path, I stop to collect berries and apples. They're placed in a silken scarf, twisted and tied around my waist like a pouch. I'm on a mission for someone, the thought running circles in my head. Either they're very young, with a high risk of distraction, or they're very old with a poor memory. Judging by the hands, this is just a child. Perhaps between six and nine.

As I wander, I stare at the path. It looks so familiar, yet I can't place it. All this foliage is bright and thriving, a far cry from the orchard I know. Overhead, the sun is beginning to set. It brings a chill of night with its disappearance. My shell doesn't seem bothered by the dimming light. Not much longer, and I see a blurred figure up ahead.

"Well, hello, Ioana. What have you brought us today?"

"Mommy sent food," I state, though with a child's voice.

I pull the package from my back and hand it to a woman. A small group has begun to gather. I wave to the kids playing a few feet away. After speaking to the villagers, I turn to walk away. Through the child's eyes, I see log cabins and a fire pit. A few tables are set up, filled with food and empty plates. I realize this is the settlement I saw in ruin. The realization catches me off guard. I almost miss when my feet come to a stop.

She stands, completely still in curiosity. A bunny hops past, and then I hear it. Somewhere in the trees, a soft music calls to me. The curiosity of a child is both a blessing and a curse. Small feet carry me off the path. She doesn't seem bothered by the twigs in the grass, too focused on the music. It's like a lullaby, so soft and inviting.

The trees part their branches, revealing a hidden cabin. It's small, probably one room, and it looks to have been built in haste. This was likely the first building erected by the settlers. A temporary shelter, meant to be discarded as they built their more permanent fixtures. A tiny garden of herbs sits alongside the cabin, a small ring of rocks for a fire pit is in front, and a well is off to the side. The music comes from there.

By this point, even *I'm* curious. She takes me to the well, peeking over the side. There's no rope or bucket, so nothing obscures my vision. Along the side, there's a rope ladder. Deeper down a waning light spills from a hidden door. The girl takes a step back, and then climbs over the edge of the stone well. I immediately know she's making a mistake. As hard as I try to dissuade her, this choice was made hundreds of years ago. There's no stopping it.

She leaves the ladder, sinking beneath cold water. It's then I note the wooden planks set at the walls of the well. Someone put a lot of thought into this hideaway. My vessel climbs onto the ledge, heading for the light. It spills through a door, inviting to her and ominous to me. Then again, I know how her story ends. With bated breath, she steps past the threshold. The room is very small, with only the necessities. There's a small bed, a bucket, wash basin, and a desk. Cautious of her footing, she looks around. The music is coming from a box on the bed… at the very back of the room. Picking up the box, she gasps when the door slams shut. The click of the lock cements my theory. This child didn't just disappear, she was kidnapped. Tiny fists slam against the door, the girl screaming pleas. They go unanswered. She curls up in a corner, the sound of her frightened tears burning into my mind.

Chapter 14

I open my eyes to stare into Nixie's. For only a moment, I forget what led up to this point. I sit up, confused, and then I notice I'm wet once more. Growling in irritation, I allow Nixie to help me stand. Glancing around, I note this is where I was standing when everything went dark. There's water damage on the carpet, yet it vanishes after I see it. Nixie has worry in her eyes.

"I'm fine," I assure. "What happened?"

"The lights went out," she explains. "You said something about water on the floor, and then the lights came back on. I found you out cold on the floor. The water seemed like it was coming from your pores, it was really weird. What happened to you?"

"… I know what happened to Ioana, the girl in the well," I utter, quiet. "Or, at least, how she disappeared."

"What are you talking about? The lore is that she fell in the well and drown… right?"

"That's what everyone believes, but… she didn't fall down that well. She was lured. I didn't see who it was, but I think this bad blood happened the moment she vanished."

"So, you think finding her will fix it all?"

"I think I already know where she is. The only problem I have is getting to her."

"Any plans coming to you?"

"… Nope. I do, however, feel as though I'm forgetting something. A missing piece to help."

"You'll think of it, I'm sure. Right now, we need to get some sleep."

I agree, however my nerves are shot. If I'm going to get to sleep, I'm gonna need a sedative. She must see it, as she returns to the kitchen. When we were stocking the cabinets, Nixie added potion ingredients… just in case. You can never be too prepared when facing the supernatural. I don't often need her special brews, but since the store… I've been having difficulty sleeping through the night. Every job I've taken since has only added to my insomnia. I watch her boiling herbs in water, and then down the tea when it cools. The affect is immediate.

Not wanting to drag me into the room, Nixie leads me to the bedroom. She helps me change, cursing herself for making it too strong. I'm asleep before my head hits the pillow. The last thing I hear is Nixie's voice. The last thing I see… is an ominous figure cloaked in the pitch of the doorway.

I can't wake myself, trapped under the potion's effect. Nixie can hold her own, though, and that knowledge is all that calms me. I find myself in the dark, that small wisp floating nearby. Walking up to it, the light reveals the Gateway's entrance. I do have questions for Meli, so I walk through the doorway. The garden on the other side seems to have grown. Turning around, I see an expanse of greenery… the doorway cut from the air. Once more, when I walk around it, it disappears on the other side. I grumble to myself, wondering if this bizarre occurrence is the way it's supposed to be. If it's just in my mind, I may need to schedule a therapy appointment after this case is solved.

The tree reaches out for me. A long, thin, branch caresses my cheek. It's leaves are cool against my skin. There's so much love emanating from her, I can see her as a mother. She really cares for her 'children'. I smile and run my hand down the limb. Afterward, I pass into the Gateway. Its doors are still active, aside from the two blocked off. Without hesitation I walk into the falling waters.

"Meli?" I call. "Meli, are you here? I have some questions, I thought maybe…"

My words go silent, eyes falling on a wooden sign. Apparently, my fellow Roots don't *need* to stay in their gate. Grumbling in frustration, I fall to the sand and look toward the sky. it's sunny and warm, yet so empty. As my mood begins to dampen, I note clouds are moving in. this would be the ideal place to practice. With that in mind, I sit up to look upon the ocean. I've never seen water lay so calm.

As beautiful as the scene is, I can sense an underlying layer of the grave. I feel like I'm walking through a cemetery, knowing there are bodies beneath my bare feet. So ominous. The salt water begins to creep onto the beach, reaching for my toes. Despite the chill in the air, the water is warm. A wash of relaxation fills me, a deep breath soothing frayed nerves. I extend a hand toward the sea, smirking when the liquid streams over my hand.

"You don't seem in danger, so what brings you?"

"Meli," I grin, the water returning to its home. "I had some questions for you."

"I thought so," she sighs. "Unfortunately, I've given all the answers I have."

"But… who am I fighting? How am I supposed to do this on my own?"

"You were never taught this, but… there are rules laid down for those that touch immortality."

"What do you mean?"

"After mother separated the worlds, each were given rules to follow. Mortals were the hardest to care for, as they wanted to *believe so badly. The gods and goddesses used them as slaves and armies, taking advantage of their trust and naivety. When the worlds parted, mother needed them to care for themselves. She appointed gods and goddesses to different areas, allowing them to gift the mortals with knowledge,*" she explains. "*But they started interfering in other sections, causing chaos and war. Because of that, mother placed a spell upon them. They're unable to interfere directly in each other's business... but they can manipulate others to, if the balance is threatened. No one can tell you who we fight, because we never actually faced them. We faced those fighting in their name.*"

The news is troubling; it shows on my face. Meli sits next to me, eyes on the sea as well. Her presence is as calm as those waters. I can't get the answers I'm looking for, however I really don't want to leave. With nothing left to do, I glance at Meli. Her eyes are distant, yet I feel she's waiting on me. By now, I'm too tired to worry. I turn to small talk, hoping to ease myself into slumber.

"Have you met Styx?" I question.

"*Isn't that a river?*"

"No… Well… yes, but I'm not talking about the river. He's a Charon. Well, he's *the* Charon; the first. He trained my girlfriend."

"Girlfriend? I'm so happy for you! It's very rare that a Root lives long enough to date! Well, even if they do, nothing comes of it. We're not exactly normal, and our... uh... condition needs to be kept secret."

"She's an Envoy."

"Makes sense. Who's Styx?"

"Her teacher. He's immortal, ferry's the dead across the river Styx. He's a super nice guy, but his appearance is… unconventional."

She hums in understanding, exhaling a calming breath. I have to admit to liking this gate. The rhythmic sound of waves crashing on the beach; it's so tranquil. This isn't the time to relax, though. I can't afford that luxury. In truth, I should be in the orchard. Steps need to be taken to stop the abductions this month. Perhaps the lack of prey will push the gypsy to abandon her curse. I sigh in reluctance and sit up. Meli doesn't bother, too comfortable upon the sand.

"There's a Gateway for the soul in the tree," I remark. "Why is that gate available if it's in my head?"

"You haven't mastered the soul yet, and these are sort of like our bedrooms. We choose what they look like, but the element represented never changes. I've never been in your room... it creeps me out. No offense. Besides, who said this was in your head?"

"None taken," I wave off, ignoring the last remark. "How do you master your element?"

"We all have different ways to do that. When you do master it, though, you won't really need to eat or sleep. We like to indulge, but we don't need to. The best I can tell you, is to listen to your soul. It knows what it wants."

"How does my soul talk to me?"

"How does anything talk to you?"

"With words," I frown.

"Your stomach tells you it's hungry with words? You could make millions in scientific research."

"You know what I mean," I grumble. "I see your point, though. I guess I just have to learn it's language. I should be going, I'm not sure being here while asleep gets me rest."

"Good idea. And don't forget... to master anything you need inner balance."

I stand up and head for the exit. Meli waves to me and smiles, watching as I leave. Back inside the Gateway, my eyes can't help sliding to the door surrounded by mist. Without hesitation, I enter the parting fog. At first, that's all I see. When it begins to clear, however, I take a step back. An endless plain of gravestones surrounds me. The mist lays upon the ground in a thick blanket, the vegetation all dead. It's a scene from one of Nixie's favorite horror movies.

I hear eerie moans and uncontrolled sobbing. It's coming from everywhere all at once. Finally, I see a hint of someone in the fog. Following them, I'm led to an ornate headstone. The man places a hand upon smooth granite, and the stone glows red hot before rising from the grave soil. Now it sits upon a casket, which opens like a doorway. The man walks through and the coffin sinks back below the dirt. Upon closer inspection, I realize there's more to this stone than it appears. The inscription holds the man's name, birth and death dates, and address. At the top is a religious symbol, and at the bottom there are flames. When the stone stops glowing, everything fades away and the name of a cemetery surfaces. My room is a room of doors.

"I must've kept track of souls from here," I muse aloud.

There's a bright light shining to my left, so I wander closer. As I near, the vegetation begins to comes to life and flourish. I find a good sized well in its center, so big it could be a pool. Although it's large, it doesn't seem very deep. From the bottom of this pool, I sense underground channels. As I gaze upon the luminescent liquid, silver and thicker than water, a form gathers. A tiny child coos up at me, disappearing into one of those channels.

"… Did I *manage* new souls, too?" I gasp in awe. "I never would've guessed. Spirits aren't usually associated with the living."

I reach a hand forward, smiling when the next child grips my finger. The sensation is so serene, and then a sharp pain in my mind breaks it. A flash of sky, a world of greenery on the edges, and I feel nostalgic. I see a face move into view, hear a voice whispering in my head, and I remember that day. When I come back to myself, my heart aches and tears fill my eyes. It can't be true… it just can't.

Chapter 15

My eyes open to pitch. I'm lying in bed, the moon still dominating the sky, and Nixie is beside me. I don't move, barely breathe. Blank eyes stare up at the ceiling. That memory is so fresh in my mind, so painful. Slowly, careful not to wake Nixie, I slide from bed. There won't be anymore sleep for me tonight. My feet carry me to the front door. I feel so detached, trapped in an out-of-body experience. All I can do is watch.

On the way, I stop to grab my phone from the charger. My heart heavy with revelation, I automatically

The cobblestone path is cool beneath my feet, smooth and firm. A whisper calls my name, sent on an ominous wind. When I turn toward it, I see a figure with long hair. It obscures her face, but she's too familiar by now. With a forlorn sigh, I walk over to her. Ioana stands, as still as the grave she never received. Since she's by the bench, I take a seat and hum.

"You can't sleep either?" I muse. "I don't suppose you had a nightmare, too, right?"

There's no answer, not that I expect one, however she *does* move. Her frame turns and floats toward the trees. When she stops at the edge, I note she wants to be pursued. Since I haven't anything to preoccupy my mind, I give her what she wants. The walk isn't too far, but still qualifies as exercise. The trees give way to grass, land sloping to create a rather out-of-place hill. I've seen the peak over the treetops from the road, yet didn't realize how close it is to the cabin.

Ioana stops at the edge, hovering a few inches above the ground. When she spreads her arms wide, as though welcoming the night's embrace, I can't help the confusion. This isn't like previous encounters. Where she normally pleads for help, now she's leading. This place must have special meaning to her.

"What happened here?" I wonder, stepping just out of her reach. "Why brings me here?"

"*Always here,*" she states. "*Always... waiting... Find her, help her... Bring her... Save them all.*"

"Her? Are you talking about me?" I gasp. "Who told you to do that?"

"*Whisper Hill,*" she comments, slowly disappearing into the night. "*Can you hear it? Listen... hear it... the whispers...*"

"Wait! I don't get it, what are you talking about? What whispers?"

I'm speaking to the stars, though, as she's already gone. This strange twist has me feeling a mixture of dread and... excitement. The later throws me off, as unexpected as it is. Frustrated and tired, I go back the way I came.

The night is listless, clouds obscuring the moonlight in intervals. It doesn't take me long to realize things aren't what they seem. The trees have changed and the path is overgrown. Without even being near it, the orchard has swallowed me. Small groups of shriveled leaves grow now, the buds of fruit blooming. Last I was here, these trees were dead and bare. Barely a week into this month, and already there are blossoms. I trip over a root, nearly crashing to the ground. Something holds my waist and shoulders, keeping me upright. Breaking away, I note the branches of one tree caught me.

"Thank you," I comment. "I'm sorry if it was you I tripped over. It's hard for me to see in this darkness."

"*Be careful you don't get lost, or you'll share our fate,*" a male voices, drifting from the bark on the tree.

My hand immediately clutches the amulet around my neck. I haven't taken it off since Styx gave it to me. Holding it for the compass, I begin to follow its light. The air is so still, I can hardly breathe. A chill runs along my skin. It feels so much darker. Not so much the pitch, but the energy that flows through the trees like fog. I've never been this nervous before. I jump at every sound, altering my route by steps before getting back on course. Paranoia fills me to the brim.

Lost within the trees, I take a moment to study the area. An owl swoops down, brushing past my face. Its feathers glide over my skin. My heart hammering, a terrified squeak has me sighing in relief. It was only after a mouse. Moving forward, I run into that invisible force. The compass still points ahead and I can see on the other side. Unable to get through, I decide to go around. There's no way an entire half of the orchard is blocked.

One hand trails along the transparent wall, hoping for the end. Even a weak point would do. On the other side, I see nothing but overgrowth. I lean on the barrier stepping over a fallen branch. Instead of a solid surface, however, my hand slides along a curve. With a surprised yelp, I tumble into some bushes. Nothing catches me this time, and I'm almost positive I heard a chuckle upon the wind. Brushing it off as a hazard that comes with any job, I get back on my feet.

Working my way around the dome, I catch sight of small hints. The remnants of a picnic table hides in bramble bushes, a hole dug for a pond is nearly empty of water, and a porch has collapsed. The later I barely make out between trees. As I thought, this area matches the one I saw in another's skin. This has to be where the well is located. I walk to the other side, gasping at the sight of a figure in the trees. They're gone just as fast as they appeared.

I'm suddenly very anxious about being alone. Whoever that was, their presence is steeped in mal-intent. Carefully back away, I grip my amulet tightly. Eyes locked on the trees hiding that figure, I back into something solid. My body freezes, breath trapped in my lungs. Ever so slowly, I turn to face what I hope is a tree.

"Styx?" I utter in surprise. "What are you doing here?"

"You called me," he points out. "When I gave you that amulet, I thought you'd only call me when you were in danger."

"… I don't know *how* to call you," I protest. "Unless it involved creepy people with malevolent energy."

"That would do it," he smirks. "Where is this malevolent spirit?"

"That's just it… I don't think it *was* a spirit."

He waits for me to explain, but I can't put it into words. There's little to no evidence what I say is true, yet I believe it. It may be dark, I may have only glanced him, however the feeling is still there. That unnatural sensation of clammy hands on the back of your neck. I've learned to associate it with death… but it's different this time. Too unnatural, too dark, and filled with promises of eternity. The later is what I fear. That sensation of death normally accompanies the threat of finality. Although I begin to explain, Styx holds up a hand to shush me. His eyes are narrowed, sliding to glance past me. His expression is blank, but his eyes shimmer with threat. Goosebumps break out on my skin. There's no doubt he's not only old… he's also quite feral. I don't dare move, holding my breath until his focus shifts.

"You might be right," he states. "I feel death beyond this barrier, but also… a soul trapped in its shell. It's been a long time since I've come across this. I thought we got them all during the plague."

"Got what?" I question. "Did you see it, too?"

"… I need to get you out of here," he comments, tone silk with an underlying steel.

Without warning, he grips my wrist and starts to pull. His strength catches me off guard, yet I manage to stay standing despite the branch I trip over. This seems like a side of Styx he hides well, so it's beginning to unnerve me. A couple yards from the barrier, he opens a doorway with his lantern. I'm pushed through, spying him looking over his shoulder before following.

I'm standing back at the cabin, confusion obvious on my face. Styx is about to make his exit, when Nixie steps out of the cabin. Her eyes are murderous at first, and then she sees the look on Styx's face. The fear that overcomes her has me sweating bullets. She calls out to Styx, running up to us with bare feet. He stays, yet I know it won't be for long. He's a man on a mission, and I pity anyone foolish enough to get in his way.

"Styx, what's going on?" Nixie asks, a soldier ready for orders.

"Something is lurking in the orchard, keep Catori away from there until I give the okay."

"What is it?"

"… It's from the plague."

She takes in a sharp breath, telling me this is likely worse news than I thought. Personally, I couldn't imagine anything worse than what was in my mind. This just winds my nerves all the more. It's at that time my brain catches up with the conversation. I'm being banned from the orchard. Without it, I chance missing my window of opportunity. There's no way I'm leaving these souls to suffer another year.

"No way," I frown. "I have a job to do, you can't keep me out of the orchard! Those souls need to be set free!"

"They have an eternity to be set free," he huffs. "I'm more worried about you. Now, *please* stay put… or I'll bind your soul to this cabin until I finish dealing with this threat."

"… Can he do that?" I whisper to Nixie.

"Yep. I've seen it. I've also been victim to it," she mutters. "That's his idea of being grounded."

"That's playing dirty," I hiss.

"You're not telling me anything new," she scoffs. "I grew up with him."

I can't afford the price he's offering, so I send a petulant glare his way. As I hoped, he takes it as a win and leaves. In truth, I have no intention of doing as he says. It would seem Nixie knows this as well, because when I look her way… she's giving an expression of suspicion. I've ignored her warnings multiple times, she's not fooled. Though she doesn't call me out on it, I know it's coming. As soon as she closes the door behind us, she levels me with a glare.

"What?" I question, innocent.

"Don't even *think* it," she warns. "Styx doesn't pick a fight unless he's positive no one else can get the job done. Whatever he found isn't likely to go away without a serious battle."

"I've defeated malicious spirits, vengeful wraiths, and multiple demons. How is that not serious enough?"

"Just… stay here," she comments. "This thing is beyond you."

"What is it? I know you know," I frown.

"… Cat, these things are too much for you, for anyone," she sighs. "They were so dangerous, it was decided they be hunted to extinction. Styx was charged with reaping their souls. He and the other Charon had to team up with the Envoys. It led to an all out war. It lasted so long. Thousands of humans were killed, just as many souls were lost to darkness."

"So… what is it?" I inquire, pointedly.

"... They're the undead army, created in the underworld to drag down pure souls."

"... Zombies!" I ask in disbelief, albeit mixed with excitement.

"No, not exactly," she sighs. "They're more like a parasite. They target mortals with darkness in their hearts, feeding on their soul and nurturing that evil within. Styx called them 'skin walkers'. I don't want you anywhere *near* that orchard. Swear to me you won't go."

"... I won't go willingly," I frown. "I have no control over the plans of others."

She has no choice but to agree. She can't stop spirits from dropping me off there, nor can she keep them from my dreams. Resigned to that fact, she follows me to the living room. I can't help but feel jealous. Fighting this zombie sounds way more interesting than getting haunted. I'm not tired, so I take up the couch. I expect Nixie to go back to bed, but she grabs a blanket and joins me. With her head using my lap as a pillow, there won't be any sneaking out tonight. With a resigned sigh, I turn on the television and turn down the volume.

Chapter 16

I don't know when I nodded off, the sun's light waking me. Nixie isn't with me anymore. I can only assume she went to work. This discovery gets me a mix of eagerness and resignation. It's a temptation to explore, yet I have a feeling Nixie's still watching me. Playing it safe, I grab the keys and head into town.

Outside, a strange feeling washes over me. The weather was supposed to be sunny, yet gray clouds clutter the sky. If I didn't know any better, I would say it was a coincidence. Unfortunately, I might just end up in the orchard after all. As soon as I get in the truck, I drive off in hopes of more answers. The road is strangely busy, especially for being in the middle of nowhere. Coming up on the many vehicles, I realize they're police cars and paramedics. One of the boys in blue flags me down upon approach. I stop and roll down the window.

"What's going on, officer?" I inquire.

"Are you the one staying in the cabin down the street?"

"Yes, did you need something?"

"A vehicle was found here early this morning, did you see or hear anything strange?"

"Not concerning the vehicle. I'm sorry. Would you happen to know who it belongs to?"

"Not a local, that's for sure. Looks like a couple looking to camp from the contents. You're sure you haven't seen anyone? I think I was told you're staying with another girl, where was she last night?"

"We were both at the cabin last night," I answer. "I went for a walk, but returned long before sunrise. If you'd like to know, I went to that large hill nearby. Nixie went to work, but I'll tell her to call the station when she returns."

"I would appreciate that, thank you. Where are you off to now?"

"I'll be in town if you need me. I'm not sure how long I'll linger, but if I'm not there I'll be at the cabin."

He nods and allows me past. Driving on, I chance a look at the abandoned car. It's not familiar. Deep in the trees, however, two people stand. Their transparent forms are trapped in twisting roots, slowly devoured by the hollow grave. There's no helping them now, but those terrified expressions will haunt my nightmares. With dread in my stomach, I realize they're staring directly at me. Their piercing gaze follows the truck, and I feel another presence next to me. The truck has gone cold despite the heat outside. I pray for a docile spirit, slowly turning my head to address them. No one is there. It's impossible, though, as I've tuned in on that sixth sense. When I feel another presence, I've never been wrong. Whoever sits in that passenger seat, doesn't want me to see them. Since that's never happened before, as I've seen hiding spirits without trying, I can only assume they're very powerful.

"I don't know who you are, but I find it rather rude to hang around without showing yourself," I comment, glancing beside me. "Just because you're hiding doesn't mean I don't know you're here."

In answer, something moves my rear view mirror. In the backseat, the window fogs. An invisible finger writes in the fog, just two words… and ice runs through my veins. The words read 'Hello, Catori'. Spirits don't know my name unless I've met them previously. This presence isn't a familiar one. Swallowing nervously, I pull to the side of this deserted road. After I put the truck in park, I turn toward the passenger side.

"How do you know my name?" I nearly demand. "You're not familiar to me, and I've never felt your presence before. There's no reason for you to know me."

This time, the windshield fogs up. My only answer is written… 'Can you hear it'. Afterward, that strange presence vanishes. Ioana asked me the same question. They felt nothing like her, and yet… my gut tells me they're connected. Alone once more, I try to shake off the encounter. Although I give it my all, by the time I reach town my mind is consumed by it. That hill… it's important, and I need to know why.

Town is quiet today, an eerie blanket of tension beginning to grow. Even if they don't act it, the residences are aware of the countdown. My first thought is to visit the historian again, however I don't want to focus on one person's tale. My feet carry me to a small museum instead. I had missed it at first, it's so tiny. The outside, as it turns out, is quite misleading. Though small from the front, its length is well used. A woman in a fashionable suit dress waits for customers. When she sees me enter, her face lights up and she approaches without hesitation. Taking my hand in an enthusiastic shake, she introduces herself.

"Good afternoon, I'm Natalie," she states. "I'm the curator of this museum."

"Hello," I greet. "I was researching a few urban legends that originated from here. Would you happen to know the best displays to learn more?"

"Hmm… Which urban legends are you looking into?"

"The orchard, the girl in the well, and possibly an old hill near the orchard."

"Interesting," she muses. "Not many know about that old hill. Even the locals have forgotten it. How did you know, if you don't mind me asking?"

"As long as you don't judge me for the answer."

"Of course I won't."

"The spirit of the girl in the well," I blush. "Or rather, she took me there. I was hired by a family member to investigate that area. They fear foul play."

"I see. Well… just don't spend much time there. People find themselves lost forever in those trees. This way, please."

She heads to a door halfway through the hall. When I enter after her, I'm surprised at the décor. Pictures line a nearby wall, fake trees scattered around the floor, and replicas of the abandoned village stand. My eyes are drawn to the black and white photos. One in particular has my curiosity. It's the cabin with the well, the first structure built by the settlers. They stand out front, shaking hands with the gypsies. The chancellor seems so happy, greeting their new neighbors sincerely. He doesn't seem like someone who could commit murder. In the next, the children of both camps play together. These photos are set up like a timeline. I'm eternally grateful, as they set up images to the chancellor's slow descent. It appears to have started around the time they began construction on the larger village I wonder what may have been there before.

"He changed so much," I murmur.

"This is all I can show you, I'm afraid. If it's a story you want, you should see the town's historian."

"I was hoping for a more diverse information pool," I sigh, disappointed.

"Well, there's always… No, never mind," she amends quickly. "No one likes to go to that area. Just, talk more with the historian."

"Whoa, now I'm curious," I smirk. "What are you hiding from me?"

For a moment, she's quiet. Most likely trapped in a mental debate. I'm curious to know who she'd recommend. Whoever it is, they must not like visitors. After a couple minutes, she sighs in relent. Although few people are in the same room, she leads me to an office across the hall. Together, we sit by her desk. She grabs a pen and some paper, scribbling onto it before she can change her mind. Sliding it over to me, she gazes in warning.

"This is an address to a house in the swamp. The woman that lives there is believed to be psychic, but also dangerous. For centuries, the women in her family made brews for the town's sick. They're also known for poisons. She isn't fond of visitors, so be careful."

"Thank you so much," I smile.

"It's quite a drive, so don't thank me yet. Also, she's fond of roses."

The hint is noted and I start on my way out. She walks me to the door. Before I exit, I thank her once more. The doors swing shut between us. Not far from where I am, the truck sits waiting. I climb into the driver's seat and reach for the GPS in the glove compartment. Just as I'm about to turn it on, my phone rings. The name on the caller ID is unknown, but I recognize the number.

"This is Catori," I remark. "I'm so glad you called, I needed to speak with..."

"Did you use the GPS?"

"… Uh… no," I frown. "I did visit the orchard, though. Without a guiding spirit, you don't have a chance of escape. Once you pass into the trees, the orchard moves around. A never-ending labyrinth. Even if your son wasn't lured, just walking in would cause him to disappear."

"Oh my… Do you think… might he be… dead?"

"Actually, I can't say. Although the trees are poison, there's no proof it's as deadly as the curse. It could be a loop in time, maybe even a portion frozen in time. That would slow the aging process for sure. It's a very slim chance, but if he is alive, I'll get him out."

"… I appreciate that hope, but it's long since faded for me. I've seen too man news reports, I know how this is likely to end. Just… please, help him rest peacefully."

"Don't worry, I'll do my best."

"And remember, no GPS. That's how the orchard draws its victims."

"... I need it to get to the swamp," I frown. "Besides, the curse seems to be targeting descendants of the settlers. I'll be okay, I promise. This isn't the first curse I've faced."

"... If you feel you can overcome it, I'll trust your judgment. Thank you for the update."

I'm unable to say much in return, as I'm met with dial-tone. As strange as her timing is, I shrug it off and retrieve my GPS. It's turned on and I set the address. Just as I'm turning the ignition, the screen blinks off and back on. It looks to be a simple electrical problem, yet it's enough for me to turn it off. Just the sight has my stomach sour.

There's no doubt I need to find the swamp, so I'm forced to think of an alternative map. Just by chance, I spy a cop car across the street. It seems my streak of luck is growing. Turning off the truck and grabbing my paper, I hurry over to the station.

It's quiet inside, only a couple people waiting to make a complaint. I can't imagine what they'd complain about, this place is so peaceful. Bypassing them, I wave down a passing cop. She stops and smiles at me, joining me at the front desk.

"How can I help you?" she wonders.

"My GPS is on the fritz," I comment. "Could you please write down how I can get to this address?"

"Sure," the officer states, taking the paper I hand over. "I'm not sure why you'd waste your time, though. No one even knows if Eleanor is still alive. We haven't heard a peep from her in weeks. That's not uncommon, though. She usually gets quiet leading up to the anniversary."

"Why?"

"I asked her that last year. You know what she told me?" she remarks, ignoring my shaking head. "She said, 'honey, I've lost so many to that curse, sometimes I wish it would take me, too'. Can you believe that? She *actually* believes in that silly urban legend."

"If it's not true, where are all these people disappearing to?"

"I've been telling people for years there's likely a serial killer in those trees. You think they'd listen to me? Of course not. Here you go, hon. Be careful out there."

"Thank you, I will."

I exit the station, a bit surprised at her indifference. In a town filled with superstition, it would be easy for a killer to hide behind stories. I understand her point. On the other hand, however, one should never close their eyes to the illogical. There is, come to find out, truth to these old tales of the dead. I can feel eyes on my back as I leave.

Back in the truck, I text Nixie my plan. Not sure when she'll get the message, but at least I can blame her for not seeing it. Just in case she freaks out, of course. With a smirk at the thought, I pull out of my parking spot and head for the first road on my paper.

The road begins to thin of traffic, although there wasn't much to begin with. It almost makes me feel uneasy. The further away from town I get, the more foreboding rests upon my shoulders. It doesn't make sense to me, however something deep down tells me Eleanor is an important player. I can only hope to find a piece of this puzzle with her.

Chapter 17

The area really is a swamp. The road narrow, with reeds on both sides. I can see an old cottage in the distance. Before I can reach it, however, a massive alligator is crossing the dirt path. It comes to a halt when I beep the horn. Just to spite me, it lays down and closes its eyes. Irritated at the potentially deadly road block, I drop my head to the steering wheel. The horn blares, elongated with my frustration, and then an idea comes to me. I glance to the side, drawing the water over the road. The strong stream washes the gator back into the swamp.

With the way cleared, I move on. I'm almost to the ranch style gates when I realize I forgot roses. Hoping she won't mind, I turn off the truck and get out. Walking up to the door, I note a few gators skulking in the surrounding waters. An old cat sits on the porch roof, a litter of five kittens sleep on a small cat bed beside the door. The combination alone has me wary of witchcraft. Something is going on to sway the reptiles' hunger. I raise my fist to knock, yet before I touch the wood there I hear a voice.

"Come on in, girl. I don't have the energy to get up today."

Confused, and slightly impressed, I open the door to enter. The kittens run in before me, so I wait for the mother before shutting the door. Upon entry, I smell incense burning. A large cauldron sits above a wood fire, the smell barely covered. Although the fire burns bright at the room's center, it appears this is the living room. When I finally see the woman that lives here, I'm caught between running and attacking. The young woman, probably in her early forties, sits at the cauldron… and she's the spitting image of the orchard ghost. The chair she sits on is wicker, likely woven with the reeds outside, and her long red hair is a stain upon a colorful blanket. Blue eyes take me in, so pale I could mistake her for blind.

"Today must be a bad omen," she frowns, tone terse. "No one visits my home, *especially* during this cursed month."

"Sorry," I blush. "I needed help on my case. The museum curator gave me your..."

"Yes, yes. I already *know* all that," she huffs. "I *am* psychic, after all. Take a seat."

I do as I'm told, sitting in the chair beside hers. It seems to have been pulled over from a corner, where a third sits unused. For all intents and purposes, she seems to be as psychic as I was told. A part of me, though, is trying to break her down. It's happened many times before. Growing up, it made it difficult to fit in… the need to understand. I quickly learned to ignore it. Meli had said to listen to my spirit, though. If that's its language, I'm more than happy to listen.

It's her eyes that I focus on. Those pools draw me in until that's all I see. In those dark depths, I see a green bonfire. Figures dance around it. Those silhouettes morph into trees, and then a lone woman enters the scene. She falls to her knees, sobbing, and her form twists into the symbol for eternity. That, in turn, forms a heart before breaking it. Although this is the first time this has happened, I know what story those pictures tell.

"Didn't your mother ever tell you it's impolite to stare?" Eleanor frowns.

"… You were there," I comment, voice dazed. "You were there when the fires… No. Not when they were set… After."

"How could you possibly know that?" Eleanor gasps.

"… Who broke your heart? Was it the orchard? Why curse yourself with immortality? Is it worth the price… Calista?"

"Stop!"

Fingers snap before my eyes, breaking the hold I'm trapped in. Whoever did it is standing behind me. I know their presence, yet it shouldn't be here. When I turn around, I'm surprised by what I see. Styx is there, as I suspected, but he looks different. Dressed in ripped jeans and a graphic tee, he looks… normal. I'm almost disappointed. Around his neck is a choker, the thick black band sporting a gem akin to the pendant he gave me.

"I told you not to underestimate her," he points out. "She's stronger than her siblings… save one, I think."

"How could she see all that?" Calista demands, tone heavy with tears. "How did she know my name? I've been using my sister's name for centuries now, no one should've remembered mine!"

"Yeah, how *did* that happen?" I frown. "I've always wanted to know things, but..."

"You listened," he smiles, proud.

I stare at him a moment, mind shattered with surprise. Meli had told me that, but how could Styx possibly know that? The question must be lurking in my eyes. Although he acknowledges it with a sheepish gaze, he doesn't answer it. He walks between us and sits in that empty third chair set by the wall. Once seated, he sighs and opens the floor to questions. At first, Calista and myself start talking in unison. We both stop, and then I motion for her to start.

"How did she see my past? No one has ever been able to use their gift for that."

"Catori isn't just anyone. Psychics have never seen beyond your veil, because they choose to believe you're simply an old soul reborn. It's a common mistake for those in a mortal shell to make. Catori isn't psychic, she's open to so much more than humans are, and she's immortal herself."

I'm listening carefully, trying to understand this newly found gift. So focused and lost in thought, I miss the look given to me. It isn't until I get that eerie sensation of being watched that I look. Calista's features are a mixture of anger, confusion, and sadness. I can't quite comprehend where these emotions come from. Only a few seconds into her harsh gaze, she realizes my confusion.

"You sold your soul for immortality, and you dare judge me?"

"I didn't *ask* to be what I am," I glare. "I didn't get a choice in this matter! I was perfectly happy living a *normal* life!"

"Catori isn't human," Styx states, cutting off the woman's rant. "She's a Root. The Root of Souls. She can read them, soothe them, *free* them. And, before her mortal shell… she created them in her well of souls. Life begins and ends… with her."

My jaw drops at the admission, as does Calista's. Never in my life would I have known that. If someone told me that before the store, I would've laughed in their face. Probably before calling the asylum for a pick-up. How does one even create a soul? I thought they were just… I don't know… born in it? At my shock, Calista rethinks her position. With a reluctant sigh, she faces me.

"You came for the orchard's story," she remarks. "It's one I can give you, but everything has its price."

"… What's the price?" I wonder.

"I don't know," she frowns. "No one does. Not until it's collected."

"… They need to be at peace," I decide. "Please… help me put them to rest."

"… My parents brought us here. My sister and I were only babies at the time. We grew up where that orchard is. As we grew, we were schooled by our mother and aunts. Among those teachings, making medicines.

We weren't the only gypsies to lay down roots here either. There were two or three other camps. We made the medicine and delivered it to them. As time past, our parents died and we gained the seat at the head of our family.

When the settlers arrived, we were happy to have another village to help. The relationship soured quickly, though. We remained civil and continued to help. The first real issue was where they wanted to build.

Although we expressed our concerns, they were stubborn. The first spot they wanted was an old hill that now overlooks the orchard..."

"I'm staying near there," I gasp. "It means something to the little gypsy girl, Ioana, she led me to it."

"... It would. That's where her father used to take her. It's said that hill is where the winds gather. A god oversees their meetings, collecting the news they bring from around the world. That was her favorite story. Her father used to tell her to sit and listen. If she listened hard enough, she could hear the voices, too. Telling her the secrets of the world."

The comment is familiar, and I wonder if that's what she wanted me to hear. Perhaps she felt the wind could help me. Styx can see my mind working, a slight frown upon his lips. When I've soaked up her information, I motion for her to continue. Her eyes are sad, lost with her family in those trees. We wait until she comes back to us.

"I'm sorry," she whispers. "It's been a long time since I told this story."

"It's fine," I assure. "I'm going to help as much as I can. Whenever you're ready, you can continue. Styx banned me from the orchard, so I have all day."

"Banned you?"

"Yep. He can explain that to you, when he explains his presence here to me."

"... Okay," she says, slow. "Well, we told them about the god that lived at the hill. They didn't believe us, and started building. Coincidentally, they couldn't fight the winds, which blew down everything they put up. They would've blamed us, but the nails pulled out looked brand new. Even *they* couldn't turn a blind eye to the wind god's will.

After that, they chose an expanse of land further away. Again, we warned them against building there. We were told that, when we first arrived, our father chose to camp there. He had an uneasy feeling and they moved the caravan away from there.

Unable to get it out of his head, he searched out a native tribe we traded with. They said that they used to live there, but were forced to move. A demonic spirit had attacked their camp. They went to war with it, yet couldn't kill it. They did, however, manage to trap it. One of their men volunteered to contain the spirit in his body. They mummified him alive and tucked his body away in a special coffin. That was the only way to trap it. No matter how many times we warned them, they wouldn't listen.

After their homes were built, their leader started acting odd. It got worse with time. We went from daily visits, to monthly, yearly, and then… just for deliveries. The difference was noticed.

One day, a nearby encampment fell ill. I brewed some medicine and put my sister in charge until my return. My destination was a few days journey by horse. By the time I reached the camp, they had received a message by falcon. Ioana had gone missing. I returned immediately, but… it was too late. My family had been murdered and our homes burnt to the ground. I blame myself. If I had stayed, nothing would have happened to Ioana and the feud wouldn't have gotten so bad. I lost everything that day. So I used a spell for immortality, swearing to avenge my sister and our family."

"Where did you get a spell like that?"

"From the god of Whisper Hill. He watched over us. On the day I left, my sister asked him to follow me and make sure I had a safe journey. He didn't hear the warning sent to his hill, so he wasn't in time to save them… to save *her*."

My heart goes out to her. I feel as though she's holding back, yet I can't bring myself to dig it out. Instead, I move closer and dare to take her hand. The only thing I want right now, is for her to feel better. It seems my touch calms her, her tears lessen and her sobs quiet. I don't know what to say, what will diminish her burden.

"I'm so sorry you went through all of that. Your family obviously meant everything to you. I'm going to free them, though. Soon your sister, niece, and everyone else will be able to rest."

"Niece? She wasn't my niece… she was my daughter."

As if I didn't feel bad enough, she had to add that. Styx sits quietly, just waiting for the grief to pass. He seems awfully comfortable here. My gaze doesn't go unnoticed. He sighs and leans forward, laying his forearms across his lap.

"Calista is immortal," he remarks. "I still have to keep tabs on her. Besides, she's a valuable asset to have. The old ways are forgotten now, so any allies we made have passed. Calista still practices the old ways. She's yet to pass on that knowledge. I also needed help from her again."

"Again? No wonder you look so comfortable."

"She was alive during the war I spoke of, though she was young. Her spells and potions were strong, and she made it her goal in life to learn of every monster."

"How could she know about a monster you hunted to extinction? How could she learn about every monster?"

"She befriended the god of Whisper Hill. He's studious and inquisitive, so he passed his teachings to her and her twin sister."

"How is she supposed to help? She looks positively exhausted."

"Like I said, everything has a price," Calista sighs, tired. "Although I'm immortal, my energy goes to feeding the spell. It was a choice I made knowing the consequences. It's also a choice I was planning on making before the tragedy."

"Interesting," I murmur. "So… how do we stop the orchard monster? Uh… not your sister, she's not a monster. There's another monster hiding there."

"*We* don't," he remarks. "*You* are going back to the cabin. Calista and I can handle this, but Nixie will *kill* me if anything happens to you."

"I'm immortal, too!"

"You're a baby immortal. You haven't seen the world I have, you don't know as much as we do."

"Who's fault is that! If Nixie wouldn't keep that world away from me, I would know more. She won't even *talk* about it."

"There are more important things to deal with, but I can't help it," Styx murmurs to himself. "You're just proving my point."

"I can handle anything," I argue. "And I can't learn if I don't try. You and Nixie have to let me fall once in awhile. I won't break, I promise."

"She has a point," Eleanor states. "I would rather she fail where we can help, rather than when we can't save her. If she wants to help so badly, let her."

"Absolutely not! You got what you came for, go back to the cabin. If I see you in the orchard before we defeat this creature, I'm going to bind your soul to the cabin. End of discussion."

Frustrated doesn't even begin to express my irritation. With a huff, I storm out the front door. I can't be treated like a child, not with so many souls counting on me. As I pace beside the truck, cursing under my breath, I sense a change in the air. My eyes sweep the area. There are no animals here anymore, running from this cold. It raises goosebumps on my skin. A darkness touches the surface of the swamp water near me, slowly growing bigger. Dark hair surfaces, a body following. That familiar little girl has shown herself, now floating a couple inches above the water.

"*Can you hear it?*"

"No, I can't," I bite out. "I can't hear anything! That hill is just a story, it's not real. I know where your body is, I just can't get to it!"

"*You need to listen... listen to it... the wind... Can you hear it? Listen... hear... find me...*"

I want to scream, and open my mouth to do so. Ioana blinks out of sight, startling me when she reappears inches from my face. Her eyes are empty sockets, a glow set deep within those voids. Her frigid hand grips my wrist, the touch enough to make my skin crawl. I just want to get away from her. That in itself is odd. Just as I'm about to yank my wrist away, that eerie cold overcomes me. As I blackout, I retreat to the Gateway. Whatever this specter is, as I know it isn't the lost soul it appears, I know I'll be safe there.

Chapter 18

Silence. Beautiful, blissful silence. I'm immersed in it. Suspended in darkness, I breathe easy and relax. I've always liked the dark. My mind is empty, yet a nagging feeling rests in my stomach. That stone warns me of impending doom. Dramatic as that is, I can't figure out why. My mind is filled with a haze I can't shake. I don't remember much before waking, but I can recall Ioana. Her eyes… no… empty sockets were so off-putting. I've never seen her like that. It was almost as if she had been turned into a puppet.

As I contemplate what I do remember, I note the pitch is beginning to thin out. that's when it hits me. I'm supposed to be at the Gateway, however this doesn't feel the same. Fear rises in me like bile, yet I try to keep composed. Panic never helps in situations like this. I take a deep and exhale, calming my nerves. The ring I wear heats up, making the hairs on the back of my neck stand. there's a spark from that hand, the crackle of fire calling to me. It's a sound I've heard countless times before. This time, however, it has a strange rhythm. Almost like Morse code. Listening harder, there's a faint cry. Just as I'm about to answer it, a switch flips and the world is devoured by light.

I gasp and cover my eyes, trying to block the pain from the sudden change. Sadistic laughter sounds and my body drops onto a hard surface. I chance opening my eyes, and immediately wish I hadn't. The creature in front of me looks human, yet that shell is wrought with decay. Gray flesh is covered in holes, chunks of missing flesh has his clothes hanging str1angely, and half of his face has been eaten away. He steps closer, searching my expression for fear. Now that I have a face to my attacker, there's none present. Another step and I stand my ground. Irritation sparks in that sunken eye.

"I smell death on you," he cackles.

"We don't even *want* to talk about what I smell on you," I remark, arms crossed over my chest.

"Rude child, soaked in the blood of millions," he hisses. "Every breath you take is another life ended. Your very existence feeds the fires of Hell. Little wonder of the dead, cause of our demise. Our lives are forfeit thanks to you. But... how can such a sinful soul remain so pure?"

"You're wearing someone else's rotting corpse and *you* have the nerve to judge *me*?" I scoff. "Where am I? What do you want with me?"

"You are a strong soul, but I am stronger still. I won't let you take my food source. Just as the chancellor before you, I've trapped you in my web. This is a world of my making. All those I've trapped are here, hiding, suspended in their most painful memories. Your pain will be to watch them suffer. Your soul will never return to your mortal shell... It's a shame I couldn't possess it. I tire of this rotted flesh suit."

I'm about to question him, when he vanishes in a cloud of black. The smell of death gets stronger. I move away, coughing, and find myself in the dark once more. Within the void imprisoning me, I hear a woman sobbing. Worried for her safety, I attempt to locate her. A spotlight clicks on, the sound echoing in the dark, and I understand why this is a punishment. she's encased in a glass dome, an exhibit in a zoo. As I get closer, I find a placard.

"Beverly Walker. Murdered for beauty, but beauty is on the inside."

Curious, I gaze into the dome. I note the floor is a mirror. The woman is on her knees, face buried in bloody hands. When she lifts her face, all I see is muscle and tendon. One hand covers my mouth, silencing the gasp of surprise. Determined to help this soul, I knock on the glass. She looks up, but immediately screams in horror. it's at that point I gaze upon the glass across from me. In a sadistic twist, he's locked the vain woman in a two-way mirror prison. Her vanity led to her imprisonment, and now she must face her choice for eternity. The irony isn't lost upon me. I'm about to call out to her again, when the spotlight turns off. She, too, is gone just as quickly. Baffled by the sudden departure, I almost miss a man's scream in the distance.

I don't even hesitate, so used to jumping into the flames. Literally and figuratively. Another spotlight reveals yet another lost soul. He doesn't appear in a gruesome manner. The placard before his 'cage' reads: Adam Summers. Greed got the best of him. A pile of millions materializes in front of him. At first, he seems wary. Then he eagerly reaches for the riches. I jump when they burst into flames. His eyes go wide, crazed, and his screams are piercing. I'm forced to cover my ears, yet the sound refuses to be blocked. The fire calls to me, unable to breach this prison. Although I reach for it, I'm unable to make a connection. Incapable of quieting the irrational screams of anguish, I slam my fists on the glass. It has no effect. Before I can try again, the man dives into the flames to salvage what he can. he's overcome in seconds. His screams rise, yet he clings to that money as though his life depends on it. When they're both nothing but ash, the fire dies out. As I watch in horror, those cries echoing in my mind, the man is reformed. He looks just as he did when first I saw him. It's then I realize he's living in an endless loop. All these people are trapped in an eternal nightmare.

I can't witness his demise again, so I back away. My back hits a hard surface, the spotlight warm on my skin, and I know it's yet another victim. The light before me goes away, taking the burning man with it. With a reluctant sigh, I turn to face them.

"Henry Wilson," I read aloud. "Didn't want to see his unfaithful wife anymore. Love is truly blind."

Within the cage, a man stands. His eyes are empty sockets, blood dripping down his cheeks like tears. There's no fire, no hints of pain or torment. I wonder what nightmare has been built for him. Perhaps he fears the dark that comes with blindness. Before I walk away, however, I hear a girl's giggle. The man glances up, leading me to believe he knows the voice. Her laughter grows louder, filled with joy and innocence. Although I know better, I allow it to calm me. The man does the same. It doesn't last though. Her tiny voice sounds, curious and questioning.

"Daddy? Someone's at the door," she calls. "Daddy? Daddy. It's okay, I'll get it."

His body tenses, and then I hear the creak of a door. What ensues is enough to scar even myself. There's a shrill scream from the girl, probably between five and ten years of age. A clatter resonates in the prison, likely a table knocked over in a struggle. I cringe as a knife cuts through her skin. I can tell what the weapon is not only from the sound, but also from the phantom pain I feel from it. A hiss leaves my lips at the sensation. Pain blossoms along my right shoulder, spreading around to my back. The blind man stumbles around, searching for the child in need of rescue.

I drop to the knee when my leg is hit, the little girl's pleas almost drowned out by the pain. The man has bloody tears streaming down his face, unable to save his daughter from her attacker. His cries are filled with regret and misery, never getting used to this sadistic penance. Unable to stand the scene, the agony, anymore, I back away. I double over at a jab to my stomach, the little girl's screams finally coming to an end.

My body sinks to the floor, curling up within this haunted pitch. As much as I want to tear this horrific freak show apart, I haven't the time. Every prison has an exit, so this one should as well. I just have to find it.

Chapter 19

Time is a strange concept here, locked away in the inky depths. Surrounded by agonizing screams and crazed this misery is an effective weight upon my shoulders. This place is a void of hopelessness. I'm not sure how long it's been, nor am I certain it matters. All I know, is that I can't find the exit. I've stumbled around blindly, encountered many victims, but no door has shown itself. I couldn't even find a wall.

"This is impossible," I mutter. "There has to be a way to get out of here… but why haven't I found it?"

"*Can you hear it?*"

I gasp at the phrase, used so often by my gypsy stalker. She shouldn't be here, she wasn't possessed by that evil creature. Frantic for something familiar, I get up to search. Not even a prisoner is near me. I'm completely alone. A shiver races through me, sending a jolt of paranoia to my mind. It seems as though the screams have gotten louder, drowning out her voice. This only makes me more curious. I sit down and close my eyes, attempting to close out the chaos around me. It's difficult to reach past them, as my first instinct is to help them. I can't do that if I'm dead, though. Not unless I can be employed by Nixie. Once I dull my senses to those tortured souls, I focus on her.

"*Can you hear it?*" Ioana inquires once more. "*Listen… listen, and… live. Live… l-live…*"

"Live?" I question. "How am I supposed to do that? I'm trapped in this nightmare, my body… Wait… Is it still by the truck? Was I killed? Does that even matter?"

The questions roll through my mind. When I died on the island, my body turned into ash and rebuilt itself. If I was pulled from my body, as I assume I have been, it would decay and vanish. At least, that's what I anticipate.

Either that, or it was forced into a spirit form for this prison. that's when it dawns on me… this is a prison for *souls*. That should be my original form. If I take on a mortal shell, perhaps I can escape. The hope rekindles and I attempt to control my figure. As it becomes more solid, I feel invisible chains fall off of me. it's a welcome release.

Opening my eyes, I note I'm right back where I was taken. Unlike that moment, however, I'm not alone. The moon radiates behind Styx, his features twisted in worry and helplessness. It's not a good look on him. With a groan, as my body is sore, I sit up. He kneels beside me, hand on my shoulder. there's so much relief in his eyes, I'm sure the touch is to make certain I'm real.

"Well… I can mark off 'demon bait' from my list of 'things I want to be when I grow up'," I mutter.

"That's not funny," he frowns. "I thought you were gone!"

"I almost was," I remark.

"What happened?" he demands.

"You first. What are you doing out here?"

"After you left, I listened for the truck. When I didn't hear it, I came looking for you. I found you lying on the ground, your body was flickering between elements. All of a sudden, it burst into flames! I stayed because there were still embers burning."

"Ioana showed up, but… she didn't feel right. Next thing I know, I'm trapped in a menagerie of punished sin. That *thing* in the orchard sent me to a world it made to store the souls it possessed."

"What! It attacked you?" he asks, indignant and livid. "Why would it target you like that!"

"Apparently, the orchard is its food source and it didn't want me ruining that. On the bright side, now we know it's not a danger to me."

I'm aware that came out a little more hopeful than I was going for, and I curse mentally at the realization. Unfortunately, Styx isn't buying it. The expression he gives me rivals my mother's stern one. Even with the threat of the demon tracking me down, he won't let me help. It's a long-shot, but I'm hoping logic can help me win this battle.

"Wouldn't it be easier to keep me safe, if I were within sight at all times?"

"It would be easier to trap your soul in my pendant until I slay this skin walker, but Nixie said I'm not allowed. If you keep pursuing this foolish path, I'll be forced to ignore her request. Now go back to the cabin."

In a huff, I grumble and climb into the truck. Styx doesn't disappear until I'm driving away. Unfortunately, he doesn't know me as well as Nixie. If he did, he would've locked me up without the warning. I reach the end of the marsh, pulling to the side at a familiar chill. Frost spreads on the windshield, telling me it's my invisible stalker. Before the frost, I had assumed Ioana had returned. I can't say I'm disappointed, though I'm curious about the temperature change. Typically it writes in steam.

"Did you have a bad day, too?" I question the empty passenger seat.

It takes a moment, but 'I'm sorry' is written in the frost. I'm confused, however I try to push through. No spirit lingers without a reason. As long as I'm freeing the orchard, I might as well help them, too. The truck is turned off and I give my spectral stalker my full attention. A car beeps as it passes, yet keeps going. Now that the area is empty, I have little worry of being interrupted.

"What do you have to be sorry for?" I ask. "Wait… You're not going to kidnap me, too, are you?"

I watch the word 'no' cross the frost. I sigh in relief, yet more is being written. My eyes skim over the message 'you listened'. After that, they write 'you learned'. That lesson must have been the girl's clue to my escape. For only a moment, I wonder how they knew. It doesn't last long, as I don't know how ghostly gossip works. Instead of obsessing over it, I push the conversation along.

"Why won't you just talk to me?" I inquire. "It would be easier than writing on the car."

There's a long pause, as though they're stuck in a debate, and then the frost renews itself. Another message on glass. This time, I'm left baffled. It says, 'they listen and the winds are swift'. With a hum of thought, I turn the comment over in my mind. Obviously, they're afraid of being found. I don't know who 'they' is, nor can I begin to guess. What draws my attention, is the fact this stranger isn't malevolent. In fact, they don't feel the same as a spirit. It's difficult to explain, but the cold of death and any paranormal happenings are absent in this presence.

"You… You're not a ghost… are you," I state more than ask.

Before they can answer, someone knocks on the glass. It only takes a heartbeat for the frost to vanish, leaving me with the sensation of being a child alone. It's surprising just how familiar it feels. Shaking it off, I roll down my window. Calista looks back at me, worry on her brow. I'm about to question her, when she leaves the driver's side door. She goes around the front of the truck, getting in that side. After closing the door, I catch a sad smile flicker on her lips. I wonder if, perhaps, she knows my strange visitor.

"I thought the orchard took you, too," she remarks. "I'm glad I was wrong. Of all those who tried, I think you're the only one that can succeed."

"Thank you," I smile. "Was there some place you wanted to go?"

"If you don't mind."

"It's not a problem. Just tell me the way."

"You know where it is. I'd like to go to Whisper Hill. That's near your cabin, isn't it?"

"Yeah, it's near there… I think."

"You *think*?"

"This case has gotten me randomly relocated so much, I can't trust my memory of locations. Sorry."

"It's fine, I'll direct you. Be careful to remember the way… We might need to visit again."

the manner in which she speaks, it seems as though she's hiding something. For now, I ignore it. She's entitled to her secrets. Besides, she's already revealed enough for the day. Shifting the truck to drive, I get back onto the road.

Chapter 20

Whisper Hill really is close to the cabin, but not as close as I thought. In fact… there's a large expanse of trees around it. I park in the grass again, as there's nowhere else to go. There isn't even a rough path leading the way. Calista gets out as I turn off the engine. When I join her at the edge of the trees, she has a strange expression on her face. It's a mixture of sorrow and happiness… and love. Before she can disappear into the foliage, my hand shoots out and grips her shoulder. These aren't just any trees. Whisper Hill is encased within the orchard.

"Don't be afraid, it's not after you," she assures.

She grips my hand and heads in. though I don't want to test the waters with Styx, I'm not about to let her go alone. Taking a deep breath, I let her pull me along. Static snaps along my limbs, lighting up the dark for only a blink. The air is heavier, and the apples give off a dim glow within the leaves overhead. If I didn't know how many died to create it, I would be enamored by the illusory view.

"I come here every year at this time," Calista says. "It's just as beautiful as it is deadly."

"It's definitely more active," I frown. "Is it hitting a peak?"

"Yes. It's all downhill from here. You're running out of time, do you still think you can succeed?"

"I have no doubts," I reply.

She nods, pleased with the answer. A soft breeze circles us. That strange smile returns, her hand raising as though holding another. The trees seem to reach for her, embracing their lost leader… or pleading for help. I suppose it just depends on how old they are. The way they gravitate to her, the scene is ethereal. Though they're effected by her presence, the spirits refrain from appearing.

Calista doesn't seem to mind, so I take that as a normal occurrence. It's so quiet here. Unable to stand it, I attempt a conversation.

"What happened after the curse?" I wonder. "How did you keep people from finding out you're immortal? I mean, that sort of suspicion caused witch hunts back then. Did anyone ever find out?"

"After the fire, I was so angry. I wanted to *kill* the settlers for what they did. They took *everything* from me."

I can't blame her for her anger, it would've lit me up as well. Considering she's lived alongside them for so long without lashing out, I'm impressed. We step around a large tree, thick in the trunk, and get back on the rough path she's created. As I duck beneath a low branch, it curls around my hair. At first, I think it's going to pull. Thankfully, it seems to want only to give affection. It rakes thin branches through my hair, gentle and almost loving. I wonder, briefly, if this tree is a mother that lost her children. Perhaps even a grandmother, separated from her family.

"I went out to gather ingredients, planning on making a poison for them," Calista continues. "When I reached Whisper Hill, I knew I wasn't alone. The god of Whisper Hill sat down and talked me out of killing them."

"That's… kind of amazing," I comment. "I mean, not just the fact a god felt you important enough to show themselves to, but also that he was able to stop your revenge so easily. I would've taken a heck of a lot more than a talking to."

"I guess it wasn't so much that he spoke… it was more what he said," she offers. "He said everything that happened was a tragedy, but it wouldn't be for nothing. He promised to make sure of it, and I believe him."

"What could possibly make this less of a tragedy?"

"… He told me a great evil would spread and this place, my family, would be a large part of their downfall. It wasn't supposed to happen, but I didn't want it to be for nothing. He helped me hide among newcomers. I relocated frequently, even got married… once. My heart was never his… not completely."

I'm surprised by this admission. Marriage isn't something I would jump into with immortality. Being with someone on a daily basis, there's no way they wouldn't notice you don't age after so long. My ankle gets snagged by a thorn bush, so I stop to untangle myself. I expect her to keep walking, yet she waits patiently. Truthfully, I'm quite relieved she did. I don't want to be here alone if I have a choice.

"Did you tell him what happened?" I wonder, yanking myself free.

"I told him everything, he was my best friend," she admits. "He took it well… better than I expected. I was impressed, to say the least, especially during those times."

"What times?"

"He came with the second group of settlers. At first, I just wanted to get near them. To learn what they knew about my daughter. I wasn't aware she had passed. Eventually, I came to love him. When I told him of my deceit, his only answer was that he already knew. He chose to stay with me, because he knew my heart was broken. He wanted to mend it."

"That's so sweet," I smile. "What happened to him? Did you two have any kids?"

"Ioana was my only child," Calista sighs. "I couldn't have anymore after her. My husband, though… old age claimed him. I made sure he had a happy life, and I stayed by his side until the end. It hurt to let him go, but I knew he would be happier with his family in the afterlife."

I step over a creeping root, careful not to harm the little saplings near its base. A few thick limbs are growing in bends, almost as though they're sheltering children. The scene breaks my heart. How horrid their end must've been. Personally, I don't think I could handle something like this. Then again, I'm a human blowtorch. I highly doubt I'll ever be in such a position. As crazy as it might seem, I find a speck of misery at the thought. It's okay to be different, I applaud those that embrace their oddities. But sometimes, it hurts to not fit in. I think it's pretty obvious I don't have a chance to 'fit in' anymore.

We stop periodically, greeting a few trees and getting tabs on our skin walker. Thankfully, he seems to be preoccupied. Perhaps leaving to confront me used up a good portion of his power. With any luck, he'll be out of commission until Styx has a plan to kill him. Calista comes to a stop and I look around. The clearing is a good size, the trees keeping well away, and Whisper Hill looms over us. The sight is much more intimidating than my first visit. When we step past the tree line, the air grows warm. I can see gusts of wind by the leaves they pick up. They seem to come from every direction all at once, gathering upon the hill before disappearing. Calista smiles, walking to that ground as quickly as she can. Once we reach the top, the grass soft beneath my feet, Calista sits to lean against an old tree. The trunk is twisted and gnarled. As I sit beside her, I note a cross shaped depression in the bark.

"She loved this place at night," she remarks. "I could always find her here. After the fires, I would come every night. I hoped she would at least come here."

"Have you seen her since then?"

"No. I've heard stories of others coming across her, though. I hoped and wished, yet she's never crossed paths with me. Have *you* seen her?"

"Many times," I admit. "She's lost, but I want to fix that. She doesn't seem like she's suffering. When she talks to me, she keeps asking if I can hear something.

Until I spoke to you, I couldn't understand why. Now I think she meant this place."

The sky above is darkening now, glittering stars dull against the light still shining. It won't be long and they'll dominate the coming twilight. It's so peaceful here, erasing any anxiety I once had. It just seems as though time has stopped in this clearing. I can breathe. My eyes watch the sun vanish behind the trees here. When it's finally given its final shot at life, the moon takes on a brighter hue.

"I can see why she liked it here," I comment. "It's so beautiful."

"She didn't come for the beauty, she came for her father," Calista states, smile small. "He was always around this hill, always waiting to see her. If I let her, she would've set up her own camp."

I want to ask more about him, yet I feel that's a place I shouldn't go. He must be very special to put that look on her face, however remembering him may be painful. After all, he couldn't still be alive after all this time. I lean back against the tree, that depression coming to my notice once again.

"What is this?" I ask.

"This?" Calista wonders, running a hand over the cross. "This is for my Ioana. Her father helped me make it. I wanted to put her to rest, but couldn't find her. This was supposed to be the next best thing. Unfortunately, I just can't stop wondering where she is… What happened?"

"I know where she is," I offer.

"You do? Where?" she inquires, eyes wide and hopeful.

"Well… I had a dream where I saw through her eyes. It was the night she disappeared. She took food to the settlers, and then started home. On the way, though, she heard music playing. She followed it to the first settlement they built, that single home with a well outside.

The music came from the well. She climbed down and found a door that led to a secret room. When she entered the room, someone slammed the door shut behind her… She was trapped."

"You're positive?" Calista wonders. "If this is only a dream…"

"I've had dreams like that before, I know the difference between memory and fabrication. That was what happened when she disappeared. Unfortunately, I don't know anymore than that."

"… Thank you," she whispers, tears in her eyes. "It's been so long wondering… Thank you for giving me the answers I've been searching for."

"I'm going to retrieve her," I remark. "Nothing is going to stop me from freeing these people."

"You're a very pure soul," she smiles. "But don't be so hard on yourself. They've waited centuries to pass, a few more days won't hurt. In order to take care of them, you need to take care of yourself first."

I nod, understanding her comment. I've thought that before and I hold strong to it. If I should pass, there's no help waiting to take over for me. I need to stay alive, if only to help those trapped. I glance beside me, finding Calista with her eyes closed. She seems to be lost in a memory, face lifting to greet the wind streaming to us.

"I've missed this place," she sighs out. "It gets harder and harder to visit each year."

"You should just build out here," I comment. "I mean… it's way better than the swamp, right? Why do you live out there anyway?"

"It's away from the city, and no one bothers to visit," she informs. "Then again, I suppose they won't be too inclined to visit here either. I suppose I moved away from the memories more than the orchard itself."

"I suppose its something to think about. How late are we staying out here? Are we going to look for Styx while we're here?"

"You can go, but... I think I'll stay. It's been so long since I spoke with Whisper Hill's lone inhabitant. We're overdue for a conversation."

"Are you sure?" I frown. "I don't mind waiting."

"No, go ahead," she assures. "If you see my daughter again, could you tell her I love her?"

"Of course," I state. "And I'll be sure to tell her you're waiting here for her."

"Thank you."

Although it pains me to leave her in this haunted place, it's clear there's no changing her mind. I just pray she isn't weak mentally and she's staying for a delusion. Giving her the benefit of the doubt, I start for the truck. I'll check back in the morning, just to make sure she's all right.

Back in the truck, I take in a deep breath and relax upon exhale. I start the vehicle and check around me before shifting to drive. There's no one with me right now. No Ioana, no invisible stranger... I'm alone. It's a nice change to the chaos I live daily. Just as I'm relaxing, I feel a presence appear beside me. I groan and start to slow down. After parking alongside the road, I face the intruder. Styx looks less than happy right now.

"What part of 'no orchard' did you have trouble understanding?" he frowns.

He looks older right now, face stern and lips tight. Whereas I met him in his late teens or early twenties, he's aged to late twenties or early thirties. He's still in ripped jeans and a tee shirt, his skin without the showing bone and muscle.

"Would you have preferred I let her go alone?" I wonder.

"Is that any different from *leaving* her alone?"

"It is if I didn't know she was going to stay," I defend. "Besides, I didn't go wandering. At least give me those points. I wanted to, but I didn't. Instead, I left the trees behind me."

"And I thank you for that. But that Skin Walker has shown an ability it shouldn't have, which means its fed off more souls than I had imagined. With so long to feed and so many souls at his disposal, I fear it won't be stopped."

"You're an ancient," I point out. "It'll be child's play for you. Besides, I think leaving the orchard to find me drained it. That loss will definitely be handy once you figure out the plan."

He mutters under his breath, yet I can't make it out. Ignoring it, I start to drive once more. If he wants to continue talking, he can do so while I make headway. The cabin isn't much further. The sky has darkened now, night taking over until the dawn. The stars are brilliant against the dark backdrop. I try to focus on driving, not wanting another accident, and Styx begins to talk once more.

"If it really did risk so much power to track you down, it would've returned to its shelter afterward. If it's managed to hide this long without me noticing, I might not be able to destroy it myself."

"How would you kill it anyway?" I wonder. "I thought it was already dead before... You know... when the settlers accidentally freed it?"

"It was trapped, not dead. If it would've been dead, there would've been no chance to free it," he explains. "Back during the war, our weapons were enough to defeat them. They were forged in Helheim and cooled in the waters of the river Styx. That's what made them so effective against the dead."

"Don't you still have it?"

"Yes, but... it took a lot of punishment during the war. It might not have that same magic now. The only other way I can think to destroy it, is to drag it down into the waters of my mother's river. He would return to the death he was created from."

"How do we… I mean… not that I'm going, because I'm not allowed to help… but out of pure curiosity… How would we get to the river?"

"… That was a pathetic attempt at covering up what's obviously a way for you to get in trouble," he frowns. "I expected more from you."

"It's late, my brain shut down, and I'm focused on not crashing. That was a damn good attempt."

"Whatever you say," he scoffs. "But to answer your question, you'd have to learn how to jump wells."

"… Jump wells? What the hell is that?"

"When you find out, I'll let you help kill the Skin Walker," he states, a cocky smirk on his lips.

He's so going to regret this agreement. With an opportunity to join the hunt, I won't rest until I'm there. When I turn to tell him that, he's already gone. Rolling my eyes, I turn into the cabin's drive and park in the garage. Going through the door to the house, I almost run into Nixie. She's on the phone, stirring something in a large bowl in her arm. It looks like brownie batter.

"Oh wait! She's right here!" she states, abandoning the bowl to hand me the phone. "It's your dad."

"… Dad?" I question, throat dry. "What's wrong?"

"You haven't called us, is everything going okay? Did you get cursed again? Please tell me you didn't get cursed again."

"I didn't," I offer. "I was just… busy."

"You sound odd, are you alright?"

"I… I had a dream the other night," I admit. "It left me shaken and I hope it's just a dream, but… you and mom really are my parents, right?"

There's silence on the other end of the call, and then I hear him calling my mother over. The sound changes as

I'm put on speaker, and my stomach sinks. All this time I knew who I was, I knew where I came from. After that dream… nothing is the same anymore. I've lost my sense of identity with that simple glance from a well, and I wish I still had that ignorance.

Chapter 21

It was a short dream, set with a beautiful view of trees and sky. I stared up into that blue, blissfully ignorant to my location. I was in a well. The muffled voices are familiar to me. Ioana asks what a woman wishes for, and my mother answers. The next thing I know, her face peeks into the well. She picks me up, and the dream is over. Though I pushed it from my head, it still lingers at the back of my mind. Perhaps that's why I asked. Either that, or the oddly coincidental connection is nagging me. The store was in my neighborhood, my father investigated the island, and now this place is where I entered this world. It can't all be by chance. And how much did my parents know? They could've done more to prepare me. The silence is too much for me, so I repeat the question.

"Mom gave birth to me, right?" I wonder.

"… I'm sorry, honey," my mother remarks. "We were going to tell you, but… One of the conditions were to let you learn on your own. We were told if you learned before that, it could get you killed."

"All my life, you've disregarded magic and myth, and now I find out that's exactly how you got me? Are you *kidding* me right now!"

"I wanted to keep you safe!" she snaps. "All this supernatural chaos is going to get you killed!"

"You can't protect me anymore!" I shout back. "Can't you see that? The store, the island, this place… it's all connected. This was going to happen, there's no other path for me to take! I just wish… I wish I would've learned sooner."

"We're really sorry, sweetheart," my dad sighs. "We weren't told much about you, so we assumed you were just an abandoned child."

"What happened that day?" I inquire.

As they gather their thoughts, Nixie follows me to the living room. We sit and I put the speaker on. For this talk, I need her support. I know, in my youth, people would ask if I were adopted. I never understood why. My appearance seems to match my parents. Knowing how adamant Meli was about my origin, and having heard Ioana's voice in my dream, I'm curious to learn the significance of this connection.

"Your father was investigating that day, so I decided to take a walk," my mother begins. "So many people were out, so many stories filled the air. I found myself in the park. No one was there, which seemed odd to me. Then I turned and saw a little girl by the trees.

I don't know how, but I knew she was alone. I walked over to her, and asked where her parents were. She told me she was dead and I couldn't help her, but she could help me. She asked me what I wanted more than anything, and I told her I couldn't have children. I wanted a daughter. She walked over to an old stone well, and motioned for me to look. When I did, I found you. You were just floating in the water there. I lifted you out and looked back for the girl. She told me I could never tell you the truth, that you would learn when you were ready. She said you were special, that you had a great destiny and needed to be kept safe. After that, she disappeared. I tool you to your father to tell him what happened. When we spoke, you were laughing and reaching for something I couldn't see. I just thought that was normal for babies."

"I think you've always been able to see the dead," my father states. "When I erased your memory of the island, it may have damaged that talent. It would've, at least, made you forget having it. Maybe even how to use it."

"Okay," I breathe. "I know this is difficult for you guys, but… I'm getting a bad feeling about this mission. If something happens to me..."

"*Nothing* is going to happen to you," Nixie says, eyes almost icy. "I won't let it."

Her determination is comforting, but that feeling doesn't go away. It does, however, kill my conversation. I tell my parents I love them, just in case, and then I hang up. The revelation has left me mentally exhausted. As I sigh and stare at the abandoned phone, Nixie gives me a hug.

"It's okay," she says. "Family is more than blood. They took care of you, raised you. you'll always be their daughter."

"I know," I sigh. "I just… I'm disappointed at the secrecy. Why did I have to wait? What would've happened if they told me?"

"News travels fast in the immortal circle. Had they caught on to your lineage, our enemy would've trapped you in this world, too."

the comment strikes me, drawing up my located siblings. They were from different times, so it can't just be coincidence… right? To be killed in a manner that completely differs from their element, making it impossible for them to reform. It has to be more than a happenstance, they had to have been hunted. Our mysterious enemy sure did their homework. Through their countless encounters, noting how each attack effected them, and slowly drawing a master plan in the background. Who knows how long it took to finish. The only anomally they face, is the fact they've never encountered me. They were probably counting on our mother keeping me near. I would certainly assume that from Meli's story. If she would, and did, then… how was I brought here?

"What's on your mind?" Nixie inquires.

"I need to talk to the others," I remark. "I think the enemy never intended to face me. they've studied the others, but I was never away from our mother. I'm here because they don't know me."

"But what's stopping them from killing you as well?"

"... They... they can't."

"What do you mean?"

"I'm the Root of Souls... I'm *already* dead."

The remark stuns us both. I had never considered that before. Another thought strikes me, and I go over different ways I might be trapped. Although Meli and Shadow may have a list of their own, their unlikely resting places weren't something obvious enough to list. I have to think out of the box. Doing so, however, just leaves me remembering Styx's punishment. Even so, similar to the Skin Walker's world, I might be able to break free by taking a mortal shell.

After the short conversation, we decide to get ready for bed. I lay, staring at the ceiling for a long while. As soon as Nixie's breathing evens out, I close my eyes. In the dark behind my eyelids, I search for that strange door. it's not there. I can't even find the small wisp near it. Inside the room, however, I hear a rapping on wood. I shift, my hand coming in contact with Nixie in the process. that's when I open my eyes. If she didn't make the noise, then someone is in the cabin. I slide out of bed, creeping over to the bathroom. An eerie light shines from beneath the door, and I know our intruder is from the beyond.

"Why is it always a bathroom?" I grumble. "I swear, every area with its own name has stories of haunted bathrooms."

I open the door after a moment's hesitation. On the other side, I'm faced with a forest. Above the treetops, there's a massive tree. This is the Gateway, but... I'm usually asleep when I come here. Carefully, I enter the forest. A symbol is glowing on the door's handle, which I commit to memory. I can look it up later.

Walking through the trees, I note there seems to be a lot more. The life here is bravely pushing past flourishing, bordering on overabundance. It's difficult to navigate. My legs are cut by thorns, arms bruised from too many falls. It might just be my over active imagination, but it seems the plants are preparing for war. Uneasy about the image my brain provides, I push on through the overgrowth.

At the base of the massive tree, I find Meli and Shadow. The two are locked in a serious conversation. When they see me, they move around to make room. I sit and listen to them. It almost sounds like an uncertain battle plan. A thin limb from the tree reaches down and wraps around my waist. Three also weave into Meli's hair, slowly braiding her locks. It brings pause to their conversation, so I dare to create another.

"I think I understand what the enemy has been doing," I comment.

"*Girl, we all know they've been kicking our asses,*" Shadow points out.

"No, I mean before," I explain. "With each fight, they took notes. They learned your strengths and weaknesses."

"*There's no way they could've learned that much, they would've used it against us.*"

"No, I don't think so. I believe they deliberately lost to you. They only tested one of you at a time. Winning wasn't the goal at the beginning, just collecting information. Once they got what they needed, they started on another Root. To make sure you guys underestimated them, they intentionally used attacks that weren't very effective. Now that you've all been trapped, no one is left to stop them."

"*You're still free,*" Shadow says.

"Yeah, but that's something they didn't anticipate. I think they never intended that I get involved. that's why they're trying to act now. I'm not even sure I was sent by our mother… I think I was taken from her."

"*By who?*" Meli gasps.

"I don't know, but I think they were trying to help us."

They fall silent, both uneasy about the revelation. I don't blame them. There are already so many players in this game, another only helps the mess thicken. We don't know who we can trust, who might be helping, why they would even bother. It just makes my head hurt to think it through. Shadow and Meli aren't making me feel much better about all this. I would've thought at least one of them would've known about this mystery helper.

With nothing left to explain to them, I just sit back and wait. There isn't really much more I can do. Meli knits her brows together, deep in thought about this new information. Shadow, however, seems rather anxious. I've known him long enough to know he's holding back information. When he feels my gaze on him, he tries to escape the coming flood of questions. I don't let him.

"You know something," I point out. "What is it? Do you know who took me from our mother?"

"*No, I honestly don't,*" he sighs, defeated even before the battle. "*All I know, is that things were heating up in my timeline. We all met numerous times before, missing one more person each time. My era was closer to yours, so I was one of the last to get captured.*"

"And?" I wonder.

"*... There was talk with the Earth Root,*" he confides. "*Our other siblings were already trapped, there was nothing we could do on our own. We tried to figure out a plan to defeat this evil once and for all. One of us just weren't enough, but we knew you had all the power. You were the baby, the one gifted with an unsurpassed ability. If anyone could defeat this mastermind, you could. But... mom wouldn't let us risk it. That's all I know. The next time I went to the meet, I was the only one there.*"

The information is mind boggling, to say the least. To think that our own sibling was the kidnapper… I just don't know what to say to that. Meli also seems rather taken aback, her mouth slightly open in her shock. I'm curious to know this new sibling, what they had planned… why they would entrust so much to me. I can't comprehend what it is they saw in me, yet I have a feeling they would be rather letdown.

"I need to finish this investigation," I sigh out. "I'm growing weary of all this secrecy."

"*I thought you would've gotten it done by now,*" Meli comments. "*I mean, you work so hard to get to the truth. Aren't the spirits helping you?*"

"They are, but… Styx has forbidden me from going into the orchard for now. There's this thing called a Skin Walker..."

Their loud gasps quiet me. I gaze upon them both, their eyes large and filled with fear. That's enough to make me wish I hadn't challenged Styx for this battle. Although I have a feeling I don't really want to know, I can't help the curiosity eating away at me.

"Okay, what's so horrible about these things?" I ask. "Styx and Nix are both wound up about it. He threatened to bind my soul to his amulet until it was taken out. Why is it so damn bad?"

"Skin Walkers are damned souls too tainted with evil to save," Shadow remarks, voice quiet and cryptic. "They were handpicked by the gods of the underworld, from all religions, and shaped to be soldiers of the damned."

"They buried themselves deep into the core of a soul, whispering evil into their ears," Meli adds. "Little by little, it fed off the purity of a soul. That purity was replaced by darkness. Eventually, they would cajole a mortal into committing murder, claiming their soul as their own trophy and living on within their skin. As a 'mortal', they could commit atrocities and spread even more plague in the spiritual world."

"By the time we knew how bad they really were, they had already led the *mortals into a dark age. The Charon and Envoys were charged with their destruction. Their war lasted many years, tainting the spiritual world with pitch that clung to any living thing. It made them sick, creating a plague in the minds of the mortals. They died from it, some even falling prey to the echoes of the destroyed Skin Walkers. If there's one in that orchard, you need to stay away from it. They can only be killed by a couple methods.*"

"I've heard," I wave off. "I'm not letting Styx face it alone. Besides, it's started to hunt me outside the orchard. I was locked in its twisted zoo."

"*How did you escape?*" Meli wonders, struggling between rage and awe.

"I took a mortal form," I shrug off. "Its world was meant for the dead, not the living."

The two are impressed, but I don't feel the need to explain I had help. In the end, I still had to figure it out myself. Now that the topic has come up, however, I can't help but wonder if they can give me any clues to my given task. With their reaction, however, I'm hesitant to ask. I'm beginning to think I'm underestimating this Skin Walker. If I want to get this over with, though, I have no choice but to face it head on.

"Styx told me I can join his hunt… when I learn to jump wells. Do you know what he meant?"

"*No, I don't even like to hear about wells,*" Shadow remarks with a shiver. "*Way too much water for my taste.*"

"... *I'm torn,*" Meli sighs. "*I know what he meant, but... I don't want you fighting that Skin Walker. You may have gotten away once, but I don't know if it'll learn from that mistake.*"

"All the more reason to help," I remark, adamant. "Styx has already fought this thing, he might not be effective alone."

"*And if you're trapped once more? How are you to help him then?*"

"... I'll have to answer that at a later date," I blush. "I'm not much of a planner."

"*And that's why I can't help you,*" Meli frowns. "*You're too important to throw to the wolves.*"

"My life is no more important than his," I counter.

"*Just give her what she wants,*" Shadow sighs. "*She's going whether she's with him or not, at least we can give her a fighting chance.*"

"Thank you!" I exclaim, tossing my arms toward him dramatically. "Finally, someone understands how I think!"

"*It's not that hard, you're pretty reckless.*"

I glower in his direction, sulking at the barb. It's completely true, but still… I prefer the term adventurous. It sounds way more responsible. His comment, however, doesn't receive the desired result. Meli seals her lips and glares at the both of us. It isn't until our 'mother' pushes her closer to me that she speaks.

"I refused to teach you, but… I'll give you a clue. Nothing more," she states. "The tools you need are all in your room."

"My room is a massive cemetery!" I whine.

"That's your problem," she smirks, knowing. "By the time you actually find everything and work it out, Styx will have defeated the Skin Walker. So take your time."

I'm about to argue with her, yet she stands and walks toward her own room. Shadow and I just watch her leave. When she's no longer in sight, he settles his gaze on me in question. With a light shrug, I stand and wander closer to my door. By the time I realize he's following, I'm already opening it. He seems hesitant, so I assume he's also never visited. I understand why, however it seems rather lonely. Assured he's right behind me, I open the door and march in. Meli has set the challenge and I'm going to win it.

Chapter 22

The mood is eerie, a wash of pale moonlight the only source of illumination. Among the headstones, I can see translucent figures roaming about. Shadow gasps just behind me, so I reach back for his hand. Together, we venture further into the cemetery. The grass, dead beneath our feet, crunches with every step. I don't like the look of it. This whole place is dark and steeped in night. While I don't mind the moon and stars above, the dead foliage isn't helping lift anyone's mood. As she thinks this, the grass changes. It starts at her foot, spreading green in a ripple of life, and soon takes over the whole room. Trees have leaves and flowers bloom in abundance.

"*This isn't so bad,*" Shadow offers, though his voice trembles.

"You don't have to be here," I comment. "This is my task, I can handle it alone."

"*This room isn't just a room, it's a world made for you,*" he remarks. "*There's more to it than you think, you need my help to put up a good effort.*"

"... Thank you," I smile. "Meli said you guys don't like to come here, so I appreciate you doing this."

"*It didn't used to be so gloomy here,*" he admits. "*When we started out together, this place was a beautiful garden. Nothing seemed unhappy or out of place. We loved coming here... but then... it all changed. With every life we spent away from you, with every fight we left you for, it seemed to weigh heavily upon you. You wouldn't talk to us about it, but I think... I think you knew more than we thought you did.*"

The news is odd to me, as I have no memory of that time. It also makes me wonder what I was thinking back then. If my past life is similar to this one, I could easily pinpoint what made me withdraw. Unfortunately, I don't know how that works. If I was alive once before, would I be different every time I'm reborn? I can't help but question the little things.

"Was I different?" I ask, moving along a gravel path. "From now, I mean. Personality wise."

"*No, we're always the same,*" he offers, knowing. "*Our looks may change, but we're always the same on the inside.*"

"Then perhaps I was growing weary of being surrounded by death," I suggest. "Maybe I lost the living energy around me, so I fell into an unusual routine. Spending your life in a cemetery can effect you, just as easily as spending it in the forest."

"*... I guess we never thought of that,*" he hums, regret in his tone. "*We were so busy fighting off our unknown enemy... we forgot about you. I'm sorry, Catori. We didn't mean to.*"

"I know you didn't," I smile. "I don't blame you. Honestly, I can't even remember back then. Maybe that was affected by my dad's spell as well. Now… to find my tools. I'm gonna guess the first one is a well, although… I only know of one here."

"*You only need one?*"

"… Well… I guess," I frown. "Here, at least. Don't you think?"

"*I would think. Where is this well you know of?*"

"It's over this way."

I wave him to follow, and then head toward that strange well I found. With the new greenery still spreading, it's a bit more difficult to find my way. More than once, we almost walk through a spirit on the move. After a short while, I manage to locate a familiar headstone. Turning from there, I hurry toward the well.

A few trees have sprouted up, bushes and flowers thick along the life giving well. It looks like a silent grove, one couples might picnic in. A welcome change from the strange calm it held before. I stop next to it, glancing in curiously. Two little spirits form, twins, and disappear within a channel below.

"Isn't it amazing?" I wonder, tone soft with wonder. "To think something so important could start off in such an odd place."

"*That's where you created them?*" Shadow inquires. "*You never told us about this well. Then again, we didn't really ask. We all pretty much stuck to our own elements.*"

"It's a pity," I voice. "Each one has its own feeling that comes with it, or so I've noticed. I feel so powerful when dealing with fire, but very peaceful using water."

"*What do you feel when you use your element?*"

"… I feel like I'm in the center of a massive web, connected to every tiny living thing in the world. I don't think I could ever feel lonely using my element."

I sit down on the edge of the well, still watching little forms gather and disperse. This well is used to create, so I'm not sure I can use it for the purpose I need. I wonder if, perhaps, I should look elsewhere. As I wonder, Shadow moves around the area. He touches a leaf, his fires setting it aflame. Surprisingly, it goes out just as quickly as it started. Afterward, the leaf regenerates itself.

Unable to think of what comes next, I can't help huffing in irritation. Why couldn't Meli just tell me what I have to do? It would've saved so much time. Styx could be in big trouble right now, I need to reach him. My frustration must be visible to my brother, as he reaches over to set a hand on my shoulder.

"*It's going to be okay,*" he assures. "*We found the well, that's one step closer. Now we just have to think this through.*"

"I know, I know. I just wish it weren't so hard," I whine. "I'm still new to all this, I don't understand how it works. You guys act like you've always remembered your past lives, and how to use your power. Why can't it be just as easy for me?"

"*I'm glad it isn't,*" he confides. "*If it were, you'd probably be trapped just like we were. None of us would've been set free... We wouldn't even have that hope. Everything happens for a reason, and I think you were never supposed to be found by our enemy.*"

It makes sense and I'm grateful for that silver lining. Unfortunately, it's not going to help me right now. I sigh and look around. A figure appears in the night, walking over to a headstone. The religion symbol at the top opens a column of light, rising the spirit upward. I hum to myself in thought, remembering all the doors hidden in plain sight.

"Do you think this well can work?" I ask. "Or should we search for another?"

"Since this is the only one you know of, maybe we should try using it before looking for an alternative."

"... Okay. I just... have to figure out how."

The eternal night is cool against my skin, a soft draft blowing by. It almost sounds like its calling my name. For now, I ignore it. My mind is on the headstones, the doors they create. Maybe it isn't even a well I used. Could those doorways be the channel I'm looking for? Another breeze clings to my skin, altering to follow the last. It's warmer this time, catching my attention. This is the first time I've felt this warmth in here. Then again, it could be from the life that's begun to awaken. Nevertheless, my curiosity is peaked. I stand and move toward the direction it's gone. It weaves between memorials, trailing up a small gathering of stone steps, and then circling a tall obelisk.

"Whoa," I murmur. "This wasn't here last time. I mean... I think it wasn't. I didn't exactly go exploring. Do you know what it is?"

"Not really, but... I think its your room."

"We're *in* my room, aren't we?"

"Well, we are... but... it's like your own world in here. Every world has a 'home'. This one must be yours."

I hum to myself and reach out to touch the black polished stone. When my hand makes contact, it causes a ripple to spread along the surface. It makes the stone look like dark water. Taking a breath, I walk forward. My body passes through the obelisk, leaving me standing in a large space. Around me is a kitchen, a small living room, and a two person dining table. A beam of bluish light rises from the center of the room. When I step into it, my body is lifted to the next floor. Since it's set up like a tower, there are many floors. The light must be the elevator to them.

The second floor has a nice sitting room, a large bathroom, and a library. Another floor up and I'm looking at a decorative bedroom. There's a canopy bed draped in reds and blacks, a vanity, and even a small wardrobe. I listen for Shadow, yet there are no footsteps. Curious, I lean over the wooden rail. The area is small, like the opening for a firehouse pole.

"Shadow?" I call down. "You there?"

No answer. I step back into the light and gasp when my body drops down steadily. When my feet touch the floor again, I notice that Shadow isn't inside. Confused, I walk back over to the entrance and walk out. he's still standing beside the obelisk.

"You didn't come in," I frown. "What's wrong?"

"*I can't get through the wall*," he informs.

"Okay, well… I'll look around to see if I can find something to help us. I'll be right back, don't move."

"*I'm not exactly eager to explore*," he admits, sheepish.

I nod and reenter the home. With a directive set, I begin my search. Surprisingly, this place is set up remarkably similar to my home growing up. Not so much the layout, but where everything is stored. My personality must not have changed very much. It gives me hope that I'm, indeed, the same person I was before.

In the living room, I dig through the couch cushions. Checking beneath it and upturning pillows, I find nothing.

Not that I typically hide things in the couch. I check, because with no one else to snoop it's likely I might have. Thinking more along the line of what I would do now, I head up to the library. The shelves are full of books, a wide variety it probably took years to collect. I scan them as quickly as possible, searching for anything on well jumping. Nothing even close comes up. My last resort is the bedroom, which I go to next.

Growing up, I kept a journal. I can only hope I kept one here as well. My favorite hiding place was the pillow case, which I set beneath my other pillows. Checking there, I'm disappointed once more. I sit down and groan inwardly. From my position on the end of the bed, I note a strange sheen coming from the wall across from me. It looks so out of place, I can't help but investigate. I walk over and touch it, much like the door. The wall melts away, revealing a hidden wall of books. I'm shocked at first, my eyes taking it all in, and then I pick one off the shelf. I flip through a few pages, recognizing my own handwriting.

"These… are all my journals?" I gasp. "There are so many, I don't have the time to look through them all."

My frustration is beginning to morph into panic. Taking a deep breath, I try to calm myself. Panicking won't do anything to help. I study the collection a little closer, trying to find clues on the binding. Thankfully, I've always had a terrible habit of titling my journals. It works in my favor this time, though. A purple book has the title 'Ways of the Well' scrawled along the spine. I pull it off the shelf and head downstairs.

When I exit my home, Shadow is sitting impatiently nearby. The stone bench he waits at looks awfully uncomfortable, so I try to alter it like I did the vegetation. It goes from stone, to wicker, and Shadow jumps up from it in shock. The look on his face has me laughing, though it's probably the worst response at this moment. He glares over my way, yet smirks in humor.

"Sorry, I didn't mean to scare you," I offer. "I found the book, though! I kept journals in my last life, too!"

"*That's a stroke of luck,*" he sighs in relief. "*The sooner you learn, the sooner I can leave... No offense. It's not so much the setting, but the well that has me jittery.*"

"I know, I remember our time on the island just as well as you do," I remind, taking a seat. "Let's flip through here and find what we need."

I open the book and skim through the contents. It tells so much about the well of life, the process used to create those spirits, and the channels beneath it. Then my eyes fall upon what I'm looking for. That well isn't just to create souls. Since I'm a soul myself, I would use them to travel from place to place. Those channels all open up to a water source, which allows the spirits contact with hopeful mothers. Whether sinks, tubs, lakes, or wells. They're all connected to my well of life. I just have to know where I want to go… and I know *exactly* where that is.

Chapter 23

The map looks easy enough to read, each channel moving on an invisible route. I look into the well, curiously searching for these currents. They're difficult to see, however a slight pull draws me nearer. Shadow is standing well away from the liquid. I can feel his apprehension, yet I can't move back. Taking a deep breath, I reach in. a flash of memory strikes me, yanking my hand away from the water.

"*What happened?*" Shadow panics. "*Are you okay? Did you get bit? Was it a piranha? I knew there were evil fish in that well!*"

"What?" I frown. "No, there's no evil fish in there. I just… remembered something, I think. I saw myself as a baby, being lowered into the water. I think… this is where I started this life."

"*Don't scare me like that!*"

"Then stop imagining every bad scenario, you're making it way too easy to scare you."

"*… Sorry, I can't help it,*" he blushes.

"Okay, I'm going to try to get to the well Ioana is trapped in," I remark. "If you need me here to leave the room, you might want to go now."

"*Give me a few minutes,*" he sighs, reluctant. "*I don't need you here, but I don't want to know you're gone when I leave. It'll be easier to think you'll be here to save me if something attacks.*"

"What's going to attack you here?"

"*My imagination,*" he mutters. "*Good luck, Catori. You might actually need it.*"

"Thanks."

He hugs me, as though he'll never see me again, and then turns to leave. I wait until I hear the distant whoosh of the portal. At that point, he's exited this room and I'm alone. At least, as alone as someone can be in an active graveyard. Taking a deep breath, I reach for the water once more. This time, I ignore the impending memory and push through. Closing my eyes, I find I can see the currents below. A faint image of waterways come to mind, each different in location and style. When I find her well, however, the way is blocked by some invisible force. I chalk it up to the Skin Walker's dome.

Unable to get to her, I search for another route. Remembering that I left Calista alone in the orchard, I look for water near Whisper Hill. There's a small stream there, which I latch on to. I fall forward into the well, feeling the rush of a waterfall upon me, and then I'm on the move. Each twist and drop the channel makes takes me closer to my destination. My body rises up from a body of water. When I open my eyes, I'm not where I wanted to be. Confused, I look to the book still in my hand.

"I did exactly what I was supposed to," I frown. "How did I end up here?"

The sky is locked in a breaking dawn, but I recognize the area. I'm at the ferry from my last case. Thankfully, no one is around to notice my sudden appearance. Scratching my head once more, I try to relocate that current. I concentrate on getting back to my room, making the leap into the path. Once again, I feel that strange pressure.

Opening my eyes, I note I'm at the cabin. I rose from a sink filled with water. I had forgotten Nixie set the dishes in to soak. With a frustrated sigh, I walk over to the back door. Recalling the symbol from the bathroom door, I grab a pencil and draw it on the door. It's a simple crescent moon on it's curve, three teardrop shapes beneath it. A strange light peers through the cracks and I open the Gateway. Meli and Shadow are sitting back where I found them last, glancing up at me in surprise.

"Okay, how do I control where I'm going?" I inquire. "You can at least tell me that much."

"*No*," Meli remarks. "*You never told me how you control it.*"

"I focused on my destination, just like I do when using water or fire. I saw myself going to that place, but when I opened my eyes… I wasn't there. I can't let Styx face that monster alone. If you can tell me *anything* to help..."

"*You found out how in a journal*," Shadow points out. "*Maybe there's another that explains the fine basics.*"

"I don't have time to look through them all!"

"*Then you'll have to learn from trial and error*," Meli frowns. "*I can't tell you what I don't know.*"

With a resigned groan, I march back into my room. It takes less time to locate the obelisk this time. As I stand in my bedroom, eyes skimming my journals, I can feel the hopelessness rising. I'm always prepared, always ready for the next few steps. There should be something here that can help me. If I was anything then what I am now, I would've prepared for this. All the titles, though, leave me no clues.

With a groan, I fall back to lay on the bed. If I were preparing for my rebirth, I have no doubt I would leave something behind. Some form of instructions. I wouldn't want to go running into something so dangerous without warning myself. I wouldn't want anyone but me finding it, though, so it has to be hidden well. Where would I hide it? Where would no one look?

Considering no one likes to come here in the first place, I can't imagine taking that extra time to hide it. Then again, there's no guarantee this room would be left alone. If I wanted to hide something that important, where only I would look, where would it be? I've never had to worry about privacy before, being an only child. That might be the only setback I face. Just as I'm about to give up, a thought strikes me. I get up and hurry to the beam of light, taking it to the second floor. Once there, I face the many shelves of books. I love to read, that's never changed, and I can admit to finding the lives within those books appealing. Being all alone here, I've no doubt they would've been a well deserved portal. Running my finger along the spines, I search the titles. So many titles, so many genres, and yet… I know there's one I would've used more than any other. I find it resting on a small table next to a reclining chair. My favorite horror story, written by one of the greats. I pick it up and note a bookmark resting near the middle. I skim over the pages there. The hero is searching for a hidden key, finding it in a most unlikely place.

I walk into the large bathroom, setting the book back on the table. The tub is a deep claw-foot built for soaking, the shower in the opposite corner, and the toilet sits across from a large vanity and sink. Like the character in the book, I lift the porcelain lid off the back of the toilet. In the water there, tied to the pump, I find a plastic bag. When I pull it out, I find a book sealed within it. it's been wrapped a few times in plastic, set in a couple bags, before sealed with what looks like a flat iron. I must've used one to melt the plastic closed.

"I'll have to remember that one, that's clever," I murmur.

I replace the lid and carry the wet bag over to the sink. A pair of scissors lays there, as though I knew I'd need them. They cut through the bag easily, and then I make quick work of the rest of the plastic. When it's finally free of it's binds, I turn it over in my hands to study it. Instead of a title on the spine, there's a note taped to the front of the cover.

"If you are reading this, then I am reborn," I read aloud. "Everything you need to know is in this journal, please save my family."

Tilting my head in curiosity, I carry the book to the recliner and take a seat. When I open it, I read into the first paragraph. I'm stilled at what I see. Not only is it written in my own handwriting, but I seem to be addressing myself. It's like a warning from the future, so bizarre and explainable.

"I'm sorry I had to pull you into this," I read out loud. "I never wanted to visit the mortal plain again, but my family is in trouble. In this book, I've written a guide to all I know. You'll probably need it. There's an unspeakable evil rising to destroy my family, it needs to be stopped and you're the only one that can do that. As such, I've recorded all my methods and talents for you to learn. It won't be easy, creating life never is, but remember… some of the best parts of a soul, are the flaws. No one is perfect, not even us, and those flaws are what make us unique. Imperfections, fears, and insecurities are the foundation of any creature. Use them to your advantage and please… save my family."

It's a heartfelt plea and I can almost feel the tears in my eyes. Brushing them away, I start reading. Everything seems to be written in perfect order, explained down to the last variable, and I can't believe how easy she makes it all seem. I learn that some wells are off limits, due to being controlled by a trapped soul. They're too small to fit many spirits comfortably. The currents are set up carefully, yet are all connected. It's difficult to end up where you want to. You have to follow the route of the map, like driving a car, in order to find the exit you desire. With this new information, I'm finding it easier to navigate. With every new bit of information, I remember who I was… who I am. On my wrist, where the symbol for fire and water rest, another appears. It's a perfect circle, and I know it means spirit. It's on the top of my wrist, beginning to wrap around like a bracelet. To the right is the water symbol, and then the one for fire.

"Okay," I remark. "Let's try this again."

I leave the book on the table, not wanting it to fall into the wrong hands. If Styx could use our power, others might be able to as well. Exiting the obelisk, I return to the well and gaze into the liquid. Determined to get this right, I picture the destination in my mind. I can see the map there, all the channels, and I plan out my route. When it's locked in my brain, I fall into the waters again. This time, I don't let the current guide me. I turn when needed and rise from the waters at my goal. I open my eyes to find Whisper Hill a few feet away.

Calista is still there, but she's not alone. At first, I think it's the god of Whisper Hill. As I move closer, however, I realize it's Styx. He's still in his jeans and tee shirt. When I join them, he sends me a cautious gaze. I take a seat next to Calista, leaning against the tree behind me.

"How did you get here?" he asks.

"There's a stream over there," I point out. "I used the well in my room to get here."

"… You well-jumped?"

"Yep. It's not that difficult," I wave off. "Apparently, my last self wasn't much different from now. I wrote instructions down in a book, and hid them where only I would find them. They were *very* detailed."

"... Unbelievable," he huffs.

"A deal is a deal, Styx," Calista smirks, obviously humored. "She'll be joining us for the hunt."

He seems reluctant, however he doesn't refuse. With the sun breaking away from the horizon, the day is about to begin. I may not have gotten any sleep through the night, yet I don't experience that lingering exhaustion. I've never been so ready before.

"So, what's the plan?" I wonder.

"That's what we were talking about," Styx sighs. "I want to lure him to the river, but I can't open a doorway for a Skin Walker. The frame is still mortal, it's not meant to go through."

"I can take care of that," I smirk. "If I can get him closer to the water, I'll be able to drag him through to the river."

"The well will be there, right?" he inquires.

"It will, but I can't use it. It's been blocked off by Ioana's spirit. Apparently, wells are too small to use if they already contain a spirit. It's okay, though, I felt a stream of water underground. I can probably use that to get through the barrier."

"I can open a door in the barrier for us," Calista states. "I suggest Catori use the stream and go straight for the well. When we enter, we'll confront the Skin Walker and push him toward you. That way we can surprise him with the attack."

We nod in agreement, yet a sour sensation appears in my stomach. The best laid plans aren't always carried out the way you want. Styx lifts his pendant up and it glows. The next thing I know, Nixie is arriving in her armored glory. She stands, ready to fight. When her eyes catch mine, however, that stance changes.

"What are you doing here?" she asks. "You need to go back to the cabin."

"I learned how to well-jump, so I'm allowed to help. Styx said so."

"Styx!"

"I didn't think she'd have an instruction manual waiting for her," he huffs. "Besides, we need that ability to stop the Skin Walker. Our gates won't work with a mortal shell."

"... Fine," she mutters. "But you'd better stay safe."

"I promise. When do we attack?"

"At night," Styx replies. "That's when the doorway to the river is strongest."

Another day to waste, and very little left to do. The orchard is thriving now, flowers slowly turning into apples. After the Skin Walker is destroyed, the spirits should be free to pass on. If that's the case, there isn't anything left to get ready for. Then again, if it's not... what would be our next move?

Unable to shake that suspicion, I walk back to the stream. Nixie follows me, curious as to where I'm going. I grip her wrist, and fall into the water. The map I build in my mind takes us back to the cabin. Water rises from the sink, a column arching to the floor and rebuilding our figures. Nixie shivers at the feeling.

"What the hell was that?" she gasps out.

"Well-jumping," I comment, inattentive. "There's a map of currents underground, I can use them to travel."

"That's actually really cool," she states. "What's wrong? You seem distracted."

"The Skin Walker is feeding off the spirits in the orchard, but I can't be certain they'll be free once he's gone. They were killed because of a curse set by Calista's sister, not the chancellor. If they don't pass on, I need to be prepared for another fight."

"I brought my books," she offers. "There might be helpful spells in them. Honestly, though, she might just need to face the truth. I've found that curses aren't always based off what they seem. Something else could've influenced her decision on using one."

"We'll find out tonight," I state. "With any luck, we'll avoid the end of the anniversary. Calista told me the trees catch on fire at the end."

"Yeah, I definitely don't want to get stuck in that."

I let her lead me to the bedroom, where she digs around in her bags for her books. I'm not sure how they can help, but I'm always willing to keep a few aces up my sleeves. We sit down and begin to go through them. It isn't long before I locate the symbol I used on the door. That crescent moon and three teardrops mean 'blessing'. Family is truly a blessing, there's no doubt about that. And I'm going to rescue mine.

Chapter 24

The books were filled with interesting information. They hold so many spells and potions, symbols and charms. We don't have everything we need, so a trip awaits us. Nixie is strangely silent. It gives me time to think, but also unnerves me. We've never really had such a tense silence around us before, we always put everything on the table. Right now, I feel like we're drifting apart. I don't like it.

"… I know you doesn't want me going," I sigh, breaking that godawful quiet. "You never want me going. Everything will work out, though, you'll see. It always does."

"Until it doesn't," she mutters. "Why can't you be a selfish asshole? Just this once, Cat. It's not too much to ask is it?"

"I'm sorry, Nix, but… the more I learn about all this, the more I realize… this is my fight. This whole thing revolves around my family, you and Styx shouldn't have been pulled in."

"Your life is more important than ours," she argues.

"I wish people would stop saying that," I huff. "My life isn't anymore important than any other."

"Uh, actually, *your* life is the only thing keeping everyone *else* alive, so… I'm gonna have to disagree with that statement."

I can't find the rebuttal needed for that point. Looking through her eyes, hearing it put like that, I understand their reasoning. Even so, I'm merely another cog in an even larger machine. The one that sustains life is the tree that calls me 'daughter'. That's one comment I'll keep to myself, though. I don't need things to get anymore tense with her. I sigh and open another book, skimming pages of ingredients. Sometimes I wonder if these books weren't written by fantasy enthusiasts high on incense.

Either that, or someone with a passion for exotic foods. I mean, what can frog legs do for a spell?

"What are you thinking?" Nixie ventures.

"… Who writes these books?"

"I don't know," she frowns. "Why?"

"When I read them, sometimes I wonder if it was supposed to be a cookbook."

She laughs and I feel the air lighten a bit. My confused tone only draws that melody all the more, my lips twitching in a slight smile. As the strain melts away, I reach over for a notebook and pen. we'll need to make a list for the store, lest we forget something important. As I scribble the first few words down, I feel her eyes on me. With a glance up, I note the worry in those pools I love.

"Cat, I really want you to stay here," she states. "I know you've been getting better controlling your fire, but… that's only one element out of three. You're afraid of water, you barely know how to use your spirit..."

"I've made a lot of progress with that one," I interrupt. "Thankfully, I was the same over prepared person in my last life. I left myself an instruction manual."

"… Right… Because you're so good at following instructions," she scoffs, monotone.

"I'm good at following *my* instructions," I point out. "That's why I left them."

"Still… Styx and I are born and bred warriors. We've been through war and fought countless battles. We have eons of experience behind us. I'm sure we'll do just fine without you."

"Don't worry," I smirk, allowing her to relax. "I'll be hidden nearby. I'm the only one that can pull that creature to the river, *that's* why I'm going. I won't have to fight."

"Thank the stars above," she breathes out in relief. "At least I won't have to worry about you getting hurt."

I want to argue, yet I bite my tongue. It won't get us anywhere. The only sound in the room is my pen scratching against paper. I reach for Nixie's book, hoping to add to my list, when I note her gaze on me again. She seems as though she's struggling with something. I can see the inner battle rage in her bright eyes. Finally, she closes them and comes to a decision.

"If you're going to go with us, I think you should be trained a little better in battle," she remarks. "You have so much potential, Cat, I know you do. I see it every time you face down the darkness. I know I haven't been the best trainer, I've been putting on kid gloves, but… I really don't want you hurt."

"What are you saying?"

"Let's get this list taken care of, and then… I'll call Styx to help me train you."

"But you said he was too old school."

"He is," she says, tone pressing certainty. "But you seem to respond well to his school of hard knocks. He'll be able to help you better than I can."

"Awesome!"

"I'll head to the store, you go to Calista's," she smiles. "As soon as we finish these charms, we'll have time to train."

"Agreed."

Nixie wastes no time getting to the kitchen for the truck keys. The few ingredients the store doesn't sell, we'll find at Calista's home. I stand and walk over to the closet door. With a pencil picked up from the nearby desk, I draw the symbol for blessing on the wood. When that strange glow shows itself, I open the way to the Gateway and walk in. I might not need to start at my well each time, however I want to assure Shadow and Meli I'm doing okay. With Shadow's imagination, there's no telling how panicked he is.

True to my thoughts, he's pacing a hole in the ground. As Meli tries to assure him, I can hear his rising voice go through countless scenarios. My eyes roll even as a smile sneaks upon my lips. When I'm close enough, Meli gives a relived sigh and stands up.

"*I told you she was fine,*" she points out.

"*Catori! Oh my god, I thought you were dead! What happened? Are you okay? Did you get lost again? Are you hurt?*"

"I'm fine," I chuckle. "I figured it out and got back to the cabin. We're waiting for night to attack, I'll just be in charge of the portal."

"*At least you'll be safe,*" Meli comments. "*We need to keep you safe, you're the foundation of life.*"

"Nixie reminded me," I sigh. "I don't like thinking that way. Every life is precious, everyone deserves to be protected."

"*You always felt that way,*" Shadow informs. "*That's why you're so important. You remind us of what we started as, of what our family means to the many worlds mother holds apart. You're as important to us as you are to the creatures you give life.*"

"Thanks. I better get going, we need to make charms for the coming fight. Never hurts to have a little extra defense, right?"

"*Too true,*" Shadow grins. "*You stay hidden. If you feel in danger, even a little bit, get out of there. Your element won't save you from the Skin Walker, it commands death. You'll be a puppet to it in seconds.*"

"Okay, I promise. I'll see you guys later."

Waving goodbye to them, I hurry into my room. The foliage is coming to life all around me, spreading in a thick cloud of vitality. It's a welcome sight in this former world of death. I walk through the dark night, the moon forever the only light source, and run my hand along an old black railing. A large statue watches me, it's wings spread wide as it guards the stones below.

When I get to the well, I take the time to study the newest soul there. It's a little girl, and I can tell she'll be a brilliant musician when she grows up. It warms my heart to bond with her at this moment in time, so close to the start of that road. When she disperses, I reach into the well and search for the right path. In just a heartbeat, I'm drawn into the waters. The channels to her swamp are wide and it's difficult to estimate where I'll end up, but I can't let that stop me.

When I rise from the murky waters, I can see her house in the distance. It's not too far away, but there are plenty of threats between us. Shaking that off, I take a deep breath and let myself fall apart. I join the water and race through this bog toward my goal. When I reform on her spot of land, I feel gross and weighed down. I didn't think the shape of the water would affect me so, yet make a mental note to check on it later. Once I'm mortal again, I walk up to Calista's porch and raise my hand to knock.

"I'm not getting up to open the door, so you might as well get familiar," she calls from inside.

Shaking my head, I open the door and enter. She's sitting back by her cauldron, looking weary and worn. When she doesn't look up at me, I take the chance to get closer. As soon as I'm seated, I take in her appearance. She's changed into some jeans and a hoodie, her hair braided along her scalp. She's definitely ready for war, if only in style. Her spirit is strong, but her shell is weak. It won't be of much help.

“I thought a good rest would help,” she comments, dry humor in her tone. “Only… I couldn’t get to sleep.”

“Nixie makes a really good potion for that,” I offer. “It knocks me out cold.”

“Have you come to gather information?”

“No, I think I’ve pried enough,” I blush. “Nixie and I are going to make charms for tonight. I was hoping you’d have some of the more… unique… items.”

“And I do,” she smirks. “How about a trade? Take what you need, but I’d appreciate that potion.”

“Of course, let me just call her.”

I take out my cellphone and dial her up, however she doesn’t answer. She’s probably still driving, I hate when she answers the phone behind the wheel. Too much can happen in that split second. I text her instead, which she’ll only check at a red light or when she parks. As I wait for her response, I take out my list.

“If you don’t mind, I’ll start to gather things now,” I offer. “No need for you to get up, though, I’ll find my way around. Nixie should be getting the message soon. She made the potion once since we got here, but I didn’t use it all. She should still have that bottle hidden away.”

“Help yourself,” Calista smiles.

As I rummage through her kitchen pantry, I can’t help but wonder what her story is. I know about her past, about her loss, but… her life since then had to have been harder. The things she’s lived through, the people she’s watched grow old and die, couldn’t have been easy. It’s almost like she’s punishing herself for surviving that awful massacre. No one should live with a weight like that on their shoulders.

My phone buzzes in my back pocket as I reach for a jar of rosemary. When I answer, Nixie is on the other line. I mark rosemary off my list and search for St. John’s wort and dragon’s blood resin.

"You wanted me to call? What's the matter?" she wonders.

"Calista wants a trade," I inform. "She's having trouble sleeping and needs the extra energy. Do you still have that potion you make me?"

"Yeah, it's in my bag."

"Great! Hopefully she'll get the sleep she needs with that. When you get done at the store, can you drop it off?"

"Yeah, I'll be there soon."

"Thanks."

I hang up and carry my basket out to the sitting room. Calista is still seated, falling lower in her chair as her weariness grows. I can't imagine how she feels, so drained all the time. She watches me cross over to the other chair and sit down. It feels nice to just relax a moment. As we sit in a companionable silence, I get a text from Nixie. She's on her way now. A portal opens up and she steps through, the vial needed in her hand.

"Here you go," she smiles. "I hope it helps."

"Thank you, I really appreciate it," Calista replies.

"If it helps out, I'll give you the recipe. It's a really old one I found in my family's spell book."

She nods, downing the drink in one go. Similar to myself, she's out in seconds. We can't just leave her to sleep in that chair, she'll be sore when she wakes. With Nixie's help, we manage to get her into her room. After tucking her in, the two of us quietly gather the rest of our list. We leave through Nixie's portal.

Back at the cabin, the two of us take a seat and spread everything out before us on the floor. We've relocated to the kitchen, the tile offering a more practical 'table'. Granted, we could've used the dining room table. This isn't our house, though, and we're not sure how messy this is going to get. The tiled floor can be swept and mopped.

"Okay, let's make these satchels first, and then we can put together the witch's bottles."

"Sounds good," I agree.

I begin to separate ingredients, moving them about into their own piles. Afterward, I set them according to what they'll be used in. We're making four of each, that way everyone will have the protection needed. Nixie gets out the cloth for the satchels, laying them flat to fill. We work in quiet for a long time.

"Tell me about the war," I say. "You were there, right?"

"I was," she answers, tone soft and filled with hurt. "It was a horrible time. The Skin Walkers were strong back then. Their numbers were large and finding them was nearly impossible."

"How did it start? Do you know?"

"At first, we didn't know what was going on. The only clue we had, was the sudden drop of souls crossing. It was Styx who caught the change, that's why he was charged with the mission. That, and he's the oldest in this profession.

When he went to investigate it, he found a rise in trapped souls. He followed the trail of one, finding it trapped in its shell. That's how he learned of the Skin Walkers."

I listen curiously, wondering how difficult it would've been on him. He seems to be a very perceptive person. It's odd to think he knows the dead so well, he can notice something so minuscule. I'm actually impressed.

"When we faced down those creatures, it was so difficult. We had never had to kill a mortal before, so those shells were protecting them better than we expected. That's when we approached the gods for our weapons. They were designed to expel the Skin Walker from its mortal shell, leaving them defenseless.

The war lasted many months, spreading a nasty plague through the mortal population. So many died as a side effect. In the end, we overpowered them. We thought they were all dead, but… one survived."

"It seems it was trapped before the war," I offer. "If the settlers would've listened to Calista's warning, it might've never been freed."

It's the best I can do for assurance. This creature is so much more than I thought, it's getting easier to see why it's so feared. If we're going to stop it, we're going to need to have a foolproof strategy. There's no telling how smart this one is.

Chapter 25

When the last bottle is finished, I find I'm getting nervous. I've been in plenty of fights, took judo and karate in my youth, and I've fought alongside Nixie before. I know what to expect from her. Styx, on the other hand, is new territory for me. Nixie is fierce enough as a student, I can only imagine how intense Styx will be. As I pack our charms away for later, I follow Nixie with my eyes. She's pacing and mumbling to herself. It's a sight I'm used to; she's rethinking her decision. As if I wasn't nervous enough.

"Would you stress sitting down, please," I comment. "If I get any more nervous, I'm going to puke."

"Sorry, I just... I'm worried he won't go easy on you."

"It's not a war, Nix," I laugh.

"*Every* battle with him is a war, that's why he's so effective."

"I'm sure he's not that bad."

"If killing you would help control your soul element, he won't hesitate to run you through," she deadpans.

"... Okay... maybe he is," I frown. "But that's all right, I can keep up. If he gets too bad, I'll just take my water form."

"... Fine. I'll go get him. It might take a while, though. Do you have something to do?"

"I was thinking about visiting my parents really quick."

"I'll get you when we're ready."

I smile, kissing her goodbye. Once she's vanished into her portal, I walk toward the kitchen. Before I do anything, I wash the dishes and set them to dry. The last time I used this exit, a soapy taste stuck to my mouth. it's not something I prefer to repeat. When the sink is drained and washed out, I set in the plug and fill it with clean water. The route firmly in my mind, I reach for a current.

I watch my fingers turn to water, tiny droplets rising to drift into the sink. That form crawls up my arm, consuming me for the ride. Relief washes over me, my eyes closing to relish it.

When next they open, I'm standing in my parents' kitchen. The water is running, which is unusual. Mom is meticulous about turning it off. Before I can do so, I hear footsteps on the wood of the hallway. She hurries in, eyes widening at the sight of me. Her mouth hangs open in shock. While she's busy absorbing this, I reach over to turn off the water.

"Sorry, mom," I comment. "I must've turned it on when I came through."

"Catori, how did you get here? I didn't hear the car pull in."

"I learned how to move between bodies of water," I attempt. "Apparently, that includes sinks, showers, and tubs."

She says nothing more, hurrying to wrap me in a hug. Our schedules always clash, so we've had little time to spend together. I didn't realize this until now. Her arms are tight around me, nearly painful. I've never felt so guilty in my life. She nearly drags me into the living room. My father is reading the newspaper there. He seems pleasantly surprised when I'm shoved onto the couch.

"Catori?"

"Hi," I smile, sheepish.

"Is everything okay? Are you in trouble?"

"Don't panic, I just dropped in to visit. I have a training session, but it's going to take a bit to get ready."

This seems to unsettle him. I can guess why, but choose to ignore the expression. My mother sits in the recliner next to him, both across from me. Unfortunately, I know this set-up well. Many serious 'talks' started this way growing up. Next is their clumsy attempts to explain something, and then I'll have to decipher hundreds of blanks and stammers. Not my idea of a good time.

"Honey, we're sorry we didn't tell you sooner," my mom sighs. "You're our daughter, you always will be. We never thought of you as anything else."

"I know. I'm sorry I didn't take it better. There's just *so* much happening all at once… I'm glad you guys found me."

"what's going on?" my dad wonders. "You don't typically have issues solving cases. You're sharp as a whip."

"It's just a few obstacles, I don't want to bore you with specifics."

"So, you're in trouble," he decides. "What kind? Normal or supernatural?"

"I didn't say I was in trouble," I press. "I'm just visiting while..."

"Supernatural it is," he concludes. "Are you going to just tell me, or are you going to make me pull it out of you? Either way, I'm gonna get what I want."

"… So that's where I got it," I mumble. "I solved the case, for the most part. The well I have to get to is being guarded by something called a Skin Walker. Nixie and her friend are going to stop it, but… I'm going to help."

"Creatures like that are very dangerous, Catori. You should never antagonize them unless you know what you're dealing with."

My eyes glance to my mom. She's not one to believe in this stuff, but lately her eyes have been open. Right now, she's worrying her bottom lip. The concern in her orbs is palpable. There isn't anything I can say to calm her. My apologetic expression is all I can offer. I know this is hard on them. It's not college and wild parties they fear, not like parents with a *normal* daughter.

"We made satchels and witch's bottles for protection," I assure. "My role is quite limited. I just have to pull it through a portal, so I'll be hidden until that moment."

"There's the best news I've heard all day," he sighs in relief.

"Why do you have to go?" my mom questions, eyes watery. "Why are you chasing after danger?"

"I don't mean to," I say, tone soft. "This is why I was given to you. My family trusted you to keep me safe, hoping I would be overlooked until I was strong enough to face our enemy. they're all trapped and I have to save them. It shouldn't be too difficult, and I have powerful help. Don't worry, okay?"

She nods, trying to dry her tears before they fall. It breaks my heart, yet there's nothing I can do. This has to be done, or all life is going to disappear. I spare them that knowledge. Now that I know the basics of things, I'm able to inform them of my task. Of course, I'll leave out anything too dangerous. As I explain, my phone vibrates in my pocket. Although I want to get it all out, I pause to check it. Nixie is on her way. The rest of my story is addressed in a shorter version. Just as I reach the end, Nixie's doorway opens in the living room.

With a sheepish smile, she enters and waves to my parents. Behind her, Styx wanders through. He doesn't notice my parents at first, too distracted by the pictures strewn about. The hood to his cloak is down for once, revealing a partial grin where skin and muscle give way to bone. The look on their faces is a mixture of shock and confusion. When he turns to see them, he quickly pulls his hood up. I watch his features change, shifting to cover his abnormalities.

"Sorry about that," he remarks, sheepish and self-conscious. "I thought you would've been through the whole 'supernatural guest' thing."

"I didn't even think of it," Nixie gasps. "I'm so sorry, Styx. I'm just so used to you being… well… you..."

"No, it's okay," my father says. "We didn't know Nixie was bringing company. Please, sit down."

"We can't stay long," he sighs. "Catori needs as much training as she can get. I want her more than ready for tonight's task."

"I thought Nixie was training her," my mother frowns.

"Styx trained me," she offers. "He's trained billions of Envoys and Charon, he'll know how to teach her best."

both my parents seem less than impressed. As such, Nixie sits beside me. After a bit of coaxing, Styx sits on my other side. I can see the tension in his frame. He must have very little experience in socializing. For a long moment, there's nothing but silence. I feel like I'm introducing a prom date. Unable to take the awkward quiet, I try to end the questioning before it starts.

"We should really be leaving."

"How are you going to train her?" my father asks. "Nixie and I are more than enough for spells and potions..."

"That's not my forte," Styx remarks. "Spells and potions are useless for me, I specialize in combat and negotiations. I also dabble in manipulating the elements."

"And how do you think you'll be able to help her?"

"Catori has much potential, I'm very impressed by her," he offers. "But she can only get so far on her own. Nixie has been teaching her with kid gloves, she hasn't even dreamed of touching her potential yet. Since I'm the only living creature that's been taught by her mother, I think I'm the best choice to help her through this."

"I'm her mother," mom glares.

"You're her guardian," he points out. "Her mother is very much alive and grieving the loss of her children."

"I just don't want to grieve the loss of mine," she challenges.

It's clear he wants to bite back, yet Nixie's hand on his stops him. These people may be mortal, but she understands their worry. Styx has never dealt with anyone on a parental level, so he'd overlook the importance a child has to one. Although I'm no longer a child, my parents still see me as one.

"I have lived since the beginning of time," Styx frowns, tone soft. "I have ferried billions to the afterlife, taught just as many for their roles, and have been in the presence of titans you believe naught but myth. I have led, battled, and won wars that would turn your hair white. I have gone up against creatures you wouldn't even see in your darkest nightmares. If anyone is experienced enough to protect Catori, I dare say they would be me. Nothing is going to happen to her, I won't allow the opportunity. Now, if you don't mind, I would like to use the rest of the day to prepare her for the most difficult battle she's yet to face."

His tone has grown an icy edge, revealing a dark side that sends shivers up my spine. He's not at his darkest, though, and it chills me to the bone to think what he's capable of. The last thing I want is for this to turn bad.

"We really should be going," I comment. "You can question him later, I promise. Right now, I'd like to get on with my training."

"Good idea," my father agrees. "Call us when your case is closed, okay? Be careful, honey."

"Thanks, I will."

I give them both hugs and kisses goodbye. I feel bad for leaving them so soon, yet this is for the best. Styx obviously doesn't appreciate being underestimated, however my mother is always willing to needle others. I save them both by standing to usher Styx and Nixie out. With one last apologetic look to my parents, I step through the doorway. It closes behind me. My eyes land on an unfamiliar scene, widening in surprise and curiosity. Night keeps the area dusky, the full moon's reflection glistening upon dark waters. I see many lanterns hidden in a thick blanket of mist. On the shore, a long pier with rotted planks sits.

"What is this place?" I ask, quiet.

"This is where I was born," Styx smirks. "I crawled from the river over by that pier. Time moves differently here, hardly passing. An hour in your world can be a day here. This way you can train as much as you need for tonight."

"So, where do we begin?"

"Since you'll need to use your spirit and water elements, I want you to walk across the river," he decides. "Not *through* or *in*, but *on*. Nixie and I will stay near in a boat."

"That's not so bad," I frown. "I thought you were supposed to be hardcore old school."

"I am," he smirks, mischievous. "Look in the water."

curious, I do as I'm told. My feet inches from the liquid, hands frantically search for my ankles. I hurry away from their grasp. Millions of souls lay beneath the glassy surface, looking for anything to pull them out. If I walk over that water, they'll pull me under. I can see Styx smiling as he walks to the pier. Nixie was right, he can be pure evil. She shrugs before following him.

At the pier, I watch Styx ring a strange looking bell. There are two on the structure, one is brass and the other… is a dark onyx decorated with bone. that's the one he chooses. A rickety old boat made of dark wood and bones floats over. When he steps in it, he hangs his lantern at the front. While the light is typically blue, it changes to white with a simple touch. He then helps Nixie in. I wait until they push away from the pier to give the water another glare.

I can approach this in multiple ways, although I can't do the majority. I can try to clam the spirits, ask them to carry me across, yet I wouldn't be using my water element. The lack of progress is grating on my nerves. I step up to them, again being forced away from their reach. Styx and Nixie are waiting patiently for me to begin. Not knowing any other way, I run forward and jump over the groping hands. they're cleared, however I fail to realize there are more of them. My ankle is grabbed by one, stopping my momentum. My body falls forward. Thankfully, I manage to find my center before falling.

"Um… I'm not sure this is a good idea," Nixie frowns. "What if she's pulled under?"

"Then she'll learn to improvise," Styx comments.

That statement makes my stomach sink. Nixie tried to warn me, but I couldn't see Styx like that. I wish I hadn't judged him by his looks. I open my mouth to comment, yet it never gets through. Those hands are beginning to pull me beneath the water. My eyes go wide, my mind racing to gather a solution. If I turn into a spirit, the river may claim me. In my panic, I start to change into water. I slip under and reform back on land. This is a situation I should contemplate a bit longer.

"If you go under, you have to start at the beginning," Styx calls. "But that was pretty good for a first try. You lasted longer than I thought you would."

"You can't just throw her into training knowing she'll fail!" Nixie shouts.

"If she doesn't fail, she'll never succeed," he counters. "Take your time and analyze your obstacle."

I sigh and take in the corpse ridden waters. they're all still reaching for something to grab. While changing into a spirit will prevent them from touching me, those waters are a spirit's prison. I can't change into water, that's not walking on it. True to his comment, I'm not going to get across without failing. There are so many results lining up in my brain, and I'll likely have to try them all in hopes of getting across.

"If I turn into a spirit, will I be trapped in the river?" I question.

"*That* is an excellent question," Styx replies, tone good natured. "I have no idea."

"Styx!" Nixie yells.

"What?" he frowns. "She's not going to battle knowing every trick that works. If she did, she wouldn't need training."

"Training isn't code for 'kill your student' either!"

I roll my eyes at them, deciding to just continue as they fight. Neither are going to be much help. The best place to start, is testing the waters… literally. I try to make it raise, getting a feel for the thick liquid. Though it's water, the consistency is more like blood. As the watercourse rises like a fountain, I note that the bodies follow. They're truly a part of this grim river. They move with the liquid as though they're one. With a glance at the boat, Styx and Nixie still arguing, I wander over and brave the shore's edge.

"Please don't grab at me," I comment, tone soft. "I would like to talk to you. You seem to be searching for an escape, can you tell me why?"

I'm surprised when they hold off on their endeavor, all of them watching me curiously. They're mostly adult men, though I catch sight of a few women. Now settled, they float beneath the water near me. Just the sight of their surprise makes me wonder if anyone really talks to them. They may be dead, but that doesn't mean they should be ignored.

"Does anyone talk to you guys?" I ask. "I mean, it's not like you're incapable… right?"

"*Most of us are,*" one of the men answers. "*Others are not. It depends on the era they're from.*"

"What do you mean?"

"*Honey, we ain't here because we're too pretty for the fields,*" a dark skinned woman states. "*We're the undesirable souls.*"

"How awful! No one should be undesirable," I gasp.

"*... Baby, are you slow in the head?*" she wonders, a bit cautious. "*Undesirable means we're killers. I offed my man during a struggle, I ain't going to Heaven. I can tell you that much.*"

"That shouldn't mean you have to be ignored. People make mistakes, they have bad judgment, that's what makes them human. You shouldn't be punished because of that mistake."

"*Tell that to the Charon,*" a man huffs. "*They're so busy ferrying 'good' souls, they don't even care if they smack us a few times with their paddle.*"

"*Only one of them takes the time to talk with us, but he's been busy lately.*"

I realize they must be talking about Styx, as he seems to like checking up on spirits. He seems the type to forgo judgment, treating everyone the same. I take a seat on the shore, content to just chat with the overlooked souls. They don't seem all that eager to pull me in now, so I can't help but question their intentions earlier.

"You weren't trying to get out, were you," I state more than ask.

"... *No. We're charged with protecting the river,*" an older male sighs. "*Anyone that doesn't belong, we're to pull them beneath the water and drown them. Since they don't talk to us anyway, we tend to drag the Charon down as well. It doesn't hurt them, but it's uncomfortable enough to border it.*"

"*We protect their moat and they give us nothing in return. How right is that?*" the woman huffs. "*All we want is a bit of attention, that ain't too much to ask, is it?*"

"No, it isn't," I agree. "They should be more appreciative of your efforts."

"*They think that just because we were killers in life, that's all we know how to do. I get that we were monsters then, but there's no point in killing when you're already dead,*" the old man mutters, bitter. "*We're trapped here 'for the safety of others'. I don't mind the job, but we can be lonely, too.*"

"*When a killer dies, they have a choice to make,*" the woman says, quiet. "*They can face their afterlife and move on, or they can* continue to kill as a wraith. you'll lose all sense of yourself, consumed with rage and blood-lust. All of us accepted our fates, passed over to start anew."

"And you've all come to terms with your actions in life," I sigh. "I understand how this can be discouraging to all of you, but you perform a very good service here. you're likely the only defense standing between the living and an eternal afterlife. You should be proud of that. I'm sure they wouldn't just trust anyone with this. If it's lonely for you, just remember you're not alone there. You could create your own community right here in the river."

They perk up at the comment, obviously not having thought it before. I'm glad I can help them, even if it's only a little bit. I'll bring up this problem with Styx after this training course. For right now, however, I need to find a way across the river. They may not pull me under again, but I doubt the word will spread through the souls here before I attempt another crossing.

"I need to walk across the river," I say. "Any ideas?"

"Therapy," the old man laughs. "Because if you think you can, you'll find yourself drowning in it."

"I'm not human," I confide. "I'm a Root, an elemental, and Styx is training me today. He told me I have to find a way to cross the river, that I have to walk *on* the waters."

"Can't you turn into water then?" the woman wonders.

"I just fall into the river when I do that," I huff. "I can't keep my form on the element I'm using, or I just merge with it. I can take a soul form, but I might get trapped in the river."

"No you won't, you're not an undesirable," she waves off. *"Only we're trapped here. You don't have the dark in your heart a sin leaves."*

"That's good to know," I sigh in relief.

"Have you ever tried freezing water before?" one man asks. *"You could walk on it if it were frozen."*

"… I've never tried," I admit. "Now that you mention it, I haven't tried much of anything with my elements. I thought I could only control how they moved."

"You should try it then, but be careful," the woman warns. *"The souls here are a part of the water, if they get frozen it might hurt them."*

"Thank you so much, I really appreciate the help."

After saying goodbye to them, I scoot away from the river. Styx and Nixie are just quieting down, curious about my lack of movement. I take in the stretch of liquid, trying to get a rough estimate of length, and then I take a deep breath. This is going to take all of my concentration, but I won't stop until I've succeeded.

Chapter 26

I can feel hundreds of eyes on me, some just waiting to drown me. Styx and Nixie have finally stopped arguing, now focused back on me. The spirits have given me useful information, so I test it out. I lay my finger on the surface, imagining ice instead of liquid. A chilly sensation runs through my veins, ice water through an IV. I shy away when my skin starts to go numb. Granted getting caught on fire is no picnic, but that was much warmer. Determined to perform my task, I try again.

So used to moving water, I find it more difficult to change its form. Eventually, ice moves outward from my finger. The frost is like a tiny map at first, just random trails that circle back and stretch out. Soon, however, the water crystallizes beneath the cold. The souls nearby move away, scared to get caught in the chill. With a quick apology, I pull away from the waters.

"I'm so sorry," I say. "I didn't think it would spread that fast."

"*You almost have it*," the old man states. "*Try again, but think... smaller.*"

With a sheepish nod, I set my hand on the water. This time, I don't just think of ice. I place a specific size in my mind. The waters freeze into a disc above the souls. it's about the size of a dinner platter. Tentative, I inch away from it. As it floats upon the water, I hop over to stand on it. With a gasp, I fall straight through. On reflex, I change into water and flow back to the shore. Back in a solid form, I kick at the dark sand in frustration. From the boat, I hear Nixie.

"Cat, are you alright?"

"I'm fine," I call back. "I almost had it!"

"No, you really didn't," Styx offers. "I mean, you're on the right track, but you're *barely* halfway."

"What the hell kind of teacher *are* you!" Nixie yells, rocking the boat a bit.

"I'll be one with one less student if you tip my boat," he warns.

Again, they're no help. Sighing in irritation, I wonder if taking on an army of Skin Walkers would be more beneficial. Putting the thought aside, I look back to the water. If i'm too heavy for the ice to hold, there's a chance I won't be in my spirit form. Unfortunately, I've never tried to use more than one at a time. I don't even know if I can.

"You look worried. Don't get discouraged, there's always another way," the woman assures.

"I can walk across on the ice if I were a spirit," I sigh. "But I've never used two elements together."

"So don't," she shrugs. "Ain't you ever heard of the ghosts that stand on lakes, or wraiths that died in fires? Just because we're ghost don't mean we can't go hand-in-hand with an element. You just got to be one of the lake ghosts. That's all."

It's easier said than done, but she makes a good point. Some spirits are trapped in their death, a victim to one element or another. If that's the case, I just have to combine one element with my spirit. With eyes closed, I bring up the scene of a book I read. The story was of a lake maiden in white. She would appear at night, leaping about in play. I learned the girl, who was playing on ice in the winter, fell through a thinned spot. In my mind, the vision is so clear. I begin to feel weightless and cold.

My body is transparent when I finally look, tinged with frostbite. When I exhale, a plume of steam leaves my lips. It's a strange sensation, being a frozen soul. Throwing caution to the wind, I take a running leap toward the river. I've never been much of a dancer, but my movement is fluid enough. The strain of multiple elements is leaving me shaky. I can feel the sweat beading on my forehead. Closer to the boat, I stumble. Hands lift from the water, reaching eagerly, however I manage to find my center.

"Not bad," Styx comments. "I didn't expect you to figure it out so soon. I mean, you're obviously struggling with it, but your hold is strong."

"We'll meet you on the other side," Nixie assures. "It's not too far from here."

All I can do is nod. The bitter chill of frost and the weight of death is a haunting mixture. I doubt it'll go away after I shed this disguise. The boat glides along the waters, the only one these resentful dead ignore, and I'm left alone with them. So many voices call out, so many languages, and my ice is the only thing between us. Ice that seems to be cracking with my distraction. I focus again, jumping to the next spot. My effort is slowed, as I search for a spot empty of souls. they're closing in, though, and those spaces are few.

"Please let me pass," I say. "I'm doing my best to not hurt you, but you're all too close."

They're surprised for a moment, yet it passes. Unlike the others, they continue to close in. it's more hesitant, as though they're not sure what to make of me. I need a way through, and if they won't cooperate… I'll have to chance the ice catching them. it's not an ideal solution for me, but my hold is already shaky. If I stand out here any longer, I won't be able to maintain this form. Taking a deep breath, I charge forward. My body throws itself to the right upon landing, dodging the hands near my ankle. What started as playful leaping about, has turned into a deadly game of chase.

The other shore is within sight, Styx's lantern illuminating where they stand. I aim for it, stumbling and dodging as I go. When I'm nearly there, a hand catches my sneaker and I take a dive. In a heartbeat, I bring up a cute kitten video in my head. Instead of hitting water, I land on a sheet of ice. My body spins about, me on my stomach, and then I feel the shore. Styx steps up beside me, his face twisted in mirth.

"Lovely dismount," he laughs, reaching to pull me to my feet.

"Thank you social media," I snort in humor. "That was horrid. I'm glad it's over. So… are we going to meet Calista in the orchard, or at her place?"

"Training isn't over," he points out, an amused smirk on his lips. "It hasn't even started."

"But… that's… you told me that was it!"

"No, I didn't. I said that's where we'll begin. I wanted to see how far you've gotten."

"How far have I gotten?" I inquire, cautious.

"… Further than I expected."

Not the best answer, but I have a feeling it's his nicest one. With a wave of his lantern, he motions me to follow. We walk over to Nixie, and toward an ominous cavern. A thick layer of fog, about knee high, trails from the mouth. When we reach it, Styx turns to the left. that's when I notice the strange depression in the wall. As natural as it seems, it resembles the holy water font in a church. The lantern is dipped in, the liquid inside bursting to flame. Afterward, Styx places his hand inside it. The blue fire turns red, and then green. Finally, he settles for black.

Before I can question him, he starts walking into the cavern. The mouth is lined in large black stones, each with strange symbols carved on their surface. I'm finding myself more curious than hesitant. This isn't the most ideal place to raise a child. I'd like to ask, yet I hate being intrusive. Whatever happened here molded him, so it can't be too bad. I'm coming back to myself as the tunnel ends.

We step out into a vast field, a light drizzle moistening our clothes. It doesn't appear threatening, just a normal meadow filled with glowing flowers. We come to a stop next to a small stream. Lightening flashes overhead, turning the night into a nightmare. The ground is littered with bones and corpses, the stream dyed crimson with blood. My jaw drops at the difference.

"What… the..."

"This is the boneyard," Styx interrupts. "It's usually a lively place, but the spirits prefer to come here when it's not raining."

"… Who, in their right mind, would come here when it's filled with bones?"

"No, that's how it usually looks," he waves off. "The rain makes it green and peaceful. Not many want that reminder. This acts as a training ground, where all the most infamous warriors of time gather. They get bored easily, so this is where they keep their skills sharp… and that keeps them out of trouble."

"I practically grew up here," Nixie sighs.

"I asked a few people to help me out, they should be here soon," he informs. "This is going to be your introduction to combat. Those we wait for are heroes of the past, born and bred to battle. If you feel you can't handle them, they won't stop until *I* tell them."

"That's your only opportunity to back away," Nixie murmurs beside me. "You won't get a second chance."

"… At what point would you call them off?" I ask.

"… You're immortal and can reform after death," he points out. "Doesn't that answer your question?"

Sadly, it does. I'm not about to back down now, though, and he can see that. A proud smile touches him, lasting only a moment before he turns away. Four men are approaching us, each brandishing a weapon of sorts. I recognize a couple from history class, but the other two I've never seen before. They stop before us, nodding to Styx by way of greeting. Afterward, they eye me in disapproval. It's not difficult to tell. Especially when Nixie puts an arm around me, turning that disapproval to terror.

"I'm guessing this isn't the first time you've met," I sigh.

"I decimated them," she grins, evil.

"Once," Styx scoffs. "After *hundreds* of years to train."

"Once is all you need, as long as you leave a good enough mark," she counters. "In the age of war and sexism, losing to a *girl* is the most effective one."

There's not much to say about that, it's very true. I take in the four masters, realizing they all have different styles. They're not from the same era, that's easy enough to tell, and they seem to be from different ends of the world. It's no wonder Nixie is so good, they loo like a well rounded group. Styx shakes hands with two of them, and then bows to the others.

"Thank you for agreeing to assist me," he comments. "Please, ignore Nixie. You won't have to deal with her this time, I promise. Your student will be Catori."

I wave when eyes fall on me. This greeting is so awkward, I know I'm blushing. There are likely a hundred reasons this is a bad idea. Although they're apprehensive of training a female, it seems they trust Styx enough to help. He leads us all to a clearing. In the flash of lightening, it turns into an arena of sorts. A bright emotion akin to excitement fills the warriors' eyes at the sight. They lived and died for battle, now simply existing for it. I can tell what made them formidable, for I can't sense even a shred of fear.

"I need her to be skilled with the basics," the Charon comments. "She won't be an expert, but she needs enough to survive our upcoming battle."

"Defense would be awesome, but perhaps we can add a weapons class if we have time. Just one would do," Nixie adds.

"Agreed. Who would like to start?"

A tall man steps forward, dressed to the nines and brandishing a thin sword. I know him as Arnaldo Cortez, a pirate that claimed the seas. He took on a corrupted navy for thousands of innocent people. Eventually, he brought down that section of the government and pulled the citizens from poverty. he's been called a strategic mastermind. His blade bears the mark of the navy, a keepsake from the profession he fled for freedom.

"I will teach her to think on her feet. The fight won't stop for you to react, you need to think and plan ahead. It must be reflex to line up the options."

"I think I have that down," I point out.

Without hesitation, he flicks his wrist. The sword draws a thin line on my cheek. I didn't even see him move. At the pointed look he gives me, I grumble to myself. With barely a thought, they injury disappears. It's meant as an arrogant spit in his face, yet has an unforeseen effect… Now he knows he doesn't have to be careful. I curse inwardly. Without warning, he rushes me. I'm forced to dodge another swipe, tripping over a femur when the lightening flashes. As I hit the ground, that thin blade strikes for the kill. Just as quickly, it stops. The tip rests close to my skin, close enough to feel the pressure and light enough to keep from breaking skin. This man is truly a master of his trade.

"It would seem this fight has ended badly for you, young maiden," Arnoldo smirks. *"Perhaps I overestimated you."*

"No, you didn't," Styx remarks, leaning against his staff to watch. "She's not a warrior, she's an oddity. That oddity is what she uses. We just have to get her to use it in battle."

"Hm... She doesn't look like an oddity. Not like you, anyway. Besides healing her injuries, what cards does she have up her sleeves?"

"Many. She doesn't know much about her abilities, but that's what the crash course is for."

"Curiosity has always been the bane of my existence," he sighs, feigning reluctance. *"Shall we end that cursed emotion?"*

I roll away when he lifts his sword to attack once more. Back on my feet, I manage to duck a blow. Unfortunately, I'm focused on the blade. Arnoldo's boot catches me right in the stomach. My body doubles over, and I can practically hear the sword singing through the air. Just as it hits, my form bursts like a water balloon. That liquid spins about him as a funnel, coming to rest outside his reach. That gives me the opportunity to reform. His expression is one of fascination.

"My lady, the sea," he states. *"For all my life, I wondered what she would look like embodied. A blessed oddity you are, young maiden."*

I have no clue how to respond to that, but there's little time to. With renewed vigor, he's back on the attack. My automatic response is to get away. He's armed and my first priority is to remedy that. I can feel eyes on me as I move. I'm adept at dodging, as fist fights were unavoidable with my temper, but attacking isn't my strength. Especially when a weapon is involved. I seek a weak point, moving around his enthusiastic strikes in frustration. As I dive over his blade, somersaulting along the ground, I hear Styx on the side lines.

"Don't just run from him," he calls.

"We *don't* want her to fight, remember?" Nixie huffs.

"Oh… Sorry, you're doing great," he amends. "Why is it so much harder to train someone to run away?"

Ignoring his question, I try to think of a way to disarm my opponent. He moves so quickly, it's hard to keep up. If I can manage to get beneath the sword, though, I might be able to grab the hilt. When he thrusts, I lean back to dodge it. One hand grabs his, heating up with a thought. The pirate cries out in surprise, dropping the hot metal. I drop and sweep his feet from under him, turning as I stand. As astonished as he is, he still manages to get to his feet. I'm much better with my fists then anything else. Now that we're on even ground, I'm not shy with my attacks. He ducks a punch, attempting to retrieve his blade. I'm not the best student, but history was one of my favorite subjects. Because of that happy coincidence, I know this fight is over… as long as I stay between him and that sword. Arnoldo was never good at hand-to-hand combat. In fact, that was how he was bested.

"*My lady, I am nothing if not a gentleman,*" he remarks. "*But this is battle, and I may have to harm you with more than a sliver of a cut.*"

"As long as you're aware I'll do the same," I answer.

He jumps back in the fray. Fists swinging and legs kicking, he attempts to move around me. At one point, he dives for the blade. My foot automatically slips beneath it, kicking it high into the air. My body rolls over his back, and then the blade rests in my hand. I bring it down just as he faces me, resting it above his heart. It's easy to see the surprise in his eyes.

"*It would appear you've bested me,*" he says. "*Congratulations, young maiden.*"

"Thank you," I smile.

"*You lack expertise and finesse,*" he reports. "*And your planning process could use more attention. However, your instincts are spot on when moved by reflex. Although you fail to plan ahead, it would seem the correct response lies in your subconscious. Do not rely upon it continuously, it's still best when fully developed.*"

"Thank you," I state. "Here's your sword back."

"*Appreciated,*" he says, bowing his head. "*However, I refuse to leave you unfinished. You have the potential to be a powerful siren of the seas. You'll report back to me for further lessons. I'll make a pirate of you yet.*"

I have no time to refuse the demand, as he walks away and rejoins the ranks. The confusion passes as the next person comes forward. I know him from class as well. He's a gladiator named Viturin Cosmin. He reigned supreme in the arena, yet the gladiators were nothing more than slaves to entertainment. Learning that those he fought were little more than poor citizens and prisoners of war, he led a revolt against the emperor.

"*You lack confidence in your abilities,*" he remarks. "*Without that confidence, you fall prey to doubt and fear. There is no room for either on the battlefield. A girl like you must be ten times more aggressive than a man, ten times tougher. Can you manage that?*"

"Hell yeah!" I cheer. "Nixie, you should take lessons from him on pep talks, he's fucking good!"

"Don't turn your back on him, he cheats!" she warns.

I no sooner turn back to him, and I'm dancing away from his fist. He's not as fast as Arnoldo, but he has a lot more power in his strikes. To even get clipped by a fist will leave me with a nasty bruise. I'm caught off guard by his reach, his large hand covering my throat as he lifts me off the ground. The strangling sensation isn't one I prefer. Angry at the treatment, my body turns to fire. I know the heat has scalded his hand, as he drops me fast.

"*Water and fire?*" Arnoldo comments. "*What a wondrous oddity.*"

Viturin isn't armed, but I'm not about to run straight at him. He's too strong to up against without some form of leverage. In this situation, my elements will likely come in handy. I have to limit his movement, keep out of his reach and attack from afar. Unfortunately, I don't really know how to do that. The thought of ice comes to me, yet

I don't have any water. Just as I think it over, I'm shoved into the river. I nearly smack my forehead in disbelief. Now with a water source, I try to lure the gladiator in. The lightening tears through the sky, turning the water to blood, and Viturin launches himself at me. I fall apart, joining the water I stand in, and the river shoots skyward. As soon as he's engulfed in a column of liquid, it freezes around him.

I rise from the water, carefully melting the ice around his face. He looks less than happy about his defeat. Just as I'm about to let him go, he starts fighting against the ice. He can't break it, it's too thick, but that doesn't stop him from trying. Rolling my eyes, I banish the ice before he hurts himself.

"You lost," I point out. "You can stop attacking me now."

"*This battle isn't about winning,*" he points out. "*It's about facing the impossible and triumphing. You won't be able to run from every opponent, you won't be able to overpower them as you are. When your back is to the wall, what will you do?*"

"I'll win," I answer, confident. "Strength doesn't matter if you can find a way around it."

"*We shall see.*"

He comes at me once again, swinging large fists in hopes of landing a mark. I can dodge without issue, but I'm quickly running out of room. The lightening flashes and I trip over a small hill of bones. That's when he manages to make contact. My body turns to water and slithers away from him in a pool. I have no time to reform, though. This gladiator is like a dog with a bone, focused solely on me. Focus is good and all, however he's ignoring his surroundings.

I lead him along the ground, waiting for the lightening. When it finally pulses in the sky, Viturin is trapped in a large web of bones. Using the blood from the river, I draw it over him in a large dome. When it freezes, it keeps the sunshine from touching the ground below.

"We can keep playing this game, or you can call it quits," I comment. "You're not the scariest thing I've gone up against, so fear isn't something you provoke."

"*You're tougher than I gave you credit for*," he huffs. "*But there will be greater foes, bigger challenges. You must be taken through trials in the future, to sharpen your edge and open your eyes to the world.*"

I release him from his second prison, wondering what the last two will be teaching me. After Viturin returns to Styx's side, the third teacher steps forward. He's a native american, dressed in leather with feathers in his hair. A quiver of arrows is on his back and a bow hangs off his frame. I'm not sure what it is he'll be teaching me, his name never came up in class, but I'm willing to learn.

"*You have much potential*," he says. "*But you need guidance. You are not physically strong, so close combat is where you will fall. What you need, is a weapon with a long reach.*"

"I'm sorry, but I don't know you," I blush. "History is one of my favorite subjects, yet… I don't think your name came up. Do you mind giving me a history lesson?"

"*My name is Inali,*" he answers. "*During my time, there was war over my clan's lands. For as long as I lived, I protected those lands. My marksmanship was feared by our enemy and revered by our friends.*"

I'm amazed by the story, wishing I had known it sooner. The lives of those that have passed have always beckoned to me. I suppose it's because my element is the soul. I'm connected to them and I love to feel that connection. It's strongest when I'm aware of their past deeds. This man before me seems weathered, having grown in a time of war, and my heart goes out to him. His life could've been so much better in another time. Though, I doubt he would have changed it if he could. I smile and wait for my next lesson, hoping it's one I haven't gotten down yet. Repetition has never been popular with my ADD.

Chapter 27

A cold wind beats against us, the last of the rain hitting our surroundings. When the last drop joins the puddles, clouds disperse. we're trapped in a meadow of bones, blood and corpses. I'm just waiting for the attack, tense and guarded. So when Inali takes a seat on the scattered bones, I'm at a loss. He sees my hesitance, motioning for me to join him. It takes a moment, but I take a seat across from him. He sets his bow to one side, and the quiver of arrows to the other. As soon as we're settled, he makes eye contact.

"*This world, like you, is not what it seems. You are both gifts from the spirits,*" he begins. "*The blessings bestowed upon you have much to be explored. The great spirits have chosen you to carry their strength, because they see something in you others are missing. It is up to you to take the path they reveal... or ignore it. Which path do you choose?*"

"... Wait... What?"

"*Which path do you choose to follow?*"

"There is no choice," I frown.

"*There is always a choice and the consequences that follow.*"

"I'm going to save my family."

"*Is that what you need to do, or what you want to do?*"

I glare at him, wondering where this conversation is heading. Before I can snap at him, the fourth master joins us. As though ready to mediate, he sits on the side to face us both. His presence is strangely calm, radiating peace and relaxing my guard. His sheathed blade rests over his lap.

"*If your quest is solely for destiny, you will fail,*" he comments. "*Many samurai lived for duty, nothing more. When faced with another of equal skill, they failed to overcome those with heart and conviction. This is not a task to challenge without heart. Why do you take on this fight? Why place yourself in danger for people you've never met before?*"

"Someone has to save those lost souls," I answer, unflinching. "I have the ability, there's no reason for me to ignore their pain. I'm not scared and I know that's not a normal response in the face of the supernatural, but… that just means if I don't do this… all those people will be trapped forever. I can't stand by idly as that happens."

The two seem pleased with my answer, though I can't understand why. I should be training, not talking. Even if there's a time difference, this is wasteful. The frustration must be written on my face, as Nixie clears her throat to distract me. I force a deep breath to calm myself. The duo take their time, watching me for something. If I'm completely honest with myself, I don't have the patience for this.

"How is this helping?" I frown.

"*Patience is a powerful tool,*" Inali states. "*It's also something you lack.*"

"*Balance, inside and out, make a great warrior. If you can't bring peace to yourself, how can you bring it to others?*"

"*You must master yourself. This blessing bestowed upon you, can be as powerful as your imagination. You should never assume something is impossible until you have tried it without success. Now, grab your bow.*"

"Uh… I don't have one," I point out.

He doesn't answer, instead picking up his own. The two stand, one rejoining Styx, and then an arrow is notched. The second he aims, I'm scrambling out of the way. Letting my guard down was foolish. The arrow sticks out from the ground, right where I sat. another is drawn back, forcing me to get to my feet to dodge. Inali shows no emotion on his face, concentrating on nothing but the kill. I need something to fight back with, yet the only things available are bones. My hands dive inot the nearest pile, pulling out a skill and a femur. Both are sent his way, however they're knocked from the air by his arrows.

"*You will not overcome me with pebbles,*" he remarks.

"I *have* no weapon!" I shout.

"Cat, you *are* a weapon," Nixie calls.

"No helping from the peanut gallery!" Styx huffs.

I feel so stupid, I can't help but palm my face. My hands burst into flames, as though back on my childhood baseball team, I wind up and pitch him a fire ball. it's not even close to getting him. So marksmanship is a fail. that's what these lessons are for. A few more are thrown, yet he dodges them with ease.

"*This is not about the win,*" Inali states. "*Your mind is chaotic, your aim follows. Find peace within and trust your instincts. Do not doubt yourself.*"

His comments only serve to remind me how little I've progressed. It's irritating to miss the obvious where my abilities are concerned. How can one not doubt themselves? Every day is a battle to live life, to make the 'right' choices, to push through all obstacles. There are so many decisions to make, so many paths not taken. I dodge another arrow, diving over a pile of bones and hurling a fire ball before they hide me. Once more, Inali is missed.

"*It is not quantity,*" he sighs. "*Quality will always be worth more than any number. A thousand missed arrows can never amount to one perfect strike. Concentrate and take your time.*"

Although I grumble beneath my breath, I understand what he's trying to tell me. My attacks are nothing but random, no target in mind and thrown with a frenzy. I'll get nowhere like this, that much is for certain. For now, I just have to keep moving. My eyes stay on my attacker, my body bolting from the pile. His arrows nearly hitting my ankle, raining down from above to keep me on the defensive.

As I weave between hiding places, I try to take in Inali's movements. He's steady as he pulls another arrow from the quiver behind him, drawing it to the bow and pulling back. The string twangs as it's loosed. Again and again he repeats the movement. Finally, I notice something strange. Each time he pulls the arrow back, he pauses and closes his eyes. His lips move, almost as though in prayer, and then the arrow is let go. I dodge it, leaping between piles. Midway, I throw my hand toward him and a jet of water knocks his arrow back at him. It wasn't dead center, but it was close enough to send it back. The arrowhead grazes his cheek.

"*You are starting to understand,*" he comments. "*You have the heart of a warrior, young one. I have faith in your abilities. You, however, do not. The spirit within you is too kind in the face of monsters. That will destroy you more than standing your ground to fight. Letting a monster live, is agreeing to kill your loved ones. Never forget that.*"

"That's sort of a morbid way to think of it," I comment. "How could you say that?"

"*Because... that was my mistake in life. The one that led to death,*" he sighs. "*It is easier to win the war, if you break it into smaller battles. I did not. I allowed a monster to live, and they brought an army to my tribe. Everyone was slaughtered. In a blinded rage, I proclaimed war with my enemy. I fought thousands, killed most of* them, and died with my arrow striking down my enemy. Had I acted before, my tribe would have been spared."

"Not every story will have that ending," I frown.

"Is that what history continues to tell you?" he inquires. "When I was a youth, history told the stories of great warriors. There was always a war, there were always those who died fighting. For what? For land, or gold, or trinkets. It matters not the reason, just that war was a human act. Chaos is needed to make the living feel alive, that is what I've learned in death. Always keep that in mind."

He steps away and I cautiously stand up. As he takes a place near Styx, the last warrior steps forward. His frame is shorter than the others, but a bit taller than my own. He didn't seem this small when he was mediating. I looks for a weapon, yet his sword had been given to Styx before he approached. I'm curious about him, as he's the other warrior I don't know. Before he can move into a teaching mode, I can't help but question him.

"I haven't heard of you either," I state. "In my history classes, I mean."

"Of course not, I do not exist," he smiles. "I am nothing but a ghost, a wandering samurai. Since I lived the life of a ghost, I was merely a whisper. A myth."

"What did you do?"

"I destroyed empires, murdered thieves, and saved the innocent. Everything to earn a warrior a name, yet I never gave mine. I did not exist and that is the way I wanted it."

It's strange to me, as I can't really understand his motives. Back then it could've been as simple as he liked to kill. Not all of them were like that, though. I want to believe he's a good person at heart, so I go with that. It's always nice to entertain obliviousness. With nothing to call him, I'm forced to wait until he's ready to start talking. I don't have to wait long.

"*You have not mastered anything, but you have the potential to,*" he remarks. "*What I will leave you with, is the mastery of one's self. Harmony within is the key to your strengths. You harbor nature within your veins, a curse to most. Conflict is bound to happen in the face of opposites, so you must learn to harness that energy.*"

"I don't know how," I huff. "I asked the others how they did it, but they told me it's not something they can explain. That we all had our own way of learning things."

"*Your mind is not cleared of all, it is foggy with doubt and fear. Fear is a natural response to that which you do not understand, but you cannot let it consume you. Strength does not come from ignoring your fear... it comes from pushing through it.*"

"What will happen if I can clear my mind?" I wonder.

"*You will see with opened eyes,*" he answers. "*A world of endless possibilities will be yours to explore. There will be nothing you cannot overcome.*"

"I just want to protect my family," I state, quiet. "How can I clear my head?"

He takes a seat and motions me to join him. After the last session, I'm not as hesitant. We lock eyes and he takes a deep breath, exhaling before closing his eyes. When he hears nothing from me, one eye opens and he frowns. Assuming I'm meant to follow his lead, I roll my own orbs before closing them.

"*This world is a symphony of nature's making,*" he states, tone calm and relaxing. "*Every breath is a gift. Take them slowly, breathe deep and exhale. Smell the grass that hides in darkness, the water seeping beneath the ground, the dirt that you now sit upon. The world is more than sight. You must use all your senses to truly appreciate it.*"

I'm lost in a trance at his voice, almost hypnotic in its dulcet tones. It helps me notice things I would've marked as trivial before. The moist earth is cool to the touch, a chill in the air that has nothing to do with weather coats my skin. I know what it's from. It's the insistent reminder that this place is for the dead. I can hear the trickle of the blood stream, smell the hint of moss from the waters, and moonlight bathes my skin in its comforting chill.

"*Let go of your doubts,*" he tells me. "*Let go of your troubles. Live in the now, treasure this time. There is nothing but you and the elements that surround you. You are a part of them, just as they are of you. Let them soothe your spirit, mold your mind, and strengthen your resolve. Without you, they are but useless tools muddling about. You give them purpose, you give them a path... They are soldiers awaiting your command. Embrace them, feel them around you."*

That's exactly what I do, reaching out with my mind to offer them a hand. There's pressure from them, all around me, but nothing that feels threatening. I feel safe and warm, as though they create an invisible barrier between myself and the world. It clears my head like never before, images coming up with each element I 'touch'. I see the chaos and destruction they're capable of, but also the life they protect and provide for. Like opening a book, knowledge pours through me. My eyes open unconsciously, catching glimpses of twisting waters and blazing fires. Styx and Nixie are stupefied by the sight, yet I'm trapped in an out of body experience. My body is transparent, waters circling me like folded wings, and tiny fires dance in the air around me.

"*This is how you clear your mind,*" the man remarks, proud. "*This is how you garner your untapped strength.*"

As my mind slowly returns to itself, the elements become less restless. When they finally fade away, I'm staring at those watching me. Their eyes are large and a strange sensation fills the air. It's almost like gravity pressing down on us. The power laying upon us is astounding. When I stand, my legs are quivering with effort. I don't know what happened to me, yet I can feel the effects. It's overwhelming to think all this power came from me.

"Cat, that was amazing!" Nixie gasps out. "How did you do that?"

"I have no idea."

"That's an amazing amount of power in such a small frame," Styx utters.

"I still don't know how to use it," I mutter. "How is that supposed to help me?"

"We have opened the doors to your potential, but you are the one that needs to reach it. After this battle, we insist you return for further lessons. You are a student to be proud of, and it would be our honor to be your masters."

"Thank you," I smile. "I appreciate your help. If I do succeed, I'll do my best to get back here. I'm sure there's still a lot I can learn from you."

Styx comes to my side and waves them off in thanks. Once they're on their way, he and Nixie lead me out of the meadow of death. As we step through the doorway that led here, I can't help but look back upon it. The meadow of greenery was beautiful, but I have to admit… it's night version might just grow on me.

Chapter 28

True to his word, when we step into the cabin time has hardly passed. It's shocking to be in sunlight again. Still weary from my training, I flop down on the couch. Nixie sits beside me. At first, I assume Styx has better things to do before nightfall. He sits across from us. His robes twist and shift around him, becoming tighter. The black seems to bleed inward, starting at the sides and retracting to his chest. In the end, he's back in jeans and a tee shirt. The gaping hole in his cheek is gone, his body falling lax with a relieved sigh.

"I need a vacation," he states.

"Careful, Styx," Nixie smirks. "Remember last time you felt this tired."

"… I would've preferred not to, thanks," he grumbles.

"What happened?" I question, eager.

"He aged so fast, some orderlies thought he was an elderly patient with dementia. He spent two months in an old folks' home."

His face is a light dusting of embarrassment as I laugh. I can only imagine his disdain. From the expression, I can tell that was an event he wanted dead and buried. With the air so lighthearted, I can pretend it's just a normal day. Or, at least, I could… if the lights didn't start to flicker. Although it's still sunny out, the room is doused in pitch. After a moment, I catch the blue fire of Styx's lantern. The light reveals our faces.

"Now what?" Nixie huffs.

A soft moan, full of misery, drifts through the dark. Styx glances around, trying to locate our intruder. It doesn't matter, I can't even sense them. Before I can say anything, he glances my way and his eyes grow wide. I feel the cold breath on the back of my neck before he rushes toward me. Arms encircle me, and then I'm yanked away in what seems to be slow motion.

I'm jarred from the fall when I hit ground. Very hard ground. My hands hold my head as I sit up. It's dark here, the smell similar to moss, and the cold is bone deep. With a groan from the headache, I force myself to stand. The back of my head is throbbing, as is my back. The fall ended on, what feels like, concrete. it's too rocky for that, though. Squinting in the dark, I try to locate something familiar. A soft sound is in the air, familiar and at the edge of my mind. That music seems so distant. Careful not to fall, I make my way to it. My hand touches a wall, so I follow it back. I attempt to make a flame to see my surroundings. it's dim and I'm quick to lose it. From what I can see, this place is sealed shut. The fire would just burn any remaining oxygen, and I have no clue where I am… or how long I'll be trapped. Hoping for a quick exit, I reach out for any other element I'm connected to. Although I sense moisture beyond this room, it's not enough to use.

Just as i'm about to take the form of a spirit, I freeze. The temperature has dropped drastically. My eyes dart about searching for friend or foe. Nothing moves within the eerie pitch. I about jump from my skin at the sound of a harsh storm. Something slams against the door I lit up, rattling it on its hinges. Against my better judgment, I step closer. It seems the struggle lessens the closer I get. The air is thinning out, making my head light, but I have little hope of escape. And then I hear a hiss of air. The struggle outside broke through the sealant. Slowly, the air returns and I'm able to use my fires.

Just to be safe, I only make a small globe. It rests in the palm of my hand, as effective as a torch. I know this room. The door in front of me is weathered, with scratches that weren't there last I saw it. I raise my free hand, tracing the marks. They belong to a child, one nail still clinging to the wood. Inspecting the creases that were sealed before, I find tree sap in the grooves. there's someone moving on the other side, so I back away in hopes they overlook my presence.

In my quest for silence, I move further… until my back hits something cold. My worries aren't of the obstacle, but from the fact it doesn't feel like a stone wall. Heart pounding loudly in my chest, I turn around. The surface is more sap, sanded into a smooth oval. I almost overlook it, but a smear of darkness draws my attention. Within the amber egg, curled into the fetal position, is a little girl's body. I stare in horror at the perfectly preserved corpse, barely registering that soft music starting again.

"*Can you hear it?*"

I can't help the scream, that whisper inches from my ear. My body whirls around, ignoring the desire to scale the amber statue for escape. there's no one there. My ear still tickles from those ghostly words. The music box shifts my attention. It's small, decorated with silver and gold. Although it's been down here for years, it still looks brand new. It's odd to see it untouched by age. I reach over to touch it, hoping it's not some random trap. When my finger ghosts along the surface, it's warm to the touch.

"*I love it, daddy! Thank you!*"

once more, I check the room over. I'm still by myself. My hand hovers over the box, cautious of disturbing anything connected to it. The shock to my system still tingles along my skin. I'm not sure what happened, however I have a feeling my spirit power is connecting to Ioana. This box is a direct connection to her memory. I take a seat on the cobblestone floor, right in front of Ioana's eternal prison. Taking a deep breath, I pick up the box with both hands. It's as though I hugged a transformer, the electricity jolting up my arms. The pain forces my eyes closed. When I open them again, I'm not in that dank little room.

“Hurry, Ioana,” Calista calls. “Dinner is ready, you’re late.”

“Daddy was here,” I state.

A glance to a nearby puddle, shows that I’m a passenger within Ioana. She’s wearing a red dress with a jingling belt of coins. Her long hair is braided tight to her head, traveling do hand in pigtails. Her mother touches the flowers entwined within her locks. Her expression is confused at first, so I can assume she didn’t do it.

“Were you with the settler girls today?”

“No, mam,” Ioana states. “Just daddy. We were listening, and he likes to play with my hair. He told me about his sisters and how he used to braid their hair. And then we talked to some bunnies...”

“Honey, you have to be careful about that,” Calista sighs. “I love your father very much, but he’s not… normal. At least, not to the settlers. They have been talking about witchcraft, and that is something they will look for.”

“I am sorry, mommy,” Ioana frowns.

“it is not your fault, honey. I know your dad would never let anything happen to you. I am just worried. The chancellor has been acting strange lately. I fear something awful will happen, but… I wish I knew when.”

“Daddy is watching him. The whispers are dark and secretive, so he is getting anxious. He doesn’t know when either.”

“Did he say anything to you about it?”

“He said it is adult stuff, but when it happens… it will be fast and unavoidable. He is afraid for us.”

“Do not worry, Ioana. I will always be here to protect you.”

her smiling face fades into nothing, like a happy spirit finding rest. The body I inhabit walks forward, leaving me behind. As Ioana skips off she, too, fades away. I’m left on Whisper Hill, completely at a loss. Unable to wake myself from this scene, and hoping I won't wake in that hidden room, I take a seat in the grass. With an exasperated sigh, I close my eyes to the world.

"*She does not love him,*" someone whispers.

The random comment confuses me, leading me to open my eye. A quick glance confirms I'm alone. Just to be certain, I search for any spirits. There's a strange sensation of paranoia, but it doesn't feel like a spirit. Wary of what may be lurking, my eyes close a second time. The sun is warm on my face, reminding me of the cold I'm actually trapped in.

"*Rude child. Your manners are vile. If my boy acted like you, he'd have his hide tanned.*"

"*So many people, so little time.*"

"*How many will die before I am suspected?*"

That last comment has my eyes wide. Up on my feet, I'm searching for the owner to that voice. It occurs to me that each comment was said in a different voice. For a moment, I entertain the idea of voices on the wind might be true. I shake my head, dislodging the thought. It's a stubborn one, though. I might as well test it out. The meditation lesson is greatly appreciated at this point in time. When my eyelids hide the orbs, I take a deep breath and exhale slowly.

"She is so pretty," a child whispers.

"So much money, but nothing to spare. What a greedy person."

"I wish mommy would let me keep the bunnies I found."

the words come so randomly, it's hard to separate them. I want that man's voice from before. I'm almost positive it belongs to the chancellor. If only there was a way to organize all this chatter. These tones are little more than disembodied spirits. I imagine them in their own separate streams, each a unique color. One hand waves a few away, the other mirroring the act. One group after another is dismissed, leaving a trail of patterns. The younger the voice, the lighter the color. It doesn't take long for the assumption of purity to pop up. The more tainted a soul, the darker the energy it creates. More focused, I search out the voice I seek. The energy is a dark and angry red, littered with flecks of black. My hand touches it, drawing it closer, and I hear a strange static underlying his voice.

"She has no father, how can that be? That child is the spawn of the devil, she has to be. A child born to lure men to their deaths. She is nothing but a little whore in waiting. I cannot save her, no one can… but I can keep her from laying out the devil's plans. I will protect my village no matter the cost."

Like a devil upon his shoulder, that demonic creature whispers in his ear. Their voice distant and underlying his own. It's as though he's a puppet playing out the skin walker's story. I can't imagine dealing with that for as long as he did. Although it doesn't excuse his actions, I understand how he could've broken. I let go of that voice, sighing in frustration. It isn't until I open my eyes, that I realize I'm no longer alone. With a surprised gasp, I scoot back until I'm pressed up against the lone tree. Seated in the grass opposite me, watching as though I can't see him, is a man I've never seen before. His appearance is strange to me, but not only because I didn't hear him. His long hair, so pale I can call it white, is braided back on one side. The rest hangs past his shoulders. The man's build is lithe, clothed in colorful silks with gold jewelry, and his eyes are a pale blue. They may be pinned on me, but I notice they're looking through me.

"What an eventful day," he comments. "What has the wind blown in for me, I wonder. You are not a typical spirit, I can sense that much. Do not be shy, I can hear you speak."

"… You're Ioana's dad!" I utter in realization. "She's a *demigod*? I can't believe it!"

"How do you know Ioana? You do not feel like you are from this time… Do you meet her in the future? How did you get here?"

"I came here by accident, I thought it was one of her memories. When she walked away, she left me behind and I didn't go back. But I can tell you..."

"No!" he says quickly. "You cannot tell me anything about the future! I cannot change anything, and I do not want to know I could have. We have rules to follow."

"Oh, right," I mutter. "I forgot, sorry. Is there anything you *can* tell me?"

"… Tell me how you got here. You were listening to the voices on the wind, were you not?"

"I… I picked up a music box. It was Ioana's. It brought me here, I saw from her eyes as she spoke to her mother. When she walked away, I stayed behind. I kept hearing about this hill, so I sat down to rest. I heard voices, and then I tried to sort through them… and there *you* were."

He hums to himself in thought, and then reaches forward blindly. His hand passes through me, sending a chill along my veins. The energy he gives off is powerful and ancient, making me feel far smaller than the norm. unable to believe the shock it gives me, I wonder how old he is. it's not until he moves back, that I realize he's speaking once more.

"Hearing the wind takes a special type," he smiles, warm and sincere. "I'm quite impressed. Your energy is boundless. Unfortunately, I found the mark of a skin walker on you. I find it hard to believe you are still alive after finding one."

"I saw one in an orchard that grows here later on," I explain. "My friends want to stop it, and I'm supposed to help. This is all still new to me, I have trouble controlling all this. If I don't get back soon, they'll have to face it without me. I can't let them get hurt because of me."

"No, we cannot," he agrees. "This talent is very rare for any human to possess, but it is one I am familiar with. When I touched your shoulder, I gave you a gift. It will help you hear the voices better. As for getting you back home, you just have to wake up."

"Wake up?"

"Not every dream is a figment," he smirks. "Just shock yourself into waking up. It has helped my siblings before. I promise you will not get hurt. Make sure it is a good shock, though."

"I don't know how to do that," I huff.

He nods, and then stands up. Before I know what's happening, I'm thrown high into the air by a violent gust. The drop is long and the ground is coming up fast. My scream barely has a chance to get out before everything goes black.

I open my eyes, back in the final resting place of my little friend. Gasping for breath, cold sweat on my skin, I stare at the ceiling. My heart races as I sit up, eyes wide and searching. As soon as I shake myself from the bewilderment, I move toward the door. It opens, but only a sliver. Something is on the other side, hindering my progress. I slip through the opening made. The moisture I felt before is mud, which a thick tree now sprouts from. It's gnarled and twisted, so it's easy to climb. As I make headway, I come across the remains of an old wooden ladder. The tree has grown around it, engulfing the evidence in its haste to reach the sun. At the mouth of the well, I peek over the edge. Nothing is moving about. A rustle from behind has me on edge, but it's just a rabbit. It's trying to move past the barrier. As quiet as possible, I scoot over to it.

One hand rests on the barrier, and then passes through. With a surprised gasp, I move through with the rabbit. Just as I move through, the skin walker slams into the barrier behind me. In its fury, it tears at the barrier. Like a wild animal, it snarls and growls. I don't even look back as I run away. The second I find an underground source of water, my body falls apart to join it.

I remember the rush of water, though vaguely, and then my body tumbles across linoleum. A footstep sounds nearby, squeaky on wet floor. Nixie shouts a curse, landing on the floor a little out of reach. I slow my panicked breathing, finally taking not of my surroundings. I'm back at the cabin, my form a twisting mass of water. The floor is sopping, Nixie sprawled across it, and Styx is in the doorway. He steps carefully into the kitchen. His approach is akin to dealing with a wounded animal in the wild.

"It's okay," he states, hands within view. "I don't know where you went, but you're not there anymore. You're safe. Please calm down."

"You won't *believe* what happened to me!" I shout, shifting between water and spirit.

If I weren't so anxious, I would think the effect is awesome. A slim stream swirling around a ghostly figure. Something like that is definitely horror movie worthy. The thoughts help to distract me. My form becomes solid once more, the three of us heading toward the living room. The couch is a welcome change. It takes a moment to calm myself, and then I tell them what I experienced.

"You *met* the god of Whisper Hill!" Nixie gasps. "*Nobody* knows him, he's kind of a recluse."

"Well, I did. He gave me the ability to listen to the voices better."

"So… he made you certified," she frowns. "How is *that* supposed to help?"

"Not those kinds of voices," I huff. "The ones on the wind. I heard them on that hill, and I know Ioana could as well."

"That doesn't make them real."

"People 'made up' the Grim Reaper, too, yet here you stand."

"… Point taken."

"It's not typical for him to take interest in this world. I wonder what changed," Styx states.

"He's Ioana's dad," I admit. "I wanted to warn him, but it's against the rules."

"It would change the future," he explains. "There's no telling what that would lead to."

"There's one more thing… when I crawled out of the well, I was able to pass through that barrier. I think it was created by the god of Whisper Hill."

"That could very well be," Styx sighs. "But at least we don't have to find a way through. I'll go get Calista, you two drive to the orchard. I don't want that skin walker noting our presence until the last moment. Wait for me outside the orchard if I'm not there first."

We both nod and Styx leaves through a quick portal. When the last bit of light vanishes, Nixie leads me to the garage. Her hand is tight around my own. In the truck, I turn the key and glance her way. She looks troubled by something. I wait to say anything until we're on the road. it's difficult to bring up this topic, as the last thing I need before battle is negativity. If she senses something off about it, though, it might be safer to trust her gut. Finally, I sigh and glance over to her.

"What's wrong?" I wonder. "And don't tell me 'nothing', I know you better than that."

"… This isn't like the demons we've fought before," she admits. "I've never feared losing you so much. And after that disappearance… I wonder how you would take losing me."

"Are you going somewhere?" I frown.

"Not by choice," she comments. "But this is some seriously old magic, who knows what will happen."

"We're going to be fine," I assure. "You're immortal, I'm a Root, and Styx mans the afterlife. I think we have it all covered."

"Still..."

She lets the comment hang there. I know she's nervous, I am as well, but dwelling over the negative won't help. The ride goes extremely quiet, a tension I've never felt with Nixie taking over. Unable to leave it be, I sigh and glance her way. Before I'm able to speak, however, there's a chill in the front seat. Since my little trip, the first signs of dusk have snuck up and the truck is bathed in a hazy light. The overhead light begins turning on and off, along with all other lights on the automobile. The radio blares, randomly changing stations and pouring static.

"This is new," I frown.

"I'm so not in the mood for this," Nixie sighs. "Which one is it?"

"… There's more than one," I murmur.

My eyes glance in the rear view mirror, landing on Ioana's dark locks. I turn my head to address her, finding her almost nose to nose with me. My heart skips a beat. In a blink, she's gone. Nixie stares at me, eyes wide, and then gasps in surprise. I know there's something behind me. I don't want to turn around, but the window begins to roll open. A shiver runs the length of my back, and I scramble over to Nixie's lap. She bravely uses me as a shield. We stare as Ioana drags herself through the window, her form dripping as she reaches for my face. A curved blade is between us in seconds. At first I wonder how she fit her scythe in this cramped space, and then I note it's different. Instead of the massive blade and long handle, she wields a small handheld scythe for harvesting.

"That's close enough," she remarks.

"Thanks, honey," I comment, sarcastic. "Nothing like the last minute."

She mutters under her breath, yet keeps Ioana's hand from making contact. Ioana pulls her hand back, blinking from sight once more. She doesn't reappear this time, but I can sense she's lingering out of sight. I move away from Nixie, noting a significant drop in temperature. She frowns, watching frost spread on the windshield. Letters are traced in it. When they're done, we gaze upon the message 'You can save them'.

"Yes, I know that. That's where we're going now," I remark.

The frost renews, Nixie watching in fascination. Once more, an invisible finger writes across it. This is the first time Nixie has come across it, or she'd be annoyed by now. She's not even fond of texting. The new message says 'No, *all* of them'. I pause for a moment, and then the frost is taking over for another scrawl. The next one doesn't clear my confusion any, though, stating simply 'the prisoner must overthrow their warden'. At first, it makes no sense. A few moments of thought, and I realize this message refers to the skin walker's prisoners. To be able to set them free of eternal punishment, that's something I can't pass up. The only problem is, I don't know how.

"How?" I question. "I tried to help them, but I couldn't get through."

the word 'prisoner' is circled and underlined a few times. Afterward, the frost returns and the word 'listen' is written in all capitals. When the car turns warm and the frost melts away, I can feel we're alone again. The engine comes to life. With a wary glance toward Nixie, I hit the gas and continue to the orchard. It isn't until we're passed by another car that she speaks.

"That presence was strange," she comments. "It didn't feel like a trapped soul, more like a wandering spirit. The way it writes, it's almost as though it knows you."

"That's not the first time we've talked," I point out. "The experience is never threatening, though."

"It's just odd to me," she frowns. "There have been very few spirits that attach themselves to a person before an object. I would've expected it to happen to someone younger. Like, a baby or toddler."

"As long as it's helpful, I have no issues."

"What does it have to gain from helping?"

"Maybe it's not that type of ghost."

the trees are coming into view now, blossoms covering the expanse. Just one more step to the endgame. We pull up to park, catching sight of Styx and Calista. They stand near the road while I park. After exiting the truck, we all meet halfway. When we're all together, the plan is laid out. With the recent encounter, however, I feel the need to rethink our approach. Since Styx has dealt with this creature in the past, I hope he can answer the questions I have.

"Will it's trophies be freed once the skin walker is gone?"

"… No. although we researched them extensively during the war, we only know for certain how to destroy them. Anything beyond that is mere theory."

The admission surprises me, as I thought more was known. I wonder who even created these awful creatures. Although it's only theory, I wait for him to continue. He doesn't seem to want to, so I'm forced to insist.

"Did they even try to free the other souls?"

"We did," he admits. "Out of the millions of skin walkers we destroyed, only a few released their trapped souls."

"How?"

"I think the only way they'll be freed is if the current shell it's in commits suicide… in a way."

"Meaning?"

"The only way to free their victims, is if the current vessel's will power pushes to take control again. That only gives a short window for them to sacrifice themselves. The act cleanses their soul, freeing the others before the skin walker is chased off."

"That doesn't kill it?"

"No. Only the water from my namesake or a weapon dowsed in it can kill them. That's why you need to get it to the river."

"… If the current vessel steps into the river, will *that* kill it?"

"What are you planning?" he frowns, suspicious.

"I think I can save them all," I reply. "If I can get through to the chancellor's spirit..."

"Souls that attract a skin walker aren't pure. They have to have some level of darkness to begin with. it's better to kill that demon right away. Giving it time to formulate a plan of attack is too risky, we only get one shot at this. Stick to the plan."

"One minute," I argue. "I have to at least *try*."

"… If you can figure out a way to trap it, I'll give you one minute," he sighs, exasperated.

it's the best I'm going to get, but as least it's something. Facing the cursed orchard, determination rising, we start in. a strange mist lays upon the ground. it's so thick I can barely see below my knees. Styx has to take the lead, as his lantern cuts through anything. Calista and I are in the middle, Nixie following close behind. The second we step into this scene, I can tell something bad is going to happen.

"We need to stick close," I comment. "It'll try to split us up."

"If it's trapped, as you mentioned, it has no power here," Styx states.

"Then how did it reach me at Calista's house?" I point out. "I think it's safe to assume it can work through spirits it's familiar with."

"… That's a safe assumption," he agrees after a moment's thought. "If that's the case, we need to find a way to..."

He stops mid-sentence, eyes wide as the fog grows. it's risen over our heads, thickening to the point of blindness. My hand reaches for Nixie's, yet comes up empty. The next thing I know, I'm in a mess of white. Like a whiteout during a blizzard, my sight is stolen and my body is wracked by a deathly chill. The ground beneath my feet trembles, almost knocking me down. When the fog clears, I'm not where I was… and I'm all alone.

Chapter 29

Alone in this orchard, surrounded by trees blossoming curious fruit, I'm at a loss. My first move should be finding the others, yet I know where our destination is. Should I go there, I may find that we had similar thoughts. Then again, there's no way to guarantee that. I'm also reminded only two of us can navigate this living labyrinth. With its random movement, it may be best to find Nixie and Calista first. Since we don't want to tip off the skin walker, Styx and Nixie are on foot. With a reluctant sigh, I grasp the pendant Styx gave me. The arrow spins a moment, and then stops to the left.

My walk doesn't last too long, hindered by a clearing of charred grass and ashen piles. The trees all look the same, blossoms almost fully in bloom. Some have begun to turn to fruit. In the center of the field, a familiar well appears. Ioana is seated on the edge of it, motioning me to join her. Wary of the endless drop pictured in my mind, I let my legs dangle into the structure.

"*This is where my parents met,*" she says, after a brief pause. "*Daddy was fighting a bad thing with his friend, and a fire broke out. Mommy was out picking herbs alone. When she got caught in this clearing, daddy saved her.*"

"That's a great story," I offer. "I met Nixie at school… She pushed me down when I chased off her bully. She said she didn't need help and stormed off. We've been inseparable since."

"*Why did you bring my mommy here?*"

"She's going to help free all of you from the skin walker."

"... *How do you know that will work?*"

"Well… we don't, but… it's a place to start. When the skin walker is gone, we'll know if it worked."

"*Daddy said to not let your guard down here. You still have to face the end of the day.*"

"The end of..?"

I'm cut off before I finish, realization washing over me at her pointed gaze. The traces of a deadly fire remind me of the orchard's endless finale. At the rate these strange apples are forming, we don't have much time. I get up from my perch, swinging my legs around before doing so, and turn to address Ioana. she's gone before I get a word out. With the distraction gone, I continue in the direction my pendant indicates.

The fog is beginning to grow again, swallowing my feet and calves. Although it's just moisture in the air, I refrain from banishing it. Whispers all around me hiss my demise, rejoicing in yet another victim to join their twisted family. it's easy to ignore their chatter. What I can't overlook, is my incessant curiosity. I keep surveying the trees, my gaze lingering on the odd apples. They're garnering a dark red color, yet have the strangest shape. At first, I chalked it up to their growth. Now, I realize they're just growing into that appearance.

One of the trees shift, bowing to check on the three small saplings at its roots. Ghostly arms rise from its bark, the spirit of a woman soon follows. Anchored to her spot, I only see from her waist up. Each sapling holds a child's spirit, all of them reaching for her reassuring touch. It crosses my mind that they might fear my presence, so I walk around them in a large arc. I'm not here to scare them, but children rarely understand such things after a violent end. As I glance back, I catch a thankful expression on the woman's pale face. I smile in return.

Further along, I catch a hazy silhouette in the fog. I don't even think when I run to it. Instead of finding Nixie, however, I find Calista. she's speaking with one of the trees, yet stops upon hearing my footsteps. Her face likely mimics my own upon seeing her figure… relief and happy expectation before it falls to disappointment. I wonder if she's been waiting for the god of Whisper Hill.

"Did you come across anyone else?" I question.

"No one living," she answers. "What about you?"

"Same. I can't believe the amount of saplings around here," I comment. "Didn't this all start because of a missing child? Why would she take more?"

"As sad as it makes me to see them, I'm sure she thought it far more cruel to leave them survive on their own. Remember, when she died this place wasn't even an afterthought of passing travelers. No one settled here, very few passed through. Back then we were lucky to get visitors even five times a year. Those children would suffer hunger and loneliness had she not taken them in."

"So… the parents were revenge, but the kids were mercy. I suppose that makes sense when you take into account when she died."

"She's not a bad person..."

"Don't worry, I know that," I offer. "I didn't mean to make her seem that way, I was just thinking aloud. Let's go find Styx and Nixie."

"I was just asking Abigail where he is. She said he's talking to a man in our old village. When I asked who it was, she said she could no longer see them."

"But Styx is in that clearing?"

"No. He's gone, too."

I'm startled by that, as he was so adamant I not come. there's no time for bafflement, though. Even with his strange disappearance, Nixie is still lost and that skin walker needs destroyed. I know how, I just need the opportunity. This just means I get a longer window to coax the chancellor out. I take Calista's hand, refusing to part a second time, and we head off to find Nixie. A part of me, however, mulls over what could draw Styx away from something so important.

It doesn't seem as though we've traveled far, though our legs and feet protest, that we stop for a break. At this point, I realize we've passed the same tree about seven times. I recognize it by the plump trunk and the second tree it twists with. A garish display of undying love until the end. It breaks my heart. Calista must see that pain in my eyes, as she searches for the cause. When she notes the pair, she sighs.

"I remember them," she comments. "I believe they were on their honeymoon four years ago. I've never seen a couple so in love. When they came up missing, I just couldn't believe it. I stopped visiting for many months."

"This place would have been so beautiful had it not been built on blood and bodies."

"I agree," she states. "This was my home once… That home has long since disappeared."

"What will you do once these people are free?"

"… I don't know, I've never considered that possibility before you," she remarks, thoughtful. "I suppose I'll finally get to rebuild out here, stay with my love and try to start a new family."

I can't help but hope for her, she deserves happiness after all this suffering. I do wonder how life with a god will be for her, I don't think she can live with them… wherever it is he lives.

"We're not getting anywhere here," I sigh, exasperated. "The orchard keeps moving around, sending us right back to where we began. If we can't figure out a way to keep it still, we won't make any progress."

"The trees can help us," Calista brightens. "Their roots are stationary, perhaps they can make the ground stationary as well."

"It's worth a shot."

The willowy woman heads over to the entwined trees, reaching out to set a hand upon one of the trunks. I watch as she whispers to them, drawing the spirits forth. After a short conversation, the souls trapped there pull away. I feel a slight tremor beneath my feet, just a subtle vibration, and then everything goes still.

"Okay, we should be good now," she smiles. "Let's keep walking."

"How are they stopping the movement?" I wonder, curious.

"They're locking their roots together beneath the soil," she answers. "Since they're unable to move, their roots will tie the ground together. It won't last long, though. If that monster can work through them, it'll likely be searching for any weak points."

"Then let's get moving."

I raise my pendant once more, pushing forward with her hand in mine. With the labyrinth momentarily still, we can make more progress toward our goal. Now unhindered, we travel further and finally come across Nixie. She's sitting beneath a tree, waiting to be found with a rather irritable look on her face. At the sight of us, she gets to her feet in relief.

"I thought I was gonna die of boredom," she comments. "It took you long enough to find me."

"Sorry," I answer, sheepish. "The ground kept moving us back to the beginning. It's stopped for now, but we have to keep going before it starts again."

"Do you know how to get to the barrier?"

"Yeah, I just have to follow Styx's pendant. Grab Calista's hand, we don't want to get separated again. Styx can navigate the orchard himself, so we'll head to the barrier. Hopefully, he'll be back by the time we reach it."

"Back?"

I don't answer her question, leaving Calista to do that. Instead, I lead them on toward our endgame. As we get nearer to it, I can feel the tension in the air increase. It's almost suffocating. By the time we finally come up to that invisible barrier, my heart is thudding in my chest. We stop at the threshold, staring with apprehension at the clutter of foliage. Behind this barrier is a creature so dangerous, its own creators issued their demise. We're all that stands between it and a world of victims.

"... I just realized how heavy this task is," I murmur. "Should we wait for Styx?"

"I really want to, but... How long will he take?"

"I don't know," I admit. "The plan was just to lead him toward me anyway, do you two think you can manage it?"

"I can, but I'm worried about Calista," Nixie sighs. "She's tired, I can see it in her body language. We should at least wait for Styx, it'll give her a chance to rest up."

"I'll be fine," she protests.

"Nixie's right, I don't want to take the chance of you getting hurt," I frown.

"I might get hurt anyway, at least if we go now we can keep the element of surprise."

Both of them make good points, so it's difficult to take sides. It seems imperative the skin walker is taken by surprise, yet we're not positive it's ignorant to our presence. Looking upon Calista, though, I know she needs to rest. Against my better judgment, I take a seat to wait for Styx. Although reluctant, my companions do the same. Thankfully, Styx wanders into the area not long after.

"Sorry," he remarks. "I had some business to take care of. Are we ready to begin?"

“We were just taking a break for Calista,” Nixie offers. “Now that you’re here, I’m more than willing to head in.”

“Catori, when you get us inside, I want you to head straight to the well,” he informs. “Even if you have to take a longer way around, it’s important you get there while we keep the skin walker preoccupied.”

“Got it,” I nod. “Don’t forget, I get time to talk to the chancellor.”

“I won’t forget.”

With that decided, I step over to the barrier and reach for them. I grasp Nixie’s and Calista’s hands. They, in turn, hold tight to Styx. As a group, we walk through the barrier that seems to part for me. Unfortunately, we’ve lost the element of surprise. The skin walker stands right before us, ready for a fight. I’m hoping our numbers will give us an edge, yet those hopes are dashed when it moves.

For a walking corpse, it certainly doesn’t move like zombies in the movies. Just a blink and you’ve missed it. I barely have the opportunity to dodge before he’s right in front of me. I roll out of the way, just missing his bony hand. When I stand, however, he’s throwing another clawed strike at me. He’s blocked by Styx’s lantern. The light flares where they connect, sending the skin walker screeching in pain. Styx takes a stand in front of us, making sure to bar the monster’s path. It glares at him, baleful, and hisses in irritation.

“*The one born of poison*,” the chancellor growls out. “*So gleeful was your hunt for my kin. Has your blood-lust not run out by now?*”

“I hunted you and your kind, because I was charged with the task,” Styx bites out, standing more intimidating than I’ve ever seen. “Had you not ravaged the world needlessly, lusting for the darkness within mortal hearts, I never would've been given the order. Blame yourself for what happened to your kin, you led them to their ruin."

As I watch the two interact, enthralled with the tension of battle, I feel Nixie's hand on my arm. She gently pushes me toward the back. The motion reminds me of my goal here, and I begin to make my exit. Unfortunately, the skin walker isn't going to have it. He moves to attack once more, again blocked by Styx. It seems to realize something with that connection, though.

"*Born of poison… yet your weapon lacks its sting*," he grins. "*You have lost your ability to destroy me.*"

"No, I just lost that weapon," he comments. "There's still a way to destroy you, and I aim to make sure it happens."

I note that the skin walker's eyes seem to be pinned on me. It's as though it knows I'm the key to its demise. With it so focused on me, I won't be able to reach the well. Calista walks forward, her figure soaked in loathing and pain. At the sight of her, the creature pauses. He saw this figure before, so many centuries ago. This was the woman he killed, the one he stole from… and yet, she's different.

"You… You stole everything from me!" Calista bites out. "My home, my family… my sister… my daughter… You deserve to be locked here for all eternity! To watch the world around you pass by, unable to move! The endless dark of death is too good for you!"

"*You died, I saw it*," the skin walker gapes. "*I set fire to your body myself!*"

"You killed my twin sister!" Calista shouts, pulling a dagger from her waistband. "And my daughter! My Ioana! You trapped them here, refusing them the peace of afterlife! I returned to find everyone dead! The fires were still glowing embers!"

"*I will not miss you a second time.*"

He rushes forward and I move to intercept. Calista, however, seems to have tapped a hidden well of energy. She moves just as quickly as he does, slicing into his side with her dagger. There's a hiss and the smell of burnt flesh, and then the skin walker is backtracking. His sunken eyes are wide in shock, one half rotted hand covering the wound.

"This dagger won't kill you," she replies. "But it *will* make you suffer, just as you made my family suffer."

"Ouch," Nixie murmurs. "Vengeful much?"

"Nix, I need to get over to the well," I hiss quietly. "Any ideas?"

"Let's just get into the fight, hopefully we can move around him to get there."

I nod in agreement, turning to face the creature we hunt. My main goal is the well, but my eyes stay on our foe. At the back of my mind, I feel a thought beg for attention. Caught in the moment, however, I push it aside. My fists burn with the fire of anger, the flames licking my skin. The chancellor dodges Styx, but runs straight into my fireball. He falls back and I'm almost hoping its that easy… and then he starts to laugh.

"*Little witch, I was born of Hell's fire,*" he cackles. "*Yours cannot harm me.*"

"No fire then," I smirk. "How about something a little colder?"

Water takes the place of fire, crystallizing upon my skin. It's heavier, but I manage to swing. He takes the blows, cutting my side with the sharp bone protruding from his fingertips. It stings and I fear it might leave infection, yet there's no time to stop. he's moving, slashing at Calista and shoving Nixie into Styx. The

Charon easily moves around her, one arm directing her motion as they spin. Like partners that have danced together all their lives, she stays on her feet and he follows through with his attack. His body goes low as he darts forward, thrusting his staff into the skin walker's gut. Nixie leaps over Styx, setting both feet in the creature's chest as it straightens. Hands planted firmly on Styx's back, she does a back hand spring to regain her footing. Just as her hands leave him, Styx is turning. He strikes the creature with his staff, the sight akin to a major league player going for a home run. I cringe at the sound of snapping bone.

Calista is there to meet him, yet I've fallen still. The onslaught is unnerving to say the least. It isn't the punishing blows, made by the hands of those I care about, though. It's the laughter of a man with a foot at the edge of insanity. I know I should use this opportunity, however a part of me demands I stop this. Something sinister is underlying this attack. The tension is building to a breaking point. Calista slashes with her dagger, directing his dodge into Nixie's scythe. That's when I notice it. A hunk of flesh from his shoulder hits the ground, turning to dust before blowing away. I take a better look at him, discarding the active surroundings. His figure is missing scattered chunks. He's *trying* to destroy his current shell.

"Stop!" I shout.

My outburst sends Nixie's blade off course, slicing the skin walker's rotting head off. Although the physical form turns to dust on the wind, that cold laughter echoes around us. It sends ice through my veins. That demon is loose, and we're all vulnerable to it. No one moves, each listening for movement. I hear a thump overhead, looking to see a ripple in the air. It can't leave this place without help from me. That alone is a relieving realization, yet it doesn't help the others.

"*The cursed god contains me still,*" it bites out. "*Yet... there are four powerful vessels below. One of you will do, but which shall I choose?*"

Ice flows through my veins, eyes darting to look at the others. They, too, survey those around them. It's times like this that I understand how distrust is born during war. From the chancellor's history, I can tell this thing can rest within the soul for long periods of time. It doesn't change you immediately, it works on you slow. It whittles away at the light within, killing it bit by bit and waiting for the perfect time to take over. Then again, just because it's waited in the past doesn't mean it will right now.

Something slips passed me, a shiver running through me. It feels like a similar energy to the wraith that was Shadow. It's malevolent and sinister. The thought that I won't be able to save those trapped souls strikes me, and I feel my hopes drop. I was certain I could talk the chancellor to the surface, if only to give him the chance of freedom.

"Control your emotions," Styx calls out. "It will strengthen the harsher ones, weakening your spirit with negativity."

"Why is everything always so negative?" I huff. "Can't I go on one mission where I find nothing but rainbows and unicorns? Is that so much to ask for?"

"Sorry, Cat, but you were meant for darker things," Nixie jokes, though anxious.

"How are we supposed to know when one of us is possessed by this thing?" Calista wonders. "I only heard stories of its capture, I never knew how they succeeded. All I remember is that someone volunteered to contain it."

"That's the problem," Styx sighs in aggravation. "We won't know until it takes them over. that's what made them so difficult to track down and destroy."

"There has to be some way to tell," Nixie huffs. "Are we able to be taken over, Styx?"

"Uh… I… have no idea," he answers, sheepish. "I thought only mortals could be possessed by them. I think we're safe, though, because we're not in mortal forms. If we were, we'd be fair game."

"So… Only Catori and Calista are vulnerable," she frowns. "What should we do?"

They fall quiet and I know the answer. There's no way to tell who is possessed, so we take out the options until there's only one. I can take the form of any element, yet… I can't allow Calista to suffer more than she has. Morality is quickly winning this inner battle. I survived being possessed once before, this shouldn't be any different. At least, I hope it isn't. That presence hovers the air between us, waiting for its opportunity. Mind made up, I begin to let my worst emotions and doubts surface. The anger at being lied to all my life, the pressure of the world upon my shoulders, the doubt of success, and the vengeance of my siblings' plight. The sudden rush of anxiety makes my head spin.

"Catori! No!" Styx cries out.

"This isn't like the store demon," Nixie shouts. "You can't overpower a skin walker, they're created to break wills!"

"The river can't hurt me," I argue. "Calista's been through enough, she can be happy after this!"

they don't get a chance to reply, as the skin walker darts toward the buffet I've set up. I hold out my arms, welcoming the creature to it's end… and then I feel a sharp pain. It goes from my side up into my lung. I loose my breath, glancing down to see the cause. Calista's dagger has pierced me. One arm wraps around my shoulders, crossing in front of me, and she helps me to the ground. Confusion is obvious within my clouding eyes.

"I'm sorry," she states. "This is my fight. Someday, you'll understand. Just keep in mind, this is what *I* chose and… you just can't save everyone."

she steps between me and the skin walker's presence. The anger and hatred pours off her in a cloud of red. My body finally answers to the call of death, turning to ash so I can rise as fire. When I do, that chilling presence is gone. there's no doubt where it went. I grip the ground in frustration, the ashes from the chancellor's body mixed in the soil. I'm overwhelmed by sadness, the feeling transforming my angry fire into water. It rushes over me like a wave, extinguishing the flames with a hiss of smoke. That sadness is quick to turn into wrath. The sudden switch reminds me of the sea. It's at this point I realize, those emotions aren't mine. I'm being controlled by something far more powerful than I can imagine.

Once it passes my mind, I begin to note obvious changes. For one, it's like an out-of-body experience. I feel larger than I should, like I'm towering over those in the clearing. I'm a titan. The entire area is shrouding in mist, the waters that are my body thrashing about angrily, and I can see a strange expression on Styx's face.

"*Vile parasite,*" the presence hisses through my mouth. "*A soul of sin reborn with my stolen tears. Never have I despised creation more.*"

The voice booms with underlying thunder, the power of the seas' fury putting pressure on my spirit. I can practically see the lightening in its eyes. As terrifying as this presence is, I can also feel an overwhelming elegance. There's no doubt in my mind this is a female being. Styx moves forward, lips parted in disbelief. His image is beginning to grow younger, shrinking down to a small child. The robe he wears moves with him, yet it's still large on his figure as he stumbles forward.

"I know that voice," he states, tone tiny and young. "Mother? How are you here?"

"*Styx, my child. Born of my defeat, and yet... you wear those scars so proudly.*"

She kneels down and reaches out to hold the child Charon, her hand the length of his height. I can feel her love toward him, the tenderness an ancient creature like her dares not show. One finger draws a line around his face, careful not to harm him. Although she keeps him seated in her palm, her attention is turned once more to the skin walker.

"*Unworthy puppet, you have made a dire mistake in your hurry to possess another.*"

"*What are you talking about?*" it bites out from Calista's lips.

"*Your intention is to possess a soul, by giving it what it desires most,*" she explains, a sick humor in her tone. "*How do you possess a soul that wishes only for your destruction?*"

It pauses and an expression of confusion passes. Obviously, that thought hadn't crossed it's mind. Honestly, it hadn't crossed mine either. This situation is so similar to my first encounter with such an evil, yet I have a bad feeling this isn't going to end well for Calista. I'm only proven right when she forces herself to the surface.

"I'm ready," she comments. "Please, end this curse upon my family. Let me join them in this orchard, beneath the watchful eye of my love for eternity."

"*Child, you befriended my only*," the river comments. "*I thank you for that. In return, I shall give you the end you so seek. Go on with the satisfaction of knowing you've ended this evil and set others free.*"

She nods, face brave as she stares down the deadly waters. The river that bore Styx grasps her in her free hand, closing her fingers over her body. She's curled up in her fist, courageously taking that one breath to end it all. Tears run down my liquid cheeks, and I know they belong to me. The only tears this being would shed are for her only child. Calista opens her mouth, a last attempt to fight for air, and then she falls still. Her eyes are wide open, mouth ajar as all her muscles relax. That image will be burned into my nightmares forever.

A horrid scream emanates from Calista's still body, a dark cloud upon her skin like slime. It flakes off into the water, disappearing within the darkened depths. That would be the final moment of the skin walker. A bubble leaves Calista's lips, growing as the river begins to open her hand. When it floats into the air, about eye level with me and the river that possess me, it pops. All those souls I found trapped in the demon's world drift away, happiness radiating off each of them as they find their peace.

"*My child*," the river comments, lifting him to nuzzle her cheek. "*How happy I am to have this moment with you. For so long I was trapped in a flowing world, watching you without the ability to speak. Only one has* the ability to channel me, yet they never learned how. I am so sorry for all the pain you have suffered, for all those moments I could not hold you and wipe away your tears. I am so proud of you and what you have become. I will always be watching you."

"Can't you stay?" he wonders.

"I am sorry, little one, but I cannot. My presence is far too powerful for this youth to hold for long. I will always be with you, though. Continue to grow and learn, perhaps I'll reach an agreement with the Roots. Should that happen, I will enjoy my time with you."

"… Goodbye, mother," Styx sniffles, tears in his youthful eyes.

"No, not goodbye. I will see you again, you are near me everyday. Even if I do not hold this form, I will always be near, always be listening and watching. Never feel alone, my child. I will always be with you."

She kisses the top of his head, so very careful to only brush his hair. Afterward, I feel my form begin to shrink. The extra water seeps into the ground. When I'm back to my original height, I feel that hold disappear. My form takes a mortal shell, one hand holding my head as I stumble from dizziness. Styx, figure going back to normal, steadies me with a hand to my shoulder. He pulls me close and embraces me.

"Thank you so much, Catori," he whispers. "I can't tell you how much that meant to me."

"You're welcome," I comment, eyes on Calista's body.

When he lets me go, I kneel down beside her. One hand reaches over and closes her eyes, a heavy weight of guilt setting upon my shoulders. Nixie and Styx stand behind me, letting this moment pass in silence. She was so brave, staring death in the face and asking for it to end. I could never imagine wanting revenge so badly, I would willingly end my life for it.

"She didn't have to die," I murmur. "I could've helped her. Why wouldn't she let me help her?"

"Cat, this isn't your fault. She *chose* to do what she did. You can control a lot of stuff, but you can't choose the path of others."

"… She could've been happy..."

"She was," Styx offers. "She was very happy, but also… very lonely and tired. This is where she spent most of her time, searching for her daughter. The man she loved was out of reach even in immortality, trapped holding a barrier to protect the world outside. He used the majority of his power for it, so he couldn't really take a physical form. With her released from her mortal shell, they can be together more. I'm sure she knew this when she stabbed you. In the end, she got everything she wanted. There was nothing you could do or say that would change her mind."

Although my heart sinks for her, I believe Styx. I lost a friend today, but that doesn't mean I won't see her again. I'm the Root of souls, I can see her in the afterlife whenever I choose to. That small consolation helps to alleviate my mourning. I hear a soft thump outside the barrier. Curious, I glance over to see another apple fall from the branches. They're ripe and ready for harvest. When it hits the ground, the sound of breaking pottery shatters my mindset. Ashes hit the ground, setting the grass on fire. I inhale sharply, eyes going wide. Now I know why the fruit looked so odd. They're urns, containing the ashes of the victim that died there. Two more tumble to the soil.

"We need to leave," I whisper.

"What do you mean?" Nixie frowns. "The curse is over… isn't it?"

"Not yet. The orchard needs to go through its last cycle. The apples aren't apples, they're *urns*. When the ashes hit the ground, it sparks the fire that consumes the orchard every year."

She tries to open a portal, yet can't seem to do so. Styx has the same issue. I look around us, searching for what blocks their power, and notice a glint of gold in the well's tree. Curious, I get up and walk closer. High up in the leaves seems to be a single fruit… a golden apple. The legends about it are true, much to my surprise. Ignoring the growing fires around a weakening barrier, I start to climb.

"Cat, what are you doing?" Nixie wonders.

"There's a golden apple in this tree," I comment. "I think it might be important."

"We need to go!"

"We will. I just need to collect it. If I don't get it now, it might not come back."

She doesn't respond, but I know I need to go quickly. Foregoing my mortal form, I turn into water and dart from branch to branch. When I finally reach it, I grasp it in my hands and draw it close. My figure drops down, landing in a puddle with my hands holding the urn heavenward. I pull myself together and change back. Tucking the urn close, I rejoin my friends. One last glance at Calista's corpse, and I head to the barrier. It finally breaks, letting the fires in. the gust circles Calista, growing in strength until she's covered in a storm of dust. When it dies down, she's no longer laying there.

Nixie grabs my hand and we start running. The three of us are forced to dodge falling branches. We're surrounded by the terrified screams of the spirits trapped here, each calling for help that never came. I trip over a rock, tumbling to the ground. In an attempt to protect the urn, I curl around it. Nixie and Styx falter, about to return for me, yet I wave them on. I'm not hurt, I just have to get back to my feet.

As I do, I realize how quickly the fire is spreading. A single trip and it's almost managed to circle me. I dart through the small opening left, continuing to run for the exit. With the skin walker gone, we don't have to worry about getting turned around. A branch falls overhead, taking a path that will collide with Nixie. I change to fire and blast myself closer to her, gaining more solidity in order to push her out of the way. She flies forward and the branch hits me across my back. Thankfully, I was already half turned to water and I break apart there. The waters that create me are pulled together once more, rolling forward like a wave before leaving me in a mortal shell. As I pass Nixie, I grab her hand and drag her to her feet.

"Thanks," she remarks.

"Don't mention it," I smile.

"You're getting really good at transforming," she notes. "It's so fluid now. Your training is really paying off."

I grin as we continue, catching up to Styx just as we all break through the edge of the orchard. As soon as we're clear, we fall to the grass and gasp for breath. The fire is raging within the trees, crackling and snapping as it devours the cursed land. Above the trees, I can see the wisps of those trapped taking their first steps toward freedom. Their glowing spirits send their thanks as they pass, swirling about in relief before vanishing into the night sky. Finally, it's all over and I lay back to take in that feeling of success.

Epilogue

The orchard burned all night long, leaving nothing but ash in its wake. As much as I wanted to wait, we couldn't stay until the end. The smoke was just too much for us. Now, standing in the cabin with Nixie and Styx, we prepare for our last trip to the orchard. Although the curse is gone and the souls are free, there are still a couple loose threads to wrap up.

"Are you ready, Cat?" Nixie wonders.

"… Yeah, I'm ready."

"Styx and I can handle this if you want to stay here."

"No, I want to see this through," I assure. "I'm still hurt by Calista's loss, but… Ioana deserves to be free."

"Bring the urn," Styx comments. "The god of Whisper Hill might know what it is."

"… It's an urn," I say.

"… Okay… maybe he'll know *who* it is."

I nod and Nixie tears a hole in the air. All of us walk through, emerging near the orchard. Well… at least what's left of it. It never came back from that fire. A small grouping of trees, however, still encase Whisper Hill. Now, a small stream trickles through. Lush green grass is everywhere, dotted with wildflowers, and the area doesn't look as foreboding as before. The ruins of the old settlement still stand as twisted and aged as it was, but it's a part of history. It will always be there, until time reclaims its entirety.

We walk until we get to the old well, the remains of that tree surprisingly gone. I called the police earlier, so they should be here soon. When I told them I solved the murder of the lost gypsy girl they were stunned, yet just as excited. Even though Ioana has no family left here, she still deserves a resting place. If that's even possible, anyway. I sit on the edge of the well, swinging my legs over and carefully testing the old ladder there. There's no way it'll hold for me.

"I'm gonna need a rope," I comment. "At least as show for the cops."

"Okay, I'll set it up," Nixie states. "Do you want to wait?"

"No, I'm gonna go down and see if I can contact her."

She nods and I leap into the well. When I hit the ground below, my body shatters into water and reforms. The room hidden at the bottom is just like I left it. The sap that sealed off the room is gone, thanks to the friendly ghost writer, and I'm able to enter with ease. The room, though trapped in a state of decay, is still dark. I light the small candles I remember being there. At the back of the room, surrounded by scattered flowers, is Ioana's tomb. It would seem she had recent visitors.

"Ioana, I'm here," I comment. "Are you still trapped, or have you managed to join your family?"

"*I am still here,*" she states, sadness in her voice. "*I could not find my grave, so I stayed here. Now... I wish I hadn't. Even my body will forever be unchanging.*"

"Don't worry, the cops are coming to collect it. I'm sure they'll give you a proper burial."

"I hope so," she sighs. "I have been waiting for so long."

"I know you have. But at least this will all be over soon. I see you had a visitor earlier."

"*The petals have my mother's energy in them,*" she muses aloud. "*And my daddy was here, too. They're finally together.*"

"And you'll be with them, too."

"*Thank you so much, Catori,*" she grins. "*I'm so excited to be with my family again.*"

"I'm glad I could help."

She fades away, leaving me with her corpse and the scattered flowers. With a satisfied sigh, look back to her body once more. it'll be difficult to move, but if I have enough rope I should be able to tie it up. As I walk back to the opening, I hear sirens wailing up top. The rope is hanging down the well's shaft, waiting for me to use it.

"Catori, the cops are here," Nixie calls down.

"I'm on my way up," I reply.

Hands on the rope, I scale the side of the well and pull myself over the edge. Three police cars are parked in the grass nearby, all of the uniformed people stunned at the change in the land. When they see me, they all gather around. There are two women and four men. One of the women I remember talking to at the station.

"What happened here?" she wonders. "We've tried to burn down that orchard for so long without success… Did you do this?"

"No. You wouldn't believe me if I told you the truth."

"… You believe in that old curse, too?" she scoffs.

"Well, an orchard that burns down every year, just to grow back the next day, burned down and hasn't returned," I remark. "I'm gonna have to say there was something to that old curse. Now it's lifted. The souls are free and you can use this land as you wish. Just don't piss off the god of Whisper Hill."

"So now that legend is real as well," she huffs, skeptical. "Wonderful. Will I be visited by my dead partner as well?"

"Do you want to be?" I question. "I'm sure I can have it arranged."

She rolls her eyes and looks down the well. It's a long drop, so I stand near in case she falls. The doorway isn't visible from here, so her questioning glare is understandable. I sigh and get back on the rope. When I slide down, she follows. As soon as her feet touch the rotting platform, her eyes note the old door. Her jaw hangs open a bit, eyes wide in surprise. Together, we walk into the small room.

"Oh my god," she whispers, horrified. "What the hell..?"

"This is Ioana," I explain. "Her mother was the gypsy named Calista, the leader of those burnt to death by the settlers. The chancellor kidnapped Ioana, believing her to be a witch, and drown her down here. When she was dead, he used tree sap to create her tomb… creating a trophy to preserve his prize. After her death, he ordered the murder of the girl's family. She's been here since."

"How did you find all this out?"

"I'm an investigator, it's what I do," I shrug. "I was exploring the orchard when I came across the well. I couldn't see the door either, but something called me down here."

"… How weird."

"I'm not known for being normal," I remark, rolling my eyes. "Please make sure she gets a proper burial. Her spirit is trapped here until she does. I would recommend burying her on Whisper Hill, she… uh… *thought*… the god there was her father."

"… I'll see what I can do," she murmurs. "We can take it from here. Another team is coming to exhume the body, so we just have to wait for them. We're only here to rope off the crime scene. Thank you for your help."

"Not a problem. I understand that you have your protocol, but… I would like to stay for the rest of this. I just want to make sure she gets out okay."

She grants me permission and we climb back up the rope. It doesn't take much longer before a couple police trucks pull up. Those officers take out a pulley system and stretcher. It looks similar to rescue equipment used to carry away injured climbers. They set it up and send the stretcher down with one of them on it.

As they carefully bring up the sap grave, I stand by and wait. We should be heading to Whisper Hill, yet I can't just leave Ioana alone. When they get her up, a couple of them use hammers and chisels to break the sap open. It's taken down piece by piece, careful to leave her in tact. That's when I notice she's curled around something.

"Excuse me, but… can I see that?" I question.

"See what?"

"She's curled around something. I think it's a book," I frown.

"Oh, yeah," the officer shrugs. "It's been long enough, I don't think we'll catch the guy behind it. They're long since dead."

He carefully slides it out of her arms and hands it to me. Although it's been trapped with her for so long, the book appears untouched. It's odd, as I don't remember her holding it when she went down the well. The cover is leather, golden letters and ornaments on the corners, and a lock is set to hold it closed. I can't imagine the secrets it might hold. When they manage to load her into the truck, covered in a body bag, we head over to Whisper Hill.

"What's that?" Nixie wonders.

"Ioana was holding it," I shrug. "It's just a book. Maybe her journal."

"Do you have the urn?" Styx inquires.

"Yes I do, right here in my backpack," I smirk, sliding the book in with it.

It's a short walk to the hill. When we reach it, I notice a difference in appearance. Instead of one tree, there are two and a sapling. The larger ones are connected at the base, their branches wound around each other. I can sense Calista's presence here. Near the top, I see her holding out her arms in welcome. I don't wait to give her a hug.

"I'm so sorry," I whisper.

"*I'm not,*" she grins. "*I haven't felt this good in a very long time. Thank you for helping me, Catori. I wanted nothing more than to be with my love and our child, and now I can be. I have no regrets.*"

"Calista, we'd like to speak with the god of Whisper Hill," Styx remarks. "About this strange golden urn from the orchard."

"You found?" she wonders. "Where?"

"It was on the tree coming from the well," I inform. "I managed to get it before we had to escape the fire."

"*So many have been after that strange urn, I can't believe it's real,*" she muses. "*But... I can't get my love for you, he's traveled to the next town over. By the time he gets back, it'll be too late for him to speak with you. He did tell me to give you a message, though.*"

"He did?"

"*Yes. He said to tell you the ashes are from the earth, and they must rejoin it. He also mentioned you shouldn't fear quicksand, it's just an embrace.*"

"... Okay," Nixie states.

I think it over for a little bit, and then realize what he's saying. I drop the urn on the ground, stepping backward in case a fire should ignite. there's no fire, but the ashes do sink into the ground. A jagged rock bursts from the soil like a flower, cracking down the middle before it falls apart. In its wake, a boy of nineteen stands. His hair is brown and his eyes are amber.

"You must be my brother," I smile. "I'm Catori, the Root of Souls. Are you feeling okay… um..?"

"Tarin. I'm fine," he yawns. "Just tired. How long has it been?"

"Probably a lot longer than you'd wish it to be," Styx sighs. "Glad to have you back, though."

"You never reached out to me," I frown. "I mean… so far, our siblings have reached out to me."

"Which ones?" he asks, cautious.

"Um… Mela and Shadow," I state. "Water and fire."

"But not wind?"

"No, you're the third. Why didn't you reach out to me?"

"I was sleeping," he frowns. "Not much else to do when you're trapped in an urn."

"I suppose that's fair."

"I see you've been gifted the power of the others," he muses, glancing at the markings that circle my wrist. "You'll come across wind soon, but along the way… you may need my help. I'll gift you my ability as well, little sister. If you need me, I'll be..."

"I know, I know," I waves off, exasperated. "You'll be with mother. That's were Mela and Shadow are, so I figure that's where you'll run to. I'll visit if I need any help."

"Don't push yourself too hard," he warns, reaching for my hand. "Our abilities are as much a curse as they are a gift. If you're not ready to face something, don't force it. The elements are meant to protect you, let them do so.

They know where you stand on your teachings, just trust them."

I nod and give him a minute smile, grasping his hand. A shock travels along my limb. Just as it stops, I feel the ground begin to sink beneath my feet. My first reaction is to panic, and then I remember the message. I force myself to calm down, closing my eyes and pretending I'm in an elevator. Lower and lower I sink. From my feet to my knees, my waist to my shoulders. Finally, I can't breath anymore. My lungs strain for air, my pores clogging with dirt. I pass out beneath the ground, buried alive.

When I open my eyes, I'm in the darkness. I bring one hand up to my face, watching in detached fascination when it crumbles. The rest of me follows suit, simply turning to sand. I fall to the ground like grains in an hourglass. Footsteps sound, echoing all around me. When I look up, I see the Root of earth.

"It's easier to pull yourself together, if you think of yourself as molding sand or a statue," Tarin states. "Earth is soft and malleable, used for pottery and statues. It helps life grow on farms, and can stand sturdy like a mountain. It isn't like fire, that only takes one form. Nor is it like water, that bends to your will. You must be soft, but firm to understand it. Try to create a shell from it."

With a soft hum, I try to do as he says. I remember photos from the internet, depicting golems and such. The sand around me turns to mud and starts to gather. Wood twists together to form a skeletal structure, vines acting as muscle and sinew, and the mud makes the skin. Branches grow from beneath the mud, reaching around and blooming leaves to create clothes and hair.

"Not bad," Tarin states, impressed. "I think you'll do just fine with it. Remember, don't force it. Everything will come to you when it's meant to, when you're ready. Until then, you'll face losses. You won't be able to save everyone, and you'll hate yourself for that. Guilt will stew within you, anger and sadness and fear will becoming close companions. Just don't let anything get you down, you can't afford to stop when walking through this obstacle. Finish your mission and deal with the damage afterward. There will always be time afterward."

"… What part of that was supposed to make me feel good about being the savior of the world?" I wonder, tone flat as I glare at my 'older' brother.

"Sorry, but I'm not the understanding one. I'm the realistic one. Water is healing and caring, Fire is energetic and warm. I'm Earth. I'm..."

"Soft, but firm," I comment, rolling my eyes.

"Exactly. I'm going to prepare you for the real world, because it's about to eat you alive," he says. "I'm sorry we had to drag you into all of this, but… it was necessary. Our family is the only thing keeping this world going. We created life, we cultivated it, and we care for it. Nothing is more important to us than keeping our family, the basis of all that lives, healthy. No matter what may happen, we're here for you. We will hold you up when you fall, guide you when you're lost, and hold you when you cry… But not everything can end the way you want it to."

"… Calista wouldn't let me save her," I whisper, quiet and guarded. "I tried. I had the perfect plan set up, but..."

"That's the perfect example then, although I didn't want you to experience it so quickly. Remember, you are the Root of Soul. It doesn't matter how many you lose, you will always be able to see them again."

"It isn't about me," I argue. "It's about them, about their families, about the life they won't get to live because I couldn't save them."

"Everyone has their time, Soul," he sighs. "You used to know that."

"My name is Catori," I huff. "And I know that! It doesn't change the fact I want to give them more time. This world is beautiful and filled with so much, why is it so bad to let them enjoy it a little longer? I won't get to do that for everyone, I get that, but… I can still do that for the ones I *do* meet."

"I know you want to give them everything you can, but you did that when you gave them life," he states, setting his hands on my shoulders. "Now it's time to let them live it… Their *own* way, not yours. Once they leave the well, they're not yours anymore. You give them life to set them free, to let them make their own decisions and live the life they dream of. They can't do that if you shelter them. Please, Catori, let them go. They don't just have a specific time that life is up, their choices are what choose that time. *They* choose that time."

His words strike me, as though I've heard them before. They make sense and I never thought to look at it that way. Although Calista's death still hurts, I did see her again and she's with her family now. Tears are in my eyes and Tarin pulls me closer, holding me as I cry. When I settle, he kisses the top of my head. The darkness begins to fade, falling from above, and I find myself growing from the ground like a flower.

Nixie is over by my bag, reaching in to get the book, and Styx is sitting by the tree with Calista. I stretch toward the sky, a tree reaching for the sun, and the mud falls away to leave my mortal shell. As I bring my hand back down, checking the new mark on my wrist. I'm surprised, however, when I find *two* of them.

"Nixie, when did I find the wind element?" I wonder.

"You haven't," she waves off, lifting the book and facing me. "Cat, this book… It's the one I was looking for! How did Ioana have it? Only something supernatural had access to it..."

I start to walk toward her when I notice a presence in the air. It's familiar to me and I can't help help but smile a bit. Behind Nixie, the older man that's been helping me appears. His clothes are still jeans and a tee shirt, his dark face hidden beneath the shadow of his baseball cap.

"You're here," I state.

"*I am*," he smirks. "*I found something I had been looking for*."

Nixie turns around to face him, her features twisting in shock. The color drains from her skin, lips parting as she inhales sharply. I can see recognition in her eyes, can hear Styx scramble to his feet. The man that has been helping me grabs the book from her hands, and then thrusts his free hand into her chest.

"Nix!" I scream, running forward. "No!"

Her heart is pulled from her, a globe of dark light encasing it, and she drops to the grass. I don't get the chance to catch her, as the man disappears and reappears between us. The dark globe floating near his head, his free hand enters my gut. The pain is unbelievable as he pulls away, a sick grin upon his lips. With that, he's gone and I'm left to drag my failing body toward Nixie's. Tears fall from my eyes as I cradle her, my heart throbbing in pain. Styx is near us in seconds, holding us both. I know he cared about Nixie as well, I can see tears of blood on his cheeks.

"It's okay, Catori," he says, his voice softer as the darkness closes in. "Everything is going to be okay. I promise. I won't let anythign happen to you, I'm going to fix this. Please… hold on… Cat..."

My eyes flutter shut and I pull Nixie closer, burying my nose in her hair. I want my last memory to be of her. I want to burn the smell of her hair into my mind, the feel of her slight form as I hug her. I can hear her laughter in the back of my mind, see her carefree smile from my memories. I want to go with her, leave this life with the woman I love. The thought of returning without her is more painful than anything I can even imagine. As I fall into death's hands, I can't help but beg her for forgiveness. This is all my fault, and I can't fix it now. I can't bring her back. I thought her immortality could save her, but I guess even immortals have ways to die. The last of my tears fall, my body growing weaker. Although it's getting harder to hold her, I can't let her go. Not when I'm still conscious. So I keep that embrace until I can't anymore. Releasing her only when I'm lost to the darkness of death.

Made in the USA
Middletown, DE
08 May 2023

30138322R00156